What the critics are saying…

"Madigan's Celtic Charms: Destined is a quick paced paranormal erotic romance that keeps the reader at the edge of her seat…..If you enjoy paranormal romance, this story is definitely for you. Do not miss it." Mireya Orsini" ~ *Dawn Just Erotic Romance Reviews*

"Destined is a blending of contemporary *Celtic* fantasy and an ancient race of shape-shifters. This is a very descriptive story of time and place, I was enchanted in the Otherworld that this author created…This is a delightful start to this trilogy. *Ms. Madigan* does a wonderful job in this debut novel. *Destined* is an erotic, fun and enjoyable contemporary Celtic fantasy that will please any fan of this genre." ~ *Luisa Cupid's Library Reviews*

"A sexy fantasy, DESTINED will keep readers laughing as they root for mDara and Rowan to get together as well as to beat the forces arrayed against them. Both characters are eminently likeable…..The sexual tension between the two is enough to make readers start gnawing on their fingernails…DESTINED nicely blends fantasy with the erotic and should not be missed." ~ *Phillipa Ann Romance Reviews Today*

"All in all I'd say that Destined is a very sexy fantasy adventure! Imagine Indiana Jones made hotter and more magical. Suspense, excitement and seriously wet-panty scenes, this book is a winner! I wouldn't be surprised if Ms. Madigan soon becomes a household name in the genre."~ *Christine Ventura Euro Reviews*

Dawn Madigan

Celtic Charms
Destined

ELLORA'S CAVE
ROMANTICA PUBLISHING

An Ellora's Cave Romantica Publication

www.ellorascave.com

Destined

ISBN # 1419952986
ALL RIGHTS RESERVED.
Destined Copyright© 2005 Dawn Madigan
Edited by: Heather Osborn
Cover art by: Christine Clavel

Electronic book Publication: May, 2005
Trade paperback Publication: November, 2005

Excerpt from *Ordinary Charm* Copyright © Anya Bast, 2004

Warning:

The following material contains graphic sexual content meant for mature readers. *Destined* has been rated *S-ensuous* by a minimum of three independent reviewers.

Ellora's Cave Publishing offers three levels of Romantica™ reading entertainment: S (S-ensuous), E (E-rotic), and X (X-treme).

S-ensuous love scenes are explicit and leave nothing to the imagination.

E-rotic love scenes are explicit, leave nothing to the imagination, and are high in volume per the overall word count. In addition, some E-rated titles might contain fantasy material that some readers find objectionable, such as bondage, submission, same sex encounters, forced seductions, etc. E-rated titles are the most graphic titles we carry; it is common, for instance, for an author to use words such as "fucking", "cock", "pussy", etc., within their work of literature.

X-treme titles differ from E-rated titles only in plot premise and storyline execution. Unlike E-rated titles, stories designated with the letter X tend to contain controversial subject matter not for the faint of heart.

Destined
Celtic Charms

Author's Note

This tale is loosely based on Celtic myths. Some of the story elements can be traced back to their Celtic roots, while others can't. There are many alternative truths out there. I chose the ones most suitable here.

"From Falias was brought Lia Fáil which is in Temair, and which is used to utter a cry under every king that should take Ireland."

Adopted from Lebor Gabála Érenn (Book of Conquests)

Trademarks Acknowledgement

The author acknowledges the trademarked status and trademark owners of the following wordmarks mentioned in this work of fiction:

Chevy Silverado: General Motors Corp.

Jell-O: Kraft Foods Holdings, Inc.

Suzuki: Suzuki Motor Corp.

Playboy: Playboy Enterprises International, Inc.

Ford Bronco: Ford Motor Company

Days of Our Lives: Columbia Pictures Industries, Inc.

Guinness: Guinness PLC Corp.

Incredible Hulk: Marvel Characters, Inc.

Chapter One
Somewhere on the outskirts of Portland, Oregon
October 31

The mother of all hellish storms was raging outside, a night truly fit for Halloween. Dara Neilan gave a short yelp as a windblown bough lashed wetly against her windshield, its muddle of dark leaves writhing in the violent gusts. She tightened her fists on the steering wheel, her slim body going rigid in the driver's seat. She wasn't cold, it took extreme measures to make her body fall ill with the shivers. Fear, on the other hand, followed different rules.

Shifting forward in her seat, her eyes tried to scan through the swirl of darkness, oil-thick raindrops and things caught in the wind—things that kept slamming against her Chevy's metallic frame and windows. She wasn't supposed to be trapped in here, so close to midnight, wading through rain-washed streets within the false security of her truck.

Trapped.

If she had only missed that damn birthday party three days ago…

She hadn't even wanted to attend a party. She had hoped it would, somehow, make her feel better…help her forget. After all, it was for a good friend of hers, and she had convinced herself it wouldn't hurt to engage in a little harmless fun. Goddess knew it had been awhile since she'd allowed herself the privilege.

Now she growled at her own stupidity, smashing a small fist against the steering wheel. Feeling bad—bad enough so that each new dawn was a struggle—*that* she could handle. Memories, dreams that jolted her awake, sheened with sweat and fumbling in the dark—in the long years to come maybe they, too, would fade.

Rowan Mackey, however...*him* she could not handle, nor make him fade from her thoughts.

Dara stepped on the brake hard, and the Silverado came to a jerky stop within the vague boundaries of nowhere. A lonely woman in a big Chevy truck, she stared blindly at the soaking darkness lapping at her windshield.

If she had only missed that party...

Slowly, she shook her head with dawning realization.

If she had, then he would have found her sometime, someplace else...

The constant chatter of the merrymakers sounded like a soft hum from Dara's place of retreat. She was wrestling with the fruit punch at a secluded table, drowning her cup in a tub of cherry-red. The fluid rippled with soft shimmers in the late noon sun, dousing her fingers with a rosy chill.

"Why don't you use this?"

A male voice, rough around the edges, flavored with a softened foreign accent.

Dara turned, clutching her dripping punch cup, and lifted her face to eyes of stormy green. Her gaze wandered up to the mop of rowdy copper-red framing a square-jawed face, brushing the man's shoulders. Then her gaze dropped to a faded t-shirt hugging long arm muscles and hard pecs.

He held out a ladle.

"Too late for that now, isn't it?" She smiled flatly, standing still since she had nowhere to go, caught between the grinning man and the punch bowl.

"We have unfinished business, Dara."

The "R" rolled on his tongue. The stranger's faint Irish brogue was now unmistakable. That alone forced stiffness into her muscles.

"*We?*" She arched her brows. "I don't know you."

"I should have introduced myself first, maybe." He studied her expression. "I'm Rowan Mackey."

As if that made a difference! Dara's knuckles were growing white clasping the punch. "Well, you obviously know *my* name, Rowan Mackey."

Mackey neglected to respond to the obvious.

"I don't recall ever having had business with you." Her tongue absently flicked over her dry lips. The punch hadn't yet touched her mouth.

"Oh?" He cocked a fiery brow. "Well, 'tis just a wee matter of life and death, Dara, nothing more. Can you drive?"

"Who the hell do you think—?"

"Aye, you can. That big Chevy parked outside is yours, isn't it? Meet me on the third night from now. You'll need to drive. You want to write this down?"

Flushing with anger, she tossed her drink in his face, watching with dark satisfaction as the punch dripped from the now-soggy curls. His eyes shut briefly as the rosy liquid hit him, then cracked open into slits of green fire. Mackey's smile broadened beneath the thin punch trickles. He gathered a stray pink droplet with a lingering sweep of his tongue.

"Sweet," he murmured.

It didn't sound like he was commenting on the punch. Dara gasped as his large fist closed on her hand clutching the cup, holding her captive with a calculated force.

"Now, now, lass." Mackey stepped forward, tugging Dara along with him. "You spilled your sweet brew. You should be more careful, aye?"

His free hand dipped the ladle into the punch bowl. All Dara was able to do was watch, caught in this man's steely, yet gentle grasp, too stunned to protest.

"Let me help you with a refill. With the blessings of County Meath." He maneuvered her captured hand closer, pouring the red liquid into her empty cup with exaggerated care.

He lowered his head, speaking softly into her ear, his mouth touching her hair. He told her where to meet him in three nights, and how she should get there. Each of his words ruffled her raven-dark locks, breathed over her skin like a warm breeze. The sensation made fine tremors course through her flesh. Mackey's scent lashed at her unprepared senses, an intoxicating, sharp blend of male-beast she had once known.

Dara now visibly shuddered, but not with fear alone.

Again she lifted her eyes to the man, unaware that he had already let go of her hand. His gaze was too close, intent on her face, as if he were about to kiss her. Dara's stunned eyes was inadvertently drawn to his mouth—to the succulent male lips whose fleeting touch had just singed her cheek.

Mackey flashed her a slow smile, letting it spill into his eyes.

"On the third night, Dara. I know about Aidan. Come to me if you value your life."

Dara's own lips parted with an unspoken question, her dark brown eyes growing wide with fear.

Mackey slowly straightened up to his full height, breaking their intimate closeness.

He turned and vanished in the partying throng with a few long, leisurely strides, gone before she managed to force her reluctant muscles to move...

A dazzle of blue light washed over the truck's windows. Dara tightened in reflex as thunder came crashing down over her, sounding as if the whole world was shattering to pieces around her. It hauled her mercilessly back to the here and now.

Why had that insolent Irishman demanded to meet her on this, of all nights, when the turbulent skies hid a ripe, perfectly round moon? It was the second full moon this month, the "*Blue*

Moon" her mother had warned her about. An uncommon occurrence that left her shaky and fizzy through all the remaining days of the month.

What other pieces of knowledge was Mackey holding about her… *From* her? The only piece she had, the one Mackey had obviously wanted her to have, was that he had come from County Meath, Ireland.

Where her parents had come from.

Where Aidan had been born.

Was Mackey…*her kind?* Not that she had a great deal of knowledge what *her kind* exactly was—her parents' skulking whispers had often slipped into Irish Gaelic whenever she'd been within hearing range.

Dara's hand instinctively dug beneath her thin woolen shirt, caressing icy steel. The concealed dagger's blade burned with cold fire against her feverish skin, reassuring her of its lethal existence.

She withdrew her hand, again clutching the wheel. Slamming a sneaker against the gas pedal, she was thrown back against the seat as the Silverado leaped forward.

Yeah, she would get there, all right. Rowan Mackey was in for one hell of a surprise.

* * * * *

Private Property.

Dara had almost run over the small signpost as her Chevy rolled along the narrow dirt road. The sign meant she was on the right track. Her heart reacted with a sudden jolt, then settled to pound wildly in her chest. She straightened up and leaned forward against the wheel, straining to keep to the murky road. It unraveled before the truck's headlights piece by broken piece, the rest of the trail swallowed by thick, inky-black darkness. When the warehouse suddenly materialized ahead, she slammed her foot hard on the brakes and then sat, staring, behind the wheel.

"Goddess," she mumbled. "You're going to pay for this one, Mackey."

Again she touched the sheathed dagger, this time feeling it through her thin shirt. The dagger was a treasured gift. The day Dara began her first monthly courses, her mother had pulled her aside, making sure the both of them had truly been alone. *"Beware of Hounds,"* she had whispered, and had forced the sheathed dagger into Dara's startled grasp, her own hands shaking badly.

Dara groaned, furious with herself for getting lost in memories. With added rancor she pushed the door open, hopping out into the storm.

Outside, the wind hummed ruthlessly. Icy gusts jabbed rain needles into Dara's eyes, snatched her thick hair and lashed it against her face. Her shirt billowed like a bell about her slim form. Gasping, she was flung back against the Chevy's metal skin. As if fighting the storm weren't enough, out here in the open every inch of her body was craving the pull of the full moon, though it was buried beneath heavy layers of black clouds.

"Oh, shit!"

She used her other arm to shield her wind-beaten face, aiming a look in the direction of the warehouse.

A little rain wouldn't kill her… One of Aidan's favorite quips had been that she was made of rainproof sugar…

Her throat clenched at the mere thought of Aidan, and she bit back the encroaching tears. Her right hand maintained a firm grip on the sheathed dagger's bony hilt. She crouched against the wind, then launched herself into the tempest.

Dara screamed as white-hot iron pierced her left shoulder from back to front, the violent blow forcing her to her knees. The raging gale smothered her cry as her body hit the muddy ground.

Mackey…Mackey shot *her?*

Coherent thought broke into jumbled fragments as the pain impossibly deepened and burrowed into the bone, paralyzing her left arm. She writhed in the mud, fumbling for her left shoulder, touching cold metal and something sticky and warm.

Arrowhead…blood…

Part of Dara's mind registered this information coolly, analyzing it from somewhere faraway and safe. She threw back her head, eyes forced shut, whimpering with each movement that jolted the arrow jammed in her shoulder. Her right hand slid over the slick blood and tore the dagger away from its scabbard.

You're going down with me, Mackey…

She closed her eyes and slackened her body with an effort, playing unconscious. She wasn't too far from the real thing.

Mackey'd tried to kill her… He'd come near her to make sure he'd got her, and then she would…she would…

Another bout of pain forced any rational thought out of Dara's mind. And then someone knelt by her side, gently drawing her hair away from her face. Squeezing out a broken cry of anger and pain, she arched her dagger into the air with a silvery flash and thrust it straight into—

Rowan Mackey's large fist caught her flying hand with ease, holding her at the narrow wrist. His green eyes, pools of mystery in the darkness, revealed surprise and…concern?

"Easy, Dara. I'm on your side."

A pair of yellow eyes gleamed in the darkness behind his back and Dara screamed again.

"Shhh, let me have a look at that shoulder, lass."

"Behind you!" she blurted with her last ounces of strength. Her fingers loosened their hold, the dagger plummeting into the mud with a soft wet sound.

Rowan sensed the searing gaze on his back and swiveled with a growl, his own eyes flashing amber.

By Danu, how much more careless could he get?

His long muscles tensed, nostrils flaring as he sniffed the hostile darkness, knowing that it was already too late. The pouring rain had already erased all the scents, wiped away all the trails.

The *Cú* — the Hound — was already gone.

Rowan crouched beside Dara, collapsed in front of the Chevy. He hoped she wasn't worse than unconscious. A stab of guilt and fear penetrated his core as he pressed his face against her cold, wet breasts in search of a heartbeat. He pushed the soaked shirt up over her rib cage and groaned with relief as he felt the quick, soft drumming of her heart against the right side of his face.

He had managed to trick her into coming to him out of her own free will, as the ancient Law had demanded, but he hadn't been betting on a Hound attack on these grounds.

Great Danu, this territory was Talamh Slán…Safe Grounds!

Not to mention that Hound hits had grown extremely rare for almost a century now. Dara should have been safe here. For that reason alone had he chosen this desolate place to be the location of their first knowing. And to think he had the nerve to consider himself a Guardian…

Hastily, he hefted her fallen dagger in his large palm. It was *Scían*, a traditional weapon made for self-defense, with a bleached-bone hilt and a blade of Damascus steel, its nearly black surface inlaid with swirling silver veins. He cursed as the silver stung his skin, and thrust the weapon through his leather belt.

Shifting, he positioned his arms beneath his destined mate's back and below the bend of her knees, and tenderly gathered her limp form into his embrace. Careful not to move the arrow lodged in her shoulder, he slowly scooped her up and sniffed the empty night air one last time. His eyes flashed golden again, attempting to slash through the shadows.

Nothing was out there but wall of solid darkness.

Rowan cradled his precious load against his chest and made a desperate run for the warehouse. Devouring the short distance in three long leaps, he bashed a steel-toed boot against the door, kicking it open.

Chapter Two

Cool, damp darkness and a stale odor greeted Rowan as he charged through the doorway. They indicated that the warehouse had been unused for a long time, just as he'd been told. This was the first time he'd ever laid eyes on the place. As the Law clearly stated, their first knowing should take place within the shelter of the Safe Grounds, in a location new to them both.

As if responding to his thoughts, Dara moaned and stirred in his arms.

He shot a quick glance around and walked deeper inside, spotting a dark corner where thick furry rugs covered the otherwise bare floor. He kicked off his boots and trod barefoot across the soft rugs without raising a single dust mote. The neatness of this hidden niche was undoubtedly the work of local Kanjali folk, pampering this area's Safe Grounds.

He knelt down, his movements both cautious and fluid, and entrusted the slack body in his arms to the rug's silky embrace. Positioning Dara on her uninjured side, he propped a blanket against her back to raise her left shoulder, hoping to prevent the arrow from sinking deeper in her flesh.

He bent closer, scrutinizing the wooden shaft. It pierced his mate's shoulder through and through, likely cracking her shoulder blade. The arrow's bloodied, silver broadhead was cruelly barbed. Its black-fletched tail had been etched with two complete circles and an inner half one, a twisted version of the ancient Celtic letters of the Ogham. The markings breathed icy darkness against Rowan's spread palm. He withdrew his hand as if singed, his fingers tightening to a fist. It was a Hound's arrow, no doubt about it, and it bore its maker's signature.

"Aidan…" Dara's eyes fluttered open. She mumbled something incoherent and fell silent again, the only sound her quick, shallow gasps.

Rowan dared not breathe himself.

Dara's dark hair spilled against the carpet in a wet, tangled mass. His fingers absently skimmed over her rain- and blood-washed clothes, which were now soaking the trampled rug. The name she had uttered had stabbed through his chest and left his mind briefly numbed. His destined mate had just called for her dead lover, a friend he'd once known… The one whose place he had been chosen to take.

By Great Danu, how he hated himself.

Rowan stirred and lifted the sodden woolen cloth away from Dara's skin. He easily tore it from around the arrow, back and front. His soggy hair tumbled in thick red knots about his face as he pulled the shredded shirt from underneath Dara's unconscious body. He bent over her again, scanning for more injuries.

She moaned again, cracking open sightless eyes. "The H-Hound…" she mumbled. "Mom says if Tara's soil touches its h-heart, it will…will…die."

"Shhh, the Hound is gone now. Don't talk, Dara," he whispered, his hands working on her—but she'd fallen still again.

She had strapped her leather scabbard over her plain, ivory-colored demi-bra as if it was a handgun's shoulder-holster. Its maroon straps circled both her shoulders and slanted against her bare back, and the empty scabbard hung beneath her left armpit, ready for a cross-draw.

Was she right-handed? At that blasted party she'd been holding her punch cup in her right hand…

Rowan shook his head, forcing out every stray thought but one. He must find a way to fix what he had carelessly wrought. He must make things right again.

Dark blood trickled from the arrow's entry and exit wounds. It streamed down Dara's rain-slick back and along the soft groove underlining her left collarbone, staining the ivory flesh crimson. Its course slanted to the valley hugged by her ample breasts, ending within the carpet's disheveled furrows. Wrenching the arrow out of Dara's body would likely turn the thin oozing into a furious gush.

Should he rush her to a hospital?

So close to the night's peak underneath the ripened moon, it was definitely out of the question. The transformation would come soon, and then… If he didn't take care of things *now*, Rowan knew, all would be lost. A soft growl of frustration climbed up his throat.

He was many things, but not a bleedin' medical doctor!

There was only one way he knew that might heal her… An ancient ritual reserved for destined lifemates, passed down through the generations. As a child Rowan had been told legends of *Slánú*…healing. What the term genuinely meant was channeling one's sexual energies to heal an injured lover. He wished he'd won Dara's consent for what he was about to try, but he was left with no other choice.

Dara stirred again, mumbling her lost lover's name. Her breasts heaved with fast, shallow breathing, almost animal-like. More than blood loss had triggered it—her body was already responding to the tangible spur of the full moon. This, along with the severe trauma she had suffered, was going to make a too-heavy load for her slender form to handle.

Rowan had come to a decision.

There was no going back. Not if he wanted her to live.

He reached down and undid the scabbard's leather rig. Next his knowing fingers fumbled behind Dara's back, unsnapping her bra.

His breath wedged in his throat as he caught his first glimpse of Dara's breasts. The ample creamy globes, surprisingly ripe for her slim figure, were topped with puffy rosy areolas. Rosebud nipples were pinched atop their velvety cushions, tight enough to stab the skin of his chest.

Had the pain brought it on?

Whatever was the reason, Rowan felt his cock grow rock hard, pressing against the rough fabric of his denim. Her blood had an enticing dark, metallic odor, both sweet and sharp, so rich he could almost taste it. Whether he wanted it or not, the unique scent of the spilled blood teased his tortured senses and intensified his arousal.

Settling himself on the rug, he unbuttoned her jeans, top to bottom. He slid his hand beneath the rough cloth, over her naked left hip. Her skin felt damp, burning beneath his palm.

"Dara."

He lowered his head to her hair. The heavy tresses were drenched with the biting aroma of fresh rain, and layered beneath it was *her*. Rowan's auburn curls swept down to mingle with Dara's dark ones. He brushed his face against the mud-caked hair, hunting for the unique scent that was all Dara, filling his lungs with it.

"You're in a bad shape, lass." His whisper slid along one burning cheek, his mouth dipping lower to kiss down her neck.

"And I am the bastard to blame for it."

Dara's scalding skin stifled Rowan's words. He determinedly dug his hand deeper beneath her jeans.

"If we don't do this, *mo cara*, you will die. I will not let that happen."

His caress delved lower, finding the smooth curve of her ass. Her waistband chafed his forearm. He splayed his fingers over a burning ass cheek and squeezed the supple flesh, hauling her body tighter against his own. The movement brought Dara's crotch close against Rowan's own aching groin.

His mate hadn't stirred.

He doubted she had even felt his touch, the way she lay unresponsive in his arms.

21

By Danu, he needed to hurry.

Embracing Dara with a muscled arm, he peeled her jeans down the swell of her thighs. Her white undies went with it. His gaze went to the dark fuzz of curls shading her sex, nested damp and tangled against her pale flesh. His cock twitched against its denim cage. Rowan stifled a groan and slid Dara's jeans all the way down to her ankles. Taking great care to move her as little as possible, he stripped her completely. Every painful moan yanked out of her throat made his heart clench with fear and regret.

He had never experienced something like this, not since…

Jaw tight, he quenched the faded echoes of a long-buried childhood nightmare. An exceptionally gifted shifter, he'd always been so sure of his ability to manipulate his feelings with the same skill he used to manipulate his body. Obviously, he'd been wrong.

Rowan uttered a soft curse. There wasn't enough time to be afraid. Not now. He pushed all irrelevancies aside with a practiced will, squeezing the frosty lump in his chest into a tight knot.

Aye, he still had the knack for it.

"You'll soon be better, Dara."

Or so he hoped. The strained words had been meant for his own ears more than for hers. He slid up Dara's body, his caressing hand matching his body's movement, outlining the soft mounds and valleys of her lush curves. Her waist was so narrow, he could circle it with his hands alone. As his head finally reached hers, her breath touched his face with hot, broken gasps. He winced as the silver arrowhead grazed his own shoulder.

Leaning on one elbow, he loosened his belt and tugged his zipper down. Pressure eased on his throbbing shaft, pushing his aching erection free against his lower abdominal muscles.

He'd wanted this to happen differently.

With a large hand he cradled Dara's raised left thigh, slinging it over his waist. He slid his own leg over the fiery velvet of her right thigh, nudging her legs further apart, gasping as her feverish flesh touched the hard length of him…

And then he instantly froze at the feel of icy steel nudging his neck.

Rowan's eyes shot up, clashing with flaming dark brown ones.

"Do not," Dara whispered roughly, "move an inch."

Chapter Three

Dara prodded her dagger's point into the left side of Rowan's neck, just beneath the hard line of his lower jaw. He cursed wordlessly, recalling how he had shoved the weapon down his belt, carelessly disregarding it from then on. All she'd needed to do, and obviously *had* done, was reach out and draw it, reclaiming it for herself.

"I'm surprised," she whispered with visible effort, "you still have a hard-on under the current circumstances."

"Let go of your weapon, *céadsearc*." He hadn't moved an inch, complying with her whispered command.

In retort she dug the dagger's point deeper into his flesh, drawing a tiny red bead. "I don't think so," she spoke hoarsely.

"Please, *céadsearc*—"

"Quit...quit calling me that. That 'kay-djark' thing."

"*Céadsearc*. Means 'sweetheart' in Irish," he said, softening the word's true meaning. *First love*. "Dara, sweetheart, you're already burning with fever. 'Tis a Hound's arrow. It carries silver. Let me heal you."

He studied her face, his uncompromising hand still resting on the swell of her hip. Her eyes blazed brightly within the paleness of her skin, a feverish blush coloring her cheekbones.

"*Heal*?" She squeezed the word out through ragged breaths. "I'd call this...many things...other than that."

The hand gripping the dagger trembled, the whetted edge dancing against Rowan's throat. His Adam's apple rose and fell as he slowly swallowed.

"Heal," he repeated softly. "You are my destined mate, Dara. Our joining beneath the moon will heal you."

"My destined mate is *dead*." Dara shivered, her face tight with pain and bottled-up fury.

"You know the ancient Law as well as I." Rowan's hand rested stone-still over her hip. "We are Kanjali. Bound-Ones. We mate for life. If one of us loses his lifemate, and has the gift of bearing young ones, then he or she is to be mated again, to a spouse chosen by the *Cainteoirì* — the Speakers."

"I d-don't know what you mean. I don't give a shit about your *Law*." Mackey's words made no sense to Dara's blurring mind. She bit her lower lip and squeezed her sweaty fist tighter on her dagger's hilt. It grew heavy in her hand, forcing her to shift its position against Rowan's neck.

He spoke again through clenched teeth. "By Danu, lass, do you *want* to die?"

"I'll be sure to take you down with me when I do," she breathed out.

A lapse of consciousness slackened her body, and for a fraction of a second Rowan felt Dara's dagger falling away from his skin.

He moved fast.

The moon, now acting as a ghostly catalyst, made him even faster than usual. His hand shot up from Dara's hip to her wrist as he smoothly arched back from her dagger's point. She let out a groan, her arms straining in his hold, then sagging. She had no strength left to resist him. Her eyes locked with his.

"Please," she whispered. "Don't…" Her voice was barely audible.

He stared down at her, then his head jerked in a brief nod. "Aye, you win. Halfway, you win." He cursed softly, his Irish brogue gathering roughness and color. "I will not take you fully, but I *will* make sure you'll end up with the living, whether you prefer it or otherwise."

Her head sagged back against the damp rug. He put her weapon safely out of her arm's reach. He then dipped his head again, brushing his mouth over hers. Wearily she turned her face away, escaping his touch. Her lashes trembled as her eyes grew heavy-lidded.

"Aye, close your eyes, sweetheart. Imagine it is *him*."

His lips trailed over the cheek she gave him, leaving soft kisses in their wake. Dara gasped as his gentle touch tingled with laden electricity, an echo of something she had known once before.

"Just get it over with." Her voice came out strangled.

In response, his fingers drew lazy circles against her back, caressing, steadying. He slowly shifted with her in his arms, sitting up, cradling her as he would a child. Her hair fell in a wet mass over the arch of his left arm. The arrow jutted from her back, icy cold against his fingertips. By now the bleeding had almost stopped. He wasn't sure whether that was a good sign. His free hand stroked down the side of his reluctant mate's face, where his mouth had just touched.

"Dara, sweetheart."

Dara's eyes were fully closed now, her lips moving silently.

Aidan, her lips were forming. *Aidan. Aidan.*

Rowan leaned his head down to trace his mouth along the delicate lines of her eyebrows. His hands caressed down her neck, searched lower and cupped the lushness of a full breast. His fingers were tinted with her blood. He felt her body going rigid again, before succumbing to his touch.

Her skin was like liquid fire. He'd never known this wealth of sensation before.

She was making small sounds as he touched her. He mumbled sweet nothings into her tousled hair, speaking the ancient tongue, though he guessed that growing up in this foreign land, Dara had no knowledge of Irish Gaelic. His fingertips circled her velvety areolas, feeling the rosy pads wrinkle and raise firm. He ached to suck the sensitive rosebuds into his mouth until they were blushed and swollen, but now wasn't the time to take her this way.

Dara moaned, her nipples tightening, as this stranger — this brazen Irishman who seemed intent on making her live — gently toyed with her flesh. This man's hand on her breast aroused an ache deeper than the one caused by the arrow wound. She felt his cock growing against her naked back, but wouldn't open her eyes. The more his hands lingered over her skin, the more charged his touch became. She let out a soft scream as invisible energy jetted between the two of them, stretching and roiling whenever his fingertips withdrew from her skin and found it again. She groaned at how alien, yet familiar, his touch was. Twisting beneath his fingers, she craved more, hating herself for it... Screaming as the movement shifted the poisonous silver wedged in her shoulder.

"Lie still." His warm hand both soothed and inflamed her, studying her body with long, sure strokes. Neck to ass to low thighs, thighs to tummy to breasts, his fingers nurtured every curvaceous detail. "Let my hands do the moving, sweetheart."

She struggled to remain still as his fingers drew burning circles over the soft swell of her abdomen, shuddering each time the circle's edge tugged at the first curls of her sex. She was weak with blood loss and maddened by the gnawing pain in her shoulder, too close to the peak of the full moon. Her mind shut down, leaving her body dazzled, every sensation raw. As Rowan's hand plunged through the fiery flesh of her inner thighs and cupped her sex, her eyes flew open. A low growl formed deep in her throat.

Rowan's gaze shot up at the sound, alarmed, colliding with the molten amber that had already flooded Dara's eyes.

"Easy, Dara." The plea was uttered like a soft command, his own voice strung tight with barely contained want. "You can't take a full transformation right now."

"Oh Goddess, then make me right!" Close to screaming, she dug her right hand into his chest, emerging claws tearing through the faded shirt. Her left arm was numb with pain, cradled below her breasts.

He sucked in his breath at the sharp pain inflicted by her clawed hand. She was losing control fast, and his brow gathered sweat as he struggled to hold on to his own restraint. His fingers slid against her soaked, heated flesh and parted her folds, finding the firm nub of her clit.

Dara's thighs slowly parted and closed around his hand as he touched her center. She arched her neck and pressed her head against his supporting arm, her eyes glowing a soft gold. Moaning, her hand clawed deeper into Rowan's chest.

"*Dara*," Rowan groaned painfully, but didn't twist away from her. Bright yellow flickered in his gaze and faded as he arduously regained control.

She raked her hand down his shirt with a sharp tearing noise as his sensitive fingers kept circling her slick clit and pressing into the engorged flesh, starting a sinuous massage.

"Goddess," she half-growled, her hips bucking to meet his moving hand.

Rowan's shirt hung in bloody strips over his chest and abdomen, the muscled flesh oozing dark red from five linear slashes. It stung like bleedin' hell, but *she* was burning even fiercer in his arms. With his palm still crushing her clit, he eased two long fingers through her entrance into her searing heat. Her walls felt puffy and drenched, lubricating his fingers with her juices as they rocked and circled inside her cunt. She felt like an oven, her sodden flesh sucking him in, making wet sounds around his moving fingers.

Dara screamed, her human cry shifting to a bestial howl as she felt him stabbing his fingers deep inside her. His touch drove fizzy energy straight through her core, stirred biting currents into her very essence. His fingers kept pumping into her, as he tightened his supporting arm about her rib cage with a steely force, keeping her from moving her upper body.

"I can't." She panted and struggled, whimpering with a harsh blend of rapture and pain. "Can't take...any more of it... Rowan!"

Her hips danced with an innate rhythm as his fingers fucked her harder, faster. And then her cunt was rippling and tightening around his buried fingers in short, quick squeezes. A violent shudder overtook her body. She was howling wildly, baying a name at the veiled moon.

Rowan shut his eyes with a sharp, brief pain, because the name she had called had not been his own.

He pulled his soaking fingers out of her rippling cunt and closed a wet fist on the arrow's tail. There was no *good* way to extract the bleedin' thing in this desolate place, far from any hope of medical aid. Steadying Dara in his hold, Rowan snapped off the arrow's fletched tail.

She groaned.

He wished he could take her pain away.

"I'm sorry, sweetheart." His jaw tight, Rowan drove the remaining shaft through Dara's shoulder with a deliberate, forceful thrust.

Her body stiffened and arched in his firm embrace, quaking with another savage howl. Her cry broke at its peak and culminated in a raw, human-sounding scream.

Rowan clutched the bloody shaft against the front of Dara's shoulder. With a clean pull he wrenched the arrow from her flesh. She had gone limp and quiet in his arms, making his heart skip a beat. His fist was still clenched around the arrow's shaft, knuckles white with strain. The silver plaited throughout it singed his palm and he growled, spreading his fingers, letting the slim lethal rod bounce against the rug.

With a mounting, sickening wave of fear, he drew Dara's body up against him. Her left shoulder was drenched with blood. He swept his hand through the still-warm liquid, exploring the skin hidden beneath. Finding it whole, he raised her further into his arms and ran his tongue over her skin in wide, quick lashes. He cleansed her with swift strokes—her blood both sweet and pungent on his tongue—then drew back.

Great Danu, she truly was whole again!

Releasing a long-held breath, he gently rotated her in his arms and studied her back.

She *was* healed.

He had healed her.

A surge of pride and relief swept through him. The fever was gone, and her pulse had stopped bouncing madly, falling into a quick, yet steady pace. She appeared closer to sleep than unconsciousness.

He laid her down atop the crushed rug and stretched alongside her, marveling at how small she was, and at how close he had come to losing her. Listening to her quick, soft breathing, he absently ran his hand over the bruised skin of his chest and abdomen, only to find the wounds she had branded him with gone. Her touch had healed him, as well.

Suddenly, an alarming thought hit Rowan.

The Hound could still be prowling out there.

He leapt to his feet, forcing himself to go over each window and scrutinize every shady corner. His pending transformation made that simple task hard to carry out.

The locals seemed to have done a formidable job on the place. Though at a glance it appeared to be no more than a deserted storehouse, each window had been well-barred. There was only a single entryway, equipped with a solid, robust door that could be latched with a heavy bolt only from the inside. Rowan lifted the bolt into its intended position with a groan and a bulge of muscles. No ordinary Mortal could have accomplished it, not without another man, maybe more, aiding him.

A sharp tearing noise followed by a low rumble made Rowan turn around carefully. A pair of golden eyes gleamed at him from the niche where he'd left Dara asleep.

"Dara?" he whispered softly into the darkness. His own eyes took on an amber glow.

The beast watching him was bathed in Dara's scent, its jaws clutched around Dara's clothing—what was left of her jeans, anyway. The quivering energy emanating from its lean, muscular body tasted like his mate's sweet and pungent life force, which he had earlier sampled. It *was* Dara, fully transformed—her injury had cost her her self-control. Her golden eyes shone amidst thick dark fur, and sharp fangs glistened within her gaping mouth.

She was approaching him slowly on all fours, shaking away fading scraps of mist. She paused to pin the jeans against the floor with a clawed paw, then rip them beyond hope of repair with a forceful shake. The torn denim dropped from her mouth as she kept stalking towards him.

Seemed like she was right vexed.

Rowan bit back an involuntary smile. Dara would be in an even worse mood in the morning when she looked for her clothes.

Rowan backed away and was stopped by the latched door. It was pressing coldly against the shirt that clung to his back. He could feel, as much as hear, the squall outside—the rain hammering in undulating gushes against the building's frame, the wind shrieking madly, crushed by rolling thunder.

The beast that was Dara halted about ten, twelve feet away from him. He gave her a soft warning growl, lashing his own Power out to entwine with the moon's cool grasp. He couldn't risk holding on to his human form for long, not with *her* gazing at him with that ominous, steady glare. Somehow, he had to get them both through this night, preferably alive and in one piece.

The moon finally answered Rowan's silent call, spilling its Power down on him. Its silvery light molded his shifter's body, sweeping him away.

Chapter Four

"I must be dead."

Dara propped her forearms against the cement flooring, coughing up a few stray dust bunnies.

"*Naked* and dead," she pointed out wryly as she glanced down at her bare breasts. She was deeply startled to get a swift answer, one sounding alarmingly nearby.

"Dead, lass? Does this feel anything like *Tír Na nÓg* to you?"

Male voice. Irish accent. Gaelic gibberish.

Her mind slowly added it all up, coming to the inevitable conclusion.

Rowan Mackey.

Along with the name surfaced some of the previous night's sizzling memories, which made her groan aloud and drop her pulsing head between her hands. It was pounding like the worst hangover she'd ever had. She had a vague recollection of what *Tír Na nÓg* meant—and no, this glum place felt nothing like The Land of the Ever-Young, the Otherworld. In fact, it felt more and more like some mild version of her friends' Christian hell.

"Did I transform?" Dara's voice rose muffled from her buried face.

"Aye, fully."

"Did we...uh..."

"No. I keep my vows, Dara. You didn't want me to take you last night."

"Well, it did feel like a bit of a stretch after you'd almost got me killed."

Remembering, Dara's hand shot to her left shoulder, finding nothing beneath the sweat and mud caking. *Goddess, the brazen Irishman must have actually healed her!* Slowly she sat up, nauseated, her mind still caught in a whirl.

"Full transformation erases one's memory," she muttered. "No wonder my mind's a black hole. Last thing I remember is…"

Your fingers inside me, she had almost blurted out.

Suddenly ultra-aware of her nudity, Dara's face heated, and she desperately hoped the flush was masked by the shadowy darkness. She let out a soft gasp and turned her back on the naked man beside her. Her frenzied gaze darted around, searching for anything remotely resembling her clothing. She found only a fairly large vacant space, its periphery darkened by solid masses. Stored equipment? Crates of some kind?

"I have never blacked out with full transformation," Rowan said softly, his subdued intonation teasing a soft tremor up Dara's spine. "Shapechanging is a knack of mine. And you won't find any of your clothes here, sweetheart. Your *mac'tir* form ripped them to shreds."

He spoke in a low, husky voice. That, along with his vibrant accent, was a heady blend. Still caught within the aftershocks of the night's transformation, Dara's painfully heightened senses could trace all-too-well his musky odor of intermingled skin, sweat, and fur, both masculine and bestial. His scent clung to her skin. It was an aroma she'd used to smell on Aidan.

"My parents told me no one could sustain any memories when turning full *mac'tir*. That's why we struggle to avoid it, to stop at mid-transformation." Dara gathered up her knees, hugging herself. Her breasts flattened beneath her thighs, cool, pebble-hard nipples peaking against her legs. *Dammit, but the obnoxious Irishman was having the most deleterious, delicious effect on her!* She was determined to keep that particular fact hidden from him, as well as shut her mind to the man's coaxing assault on her senses.

"I don't need to stop at mid-transformation in order to keep control." Rowan made no attempt to touch her. "Last night, after you had fully transformed, I had to turn *mac'tir* myself. Else your beast form would have treated *me* as nicely as it did your clothes."

Dara shuddered visibly at the notion.

"My dagger?" she inquired, not knowing what else to say.

"I'll hold on to your exquisite dagger for now, since we will be sharing a common destination."

"We're doing no such thing!"

Dara leaped to her feet and swiveled about to gaze directly down at him, momentarily forgetting her lack of clothing. She was about to yell some more, but instead fell into a silent stare. It was the first time she'd laid eyes on Rowan Mackey since the previous night's ordeal.

The man was stark naked, and obviously happy to see her.

"Aye?" He cocked a fiery brow, lips curling into a small lopsided grin.

Dara couldn't help but stare.

Daylight seeped through the elongated cracks in one barred window, throwing out diagonal shafts that streaked and softly illumined his body. He lay on his side, propped up on his right elbow, his impressive height of about six-and-a-half feet stretched fully along the hard cement.

The first thing her eyes bumped into was his long, thick cock beaming up at her. Neither the cold, nor her angry gaze seemed to have a deterring effect on the fierce erection jutting from amidst his dark ginger curls.

Next, her gaze stroked over his skin, but the room's mix of light and dark stripes made it hard to guess his complexion. His biceps bulged on the propped arm, a snaking vein cording beneath his skin. He held his left knee raised and shamelessly flexed, giving Dara a clear view of his long, hard thigh muscles all the way to his groin.

Her gaze flicked to his cock again before surfing up his narrow waist, dipping into his shallow navel, and climbing up the soft, well-defined swells of his abdominal muscles. The tour ended on the coin-flat nipples gilding the lower rims of his glorious pecs, and, Goddess, his chest looked hard and silky-smooth. Dara suddenly yearned to flatten her tongue against that slick skin.

Goddess, she'd never felt such an uncontrollable surge of passion.

Not since she'd been with Aidan.

Dara wrenched her eyes upwards and collided with Rowan's steady stare. Obviously, he had been watching her watching him. A streak of sunlight thrown over the reclining Irishman's face made his eyes catch green fire, and ignited his shoulder-length hair with a fiery copper-red.

Dara's cheeks burned. "So you're a natural redhead," she muttered.

He threw his head back, his laughter thundering around the vacant storehouse. "Would you like me to turn around for you now?" he spoke in between deep chuckles. "I mean, you did grant me a generous view of *your* backside earlier."

"I'm sorry, I didn't mean to stare."

"You hid it perfectly well, then."

Rowan slowly coiled and rose to his feet in one fluid movement. Dara had to crane her neck so she could meet his heated eyes. He reached down and before Dara managed to recover and withdraw, her left hand was enfolded between his warm, large palms. His mere touch sent a ripple of heat up her arm.

"Still hurts?" he gently inquired.

"N-no," she stuttered. "You somehow managed to take care of that tiny, fatal-arrow-wound problem."

"We both did that, sweetheart. *Slánú* works only for those destined to be together."

"Well, see, that's where *I* have a problem, Rowan. I'm not your, nor anybody else's, sweetheart." She made a futile attempt to tug her trapped hand free. "And I'd like my hand back," she demanded.

Before I'm reduced to Jell-O, her mind silently added.

"You called me by my first name." Mackey grinned with triumph and eased his grip.

Dara gave her head a desperate shake, snatching her hand back from captivity. Her arm was still tingling with a pleasant case of goose bumps. She groaned and swiveled on her heels, resolutely turning her back on the man. Her eyes darted around in another search.

"Door's that way," Rowan pointed.

She frowned with suspicion and turned, glimpsing the bolted door he'd drawn her attention to. "It had better be open when I get there," she tossed over her shoulder, already marching towards the farthest wall of the warehouse.

"Of course, you can't leave here on your own," his voice trailed lazily behind her.

"Oooooh, you just watch me."

Rowan was indeed watching her.

Most intently.

Her raven curls bounced against her bare back and her tight, full ass cheeks engaged in a sensual, rhythmic dance as she paced barefoot across the dusty floor, stamping it with clear, small footprints.

He crossed his arms over his chest and waited as she struggled to lift the bolt.

"If the door bars things such as the *Cú*..." Rowan smiled patiently at Dara's shapely back, " — do you think it will yield to your gentle tugs, lass?"

He spoke his last word just as Dara had finished a series of thundering kicks and fist-poundings aimed at the door. The darn thing didn't budge, but her hands and bare feet were hurting like hell. She was still trying to figure out a more insolent way of saying *"let me the fuck out of this damn hole"* when Mackey's words registered in her mind.

"*Cú,*" Dara repeated, her sweaty palms still pressed flat against the door. "Isn't that the Gaelic word for…for 'Hound'?"

"Aye, 'tis," Rowan replied, somewhat surprised.

Beware of Hounds, Dara. "Tell me, Rowan, what…?" Dara hesitated, head bowed. "What, exactly, is a Hound?"

"A Hound is a shifter, same as us," Rowan replied, his astonishment growing at Dara's question. *Had she no knowledge of what a Cú – a Hound – was?* "Only…not the same. 'Tis a hunter of our kind. A vileness," he added, choosing his words.

"Oh." Dara gave the door one last, violent kick just for the heck of it. She folded in two, bending to nurse her aching foot.

Rowan couldn't help but give a slight flinch at the sight. "Now that we've established that without my help you're safely locked in," he said, shaking his head, "would you *please* hear me out?"

Slowly Dara rotated away from the door, bestowing a new meaning upon the expression "if looks could kill".

"Talk," she told Rowan with a sweet smile.

* * * * *

Close to four thousand years, and counting.

He'd come close to ending it last night, so close that rage still seethed red-hot, charring his already-blackened insides. The creature currently named Adam Conway stood in deathly silence, bow and quiver slung against his back, facing an Oregon winter sunrise.

The night's thunderstorm had already died away into a steady drizzle. Adam's lithe, gaunt form was indifferent to the east wind's icy battering and to the light rain stinging his fully exposed face. Through a gap in the rain he watched the black, rough triangle of Mount Hood silhouetted against the sky's deep crimson. Blood-red, matching the burning anger inside him.

He wasn't used to dealing with scorching-hot feelings, nor was he at ease with prodding himself with questions and doubts. His life was a series of missions and accomplishments.

Finding his prey.

Making a kill.

Getting food.

Adam shoved both his hands in his pockets and sighed.

Sighing...now, that was a human habit. Walking for thousands of years among the Mortals in search of Kanjali shifters had made some of their annoying human habits linger on his skin like a bad smell. There were enjoyable habits, as well... His lips curled into a wicked, thin smile as he thought of the little street hooker he'd made use of a couple of nights before. Her terrified screams, sweet music to his ears, were still ringing in his head. He was rock-hard at the thought. His tongue flicked over his lips, tasting remembered blood.

He was tired of acquiring bad habits. Tired of walking among the Mortals. Tired of his emotions swinging between hot and cold. He missed being called by his true name, *Adhamh.* Missed the earth that had borne him. He was the last of his kind, and that felt...well...

Lonely.

The Hound turned from the bleeding sunrise and cast a hungry look in the general direction of the seemingly deserted warehouse. As the wind beat his long, night-black hair against his pale face, he sniffed the morning air. A hint of a scent wafted about his nostrils, camouflaged by the wind's interference. He could almost feel his claws lengthening in response, boring into his palms.

Only one true passion was still blazing inside him. He wanted to rest again within the Earth's sheltering embrace, knowing nothing, feeling nothing...a nameless sand grain among countless, nameless others.

And no one was going to stand in his way.

Surely not this shapechanging couple that smelled so sweetly of Kanjali blood.

Chapter Five

"I was told that you'd come here very young, Dara."

"Yeah, my parents immigrated to the U.S. from Ireland when I was about four. They chose to make Rose City the O'Shea family's new 'home-sweet-home'. What's that got to do with anything?"

They both reclined upon the spacious top of a tarpaulin-covered crate. Earlier, Rowan had shamelessly slung his leg atop it and lounged against the wall, humming some cheery Irish tune with surprising resonance until Dara had decided she had no other choice but to join him there. When she had, she'd sat rigidly as far from him as possible, her arms locked firmly over her breasts. She was not about to enlighten the man as to her nipples' constantly erect state!

"I'm trying to find out how much you know of our tradition," he continued.

"Just enough to hate the primitive mumbo jumbo," she countered.

"Yet you abided by it. Your mate was a *Chosen*," Rowan stated, ignoring her quipping.

"A Chosen?" Dara sounded genuinely confused. "I've no idea what you mean by that. My *husband*, Aidan Neilan, was Irish, born and raised. My parents played matchmaker and introduced us. I married Aidan because I was in love with him, not because of some zany, New Age 'Chosen' bullshit. Since he...died, I..." Her voice trailed off. She stared fixedly into the warehouse's sunlight-dappled dimness.

"Did Aidan ever take you to Tara?" Rowan spoke again after a slight pause. "To the Destiny Stone — *Lia Fáil*?"

"*Lia Fáil*... Oh, you mean that dick-shaped stone?"

Rowan flinched at that one. "The Speakers will be fascinated with your description of *Lia Fáil*."

"The Speakers?" Dara frowned, rocking her bare feet against the crate. "That sure sounds like one of those wacky, uh, *spiritual* terms. Who are they? Some circle of demented elders channeling higher entities and doing Chakra workouts?"

Rowan fought back a smile picturing Bantiarna Niamh's exact expression should she hear this conversation. A longtime leader of the Speakers circle, she would have cocked a sandy brow at Dara's "demented elders" designation. Niamh, his godmother, didn't look her age one bit. But what was an over nine-hundred-year-old lady supposed to look like? She certainly didn't look the motherly type, or the godmotherly type, if there was such a thing. Short-cut sandy hair and almond-shaped eyes, silvery-blue as cobalt, came to mind when he thought of the Bantiarna. She'd always been spoken of that way — as Bantiarna, the Lady — though there was no permanent Lord, or Tiarna, in her life. According to the strict Gaelic feudal system, women could not hold nobility titles in their own right. Their titles were a courtesy only, while the men were the actual titleholders. But then again, the Kanjali shifters had never claimed to be true Irish Gaelic.

Dara was eyeing Rowan with a curious stare. "So, are we done here?"

"Not quite." Rowan leaned back and watched her, his face in shadows. "Your parents were...?"

"Killed in a car accident three years ago," she answered faintly after a long pause. "I lost Aidan a couple of months later that same year. Look, I've had enough small talk, Romeo. Open the damn door!"

Dara hopped down from the crate, long past caring what the sudden jolt would do to her breasts. A soft groan coming from above told her that Rowan had noticed the way her breasts had just jiggled. Sliding down smoothly, he towered above her.

She could sense his gaze roving over her body, warming her to the core. Her treacherous nipples came to attention.

Again.

"Let's cut a deal." His eyes were still somewhat shadowed, but she could swear they held a roguish glint. "Deals, that's the American way, aye? I'll open the…er…damn door." One side of his mouth shot up in a slanting grin. "But you'll let me accompany you. I'll eventually get out of your life, but first you will indulge me with a small trip."

"I'm not playing *quid pro quo* with you."

"Of course we could just as well stay here, sweetheart."

"Goddess, you can't be serious!"

"Oh, you just watch me," he retorted.

Dara gave an incoherent scream, her hands balling into fists. She swiveled a hundred-eighty degrees and took a few fast strides away from him, then skidded to a stop and thought the better of it. She whipped around and marched back, halting no more than a few inches from Rowan.

"This is blackmail, Mackey," she growled. "A very, very primitive form of blackmail!"

He watched her face with stoic amusement, again neglecting to respond to the obvious.

Dara's fists itched with the desire to pound against his chest, but his nudity made her aim higher.

Goddess, how she ached to wipe that tiny smug smile off his face!

Her right fist flew of its own will and slammed into his hard, arrogant jaw. He gave a slight groan, but his stance didn't waver.

"I guess I deserved that." The Irishman flexed his jaw, rubbing his hand against it.

"You've got yourself a deal, Mackey." She assumed a calm voice, her teacher's voice.

"And you've got one mean right hook, sweetheart."

Rowan ambled towards the door, his back turned from her, so she could only guess as to his expression. He sounded suspiciously as if he were speaking through one of his impish grins. She silently wished him all kinds of nasty things, most of them unfortunate mishaps involving his family jewels. Her gaze betrayed her, falling to the muscles flexing in his tight buttocks as he walked. Arriving at the entrance, muscles rippled in his upper back and shoulders as he lifted the hefty bolt and lowered it to the concrete with a grunt. Dara felt her treacherous tongue run over her dry lips in keen admiration for the show, and she pinched herself once, *hard*.

"Oh, that trip you mentioned," Dara spoke, mainly to stop herself from thinking. "Where are we heading?"

"To the dick-shaped stone, I believe," Rowan answered calmly as he stepped naked into the late morning's sun.

"Oh, no! No, no, *no*! No fucking way, Mackey!"

Dara stormed out after him, and froze as bright sunlight washed down over her naked skin. Of course, Mackey was already lurking out there, leaning against her Silverado. As if to add a bit of panache, he was also ankle-deep in mud-drowned grass.

"Now that's just fucking lovely," Dara bit out, raising furious eyes from Mackey's feet to his face. "That's just fucking grea—"

She was arming her tongue with an exceptionally sarcastic remark when the words wedged in her throat.

For a frozen moment it seemed as though an Irish Apollo had alighted his sun-chariot for a brief visit.

Rowan's still, nude form was displayed against the softly rounded roll of dark green hills, and beyond that rose Mount Hood's snow-clad, sharp-angled peak, majestic and ethereal. Both Rowan's rowdy hair and his eyes were ablaze. He wasn't wearing his usual grin. Not a tiny smile, even. In truth, he'd been watching Dara so intently she thought his gaze would burn right into her.

* * * * *

The rain had rinsed clean even this forsaken patch of untamed land in the farthest outskirts of the city. The foreign soil now oozed a familiar, fresh smell—it made Rowan's thoughts drift back home, to Ireland. As Dara charged after him, the morning light showered her pale skin with a bright luster. Caught by surprise, she stopped dead in her tracks, failing to latch her hands over her breasts. Rowan looked his fill at her creamy body, from the patch of black pelt at her thighs' juncture to the round, pink nipples jutting from her lush swells.

And then she lifted fuming dark brown eyes, her gaze lashing at him from behind her tumbled raven locks. Her cheeks were an intense red. When their gazes met, his heart skipped a beat for the second time these last twelve hours.

Dara found her tongue first.

"Anything I can help you with?" she snapped.

"You're beautiful," he said simply.

"Oh." She shifted uneasily from one foot to another, averting her eyes from his furious erection, finally remembering to cross her hands over her breasts. Which left her crotch bare. Which made her frown and drop her hands to her hips while glaring menacingly at Rowan.

"Look, I'm not flying to Ireland with you."

"I said nothing of flying."

"Maybe I should rephrase that. There's absolutely *no fucking way* I'm leaving U.S. territory with you. Hey, what the hell are you doing? Move away from my truck!"

Too damn late.

His upper body disappeared behind the Chevy's front door as he leaned into the driver's seat. She'd left her car keys jammed inside.

"Just a precaution. 'Tis not safe taking your car. The Hound obviously saw you arrive." Rowan slid back out and slammed the door shut, her keys jangling in his hand.

"Let me guess." Dara's eyes were shooting daggers again. "You'll 'hold on to my car keys for now, since we're sharing a common destination'. Just like you borrowed my dagger. Say, Romeo, where are you planning to hide all these pretty metal objects, you being naked an' all. Up your ass?"

His brow quirked. "Such words from the mouth of a kiddie teacher!"

"I'm a swimming teacher," she snapped. "I care more about keeping the 'kiddies' heads above the water than my exact choice of words!"

Rowan clicked his tongue with mock reprimand as he strode straight towards her in what appeared to be a direct collision course. She scowled, deciding she wasn't going to budge for him, and he brushed just past her, skin barely touching skin.

"Our ride's just around the back, along with some food and clothing. Unless you feel you need neither."

Dara found her hands instinctively balling into fists again.

Goddess, but the guy was an impossible jerk!

An impossible, *gorgeous* jerk.

A loud yelp from the warehouse's rear startled Dara into finally following Mackey to the back of the squat building. She thought she heard him roaring something about "bold brats trying to lift a fella's motorcycle". Quickening her pace, she ran straight into the show.

A GSX-R 600 white and blue Suzuki, presumably the aforementioned ride, stood against the back of the storehouse next to a tumbledown shed. Its tires were mud-tarnished and its smooth frame still glistened with raindrops. Had Rowan actually been insane enough to ride his bike here through last night's storm?

The source of the shrieks was writhing wildly in Rowan's steely hold. His arm muscles swiftly jumped to attention as he held his captive a good few inches above the ground. It fell and curled into a scruffy bundle as Rowan abruptly let go, waving one of his hands with a curse.

"She bleedin' bit me!"

"Good!" Dara lashed out.

The bundle uncurled and leaped to her feet, swiping angrily at the mire pasted to her butt. Her hands patted and tugged, smoothing down her green woolen dress and gray cloak. She then gave a fierce shake to the golden-red mane that cascaded over her shoulders.

"I didn't bite you!" The girl brandished a condemning finger at Rowan's chest. She had obviously meant to wave it in his face, but was far too short for that. "And I wasn't stealing your metal junkpile. I was just trying it on for a fit!"

Something flashed within her gaping cloak.

"Silver," Rowan growled. "You're wearing silver in there. You didn't bite me, you just bleedin' burned me!"

"Well an' who told you to shove your hands down my dress?"

"Are you two related?" Dara interrupted.

"Related?" the girl chirped with an Irish flavor. "To this bucket of snots?"

Rowan's nostrils flared.

Dara groaned and took a step that placed her between the two. She laid a restraining hand against the fuming Irishman's chest. Goddess, his skin *did* feel velvety smooth, and beneath that smoothness rippled perfectly hard muscles…

She shook her head, hoping to shake out each and every sassy thought involving Rowan Mackey.

She felt ridiculous, attempting to stop the Irish version of the Incredible Hulk from swooping down on a sneering Thumbelina. Not to mention that both Dara and the Hulk were butt-naked.

"'Tis nothing but a birth charm." The girl closed her fingers around the silver amulet dangling from her slim neck. "A Celtic birth charm."

"May I see it, then?" Dara hoped she managed a friendly, candid smile while trying to ignore Rowan's disgruntled rumble beneath her palm. She staunched a barely controllable urge to grit out, *down, boy*.

The girl gazed back at her with light gray teacup eyes. Dara stifled a faint shudder. Within the face of a young woman, those huge eyes of shifting smoke and clouds shone with ancient wisdom. The girl shrugged, snapping Dara out of her spell. The amulet's delicate silver chain stretched as she carefully extended her cupped hand and unclasped her fingers.

"A raven," Dara mumbled, as she cautiously leaned forward to take a closer look.

Even saying the word felt like an understatement. The amulet gleamed with a silver so rich its surface seemed to flow, flashing a dazzling white with the slightest hint of sunlight. It almost hurt to look at it. The engraved bird, the work of a master craftsman, gave the disturbing impression that any minute now it was about to flap its wings and soar off its metal platform.

"'Tis my sign, since I was born on the first of November," the girl cheerfully informed Dara.

"Oh! Happy birthday then." The increasing pressure against Dara's palm told her that Rowan was taking an interest in the silver amulet as well. Her fingers fluttered against his strong heartbeat, infusing warmth up her arm. Her betraying nipples demonstrated acute awareness of the man's closeness.

She sneaked a downward glance.

At least part of him demonstrated—quite visibly—a similar, keen awareness of *her*.

Dara snatched her hand from Rowan's chest, her face glowing scarlet.

A miscalculation.

With the obstacle of her arm removed, Rowan inched closer. *Much* closer. Touchy-feely close. Dara bit her lip while trying hard not to look down. Her eyes whipped sideways in search of escape.

Rowan draped an arm around her shoulders, the surprise move briefly stunning Dara into immobility. He bit back a smile, letting his fingertips roam back and forth along his willful mate's arm.

"The sign of *Samhain*," he said at length as he studied the crafted silver, his sizzling senses finally gaining focus. "Who, by the name of the Great Mother, *are* you, lass?"

"Should've asked me that before you ate the head off of me!" The girl slipped her pendant back beneath her cloak and fastened the gray cloth over the shifting glimmer. "I'm Brighid. With an 'H' and a 'D', mind you."

"And what are you bleedin' doing here, eh, Brig-Hid?" Rowan pronounced the "H" and the "D" in a way that made the petite redhead frown deeply.

"Getting sick and tired of tracking the two of you down across two continents, both Above and Below," she growled in response.

"Hold on a minute there, Brid." Rowan's nimble fingers had just dipped into the soft, inner hollow of Dara's elbow. "Why were you tracking us down? And what's this 'above and below' rubbish?"

"Well, I was trying to warn you two against a possible Hound hit," Brighid admitted sheepishly.

"You sure blew that one," Dara mumbled. She let out an involuntary yelp as Rowan traced a particularly sensitive spot inside her elbow. Twisting desperately, she managed to break free of his embrace.

"I'm aware of my disgraceful failure." Brighid meanwhile had the decency to appear embarrassed regarding the overall state of affairs. "See, I—uh—'blew' it 'cause I miscalculated my slip Up," she supplied helpfully.

"How can you miscalculate a slip-up?" Dara wondered aloud. Her fingers absently skimmed over her abandoned elbow.

Rowan took notice, concealing a soft grin.

"I believe she means something a wee bit different than you, Dara." He brushed his hand through his hair, increasing the fiery mayhem. "She might mean she miscalculated the time, or the place, of her slipping Up here from her world Below."

"You don't mean she came from..." Dara's eyes darted to Brighid, who now bore a look of growing impatience.

"Aye, from the Otherworld. She's Sidhe," Rowan said softly. "I think she's *bean-sidhe*, judging by her looks—the cape, the green gown. Aren't you, Brid?"

"Rowan, did you just say *banshee*?" Dara sounded alarmed. "Let's put aside for a sec the fact that I *do not* believe in fairies. Being tracked down by a banshee is supposed to be good, *how*? Isn't she a foreteller of death? A bad omen?"

"Could you possibly be more insulting?" Brighid stomped a booted foot against the sodden grass, splatting mud in an impressive arc. "And 'tis truly grand hearing a shifter claiming not to believe in fairies!"

"Americans." Rowan rolled his eyes. He quickly raised both palms in a gesture of mock surrender as Dara opened her mouth to retort. "No harm meant. Listen, Dara. According to Irish tradition, a banshee is much more than a warning of a person's death. 'Tis a family's guardian spirit, an ancestral spirit bound to a Mortal family—an old aristocratic Irish family, such as the O'Neills, the O'Briens, the O'Connors—"

"I don't need a lecture in Irish genealogy, pal!" Dara was close to stomping her own foot.

"And when one of the members of the family she's attached to is dying, and she can do nothing to save him, *then* you can hear the banshee's piercing cry on the night air, rolling over the hills of Ireland. That's where the 'bad omen' legends are rooted." Rowan lowered his voice secretively, deliberately stretching the last words.

"Moron." Dara suppressed a shudder. She hugged herself, drawing in a lungful of chilly air. The sunlight was dimming, and the skies were piling up rain clouds.

"Clothes," she growled with menace. "This has all been soooo much fun up 'til now, but it's starting to rain, dammit! I don't want to get wet until I'm wearing some *fucking* clothes!"

"So, *that's* what turns you on, eh, sweetheart? I'll try to keep it in mind for our next special time together." Rowan flashed one of his roguish smiles.

Dara flushed angrily and finally stomped her foot, lacking a matching verbal response.

Brighid threw her head back and laughed, her gray cloak ballooning about her in the mounting wind and rain.

Rowan reached for the knapsack secured to the back of his Suzuki and fumbled in its depths, fishing out a rolled-up t-shirt and throwing it at Dara.

"You *must* be kidding." She'd slipped Rowan's shirt over her head and was struggling to find where the sleeves were. As expected, the XXL-sized shirt hung low, brushing her lower thighs. "That's it? You expect me to *frolic* around in *this*?"

She swiveled just in time to catch Rowan pulling a pair of jeans up his naked ass. He half-turned to face her and zipped his jeans up with a devilish smile. His glorious upper torso remained naked. Raindrops dripped from tangled, dark copper locks, hit Rowan's chest, and engaged in a slow, sinuous slide to sneak beneath the denim's waistline.

Dara found herself wanting to follow the sneaky raindrops with her *tongue*.

She drew in a shaky breath, clenching and relaxing her fists.

"'Tis only a fair split, aye?" Rowan said, not missing Dara's mesmerized stare. "I don't carry more clothes than this. So you get the upper part, and I get the lower. My jeans are much too large for you anyway." With a devilish grin he added, "Not to mention you're used to *frolicking* around in a swimsuit in your line of work."

Dara gritted her teeth. He was giving her that *smile* — and her hands were itching to wipe it right off his face. "Okay, you've had your fun, Mackey, now give me back my car keys! There's no friggin' way I'm playing *Playboy* centerfold by hopping on that bike with nothing but your shirt on!" She gave him her own sweet smile, her tone chilly enough to freeze. "Coming to think of it, there's no friggin' way I'm hopping on that bike *at all*!"

"Nice try," Rowan said appreciatively, cutting her short. "But your car keys stay with me for now, and so do you. We made a deal, remember?" He stooped down to his Suzuki and fumbled again within his knapsack's depths, wrestling something out.

That's it. She wasn't taking any more of this shit!

"A *deal*? An extortion is more like it!" Dara leaped forward like a caged tiger cut loose.

Rowan turned away from his bike, something clutched in his hand, just as Dara stormed him. Her fists were suddenly hammering at his chest, and he could do nothing but stare at the frenzied look in her eyes and the tears streaming down her cheeks.

"*I hate you!*" She gritted between broken gasps. "I…"

Her head sagged and he felt her face and her small fists pressing into his skin. She was trembling and sobbing with rage against his chest, making choked sounds like a wounded animal. He let the object clasped in his hand drop to the ground at their feet. His arms rose to hug her, hesitant at first, and then he wrapped them roughly about her quivering shoulders. She was still sobbing, and he lowered his face to her messy hair, embracing her with all he had to offer.

Her arms were suddenly circling his neck. She lifted her face to his, lips parting. Without thinking his mouth dived to seal hers and his tongue sought the alluring gap she'd opened.

Dara moaned into Rowan's mouth, kissing him back with an almost-desperate need.

He cradled her face in his feverish, large palms. Dara's floral, fresh scent wafted about him and ensnared his senses. His lips pressed harder against her soft, moist warmth and his tongue plundered her mouth. He felt her fingers tightening in his hair. Her nipples, chilly and firm, stabbed his naked chest through the thin cloth of the shirt he'd given her.

Dara felt Rowan's bulging erection pressing through his jeans against her abdomen. The naked flesh of her inner thighs was warm with a familiar, welling wetness.

Their kiss became bruising, demanding. Rowan's hungry hands roamed all over, claiming her for himself. He cupped her ass cheeks and pressed her hard against him, lifting her slightly. It made her rise on tiptoes, parting her thighs, as her arms clutched him tightly for support. It felt like he was trying to fuck her through his jeans, through her shirt. She was out of breath, on the verge of a soft orgasm.

The light sprinkle of rain became a shower, pasting hair and clothes against skin as their kiss went wild.

Dara suddenly flattened her palms against Rowan's rain-moist chest and shoved back sharply, breaking their kiss.

"Please," he whispered, complying with a visible effort. He was breathing heavily. His eyes held a need so raw, and yet something more was in their stormy depths...

She shook her head and drew back, hugging herself in a failed attempt to quell her trembling. Their eyes locked and for a while they just stared at one another, each struggling to catch his breath.

"Your *Scían*," he said.

"My *what*?"

"Your dagger," he repeated and pointed to the ritual dagger tucked in its sheath along with its rig, lying at his feet. "I was just taking it out of my pack to give back to you when…"

"Thanks," she said quickly, taking a tentative step that put her close to him again. She knelt at his feet, scooping up her dagger. Slowly she straightened, shooting a wary look up at Rowan's face.

She gasped and he inquired, alarmed, "Dara, is something wrong?"

"The sky's a perfect blue, and there's no rain," she whispered.

"'Tis *Tir Na n'Og*. Sure an' it never rains here!" Brighid's voice cheeped jovially from somewhere nearby.

Both their heads snapped to the forgotten little redhead as they spoke in unison,

"*Tir Na n'Og*?"

Chapter Six

The sky stretched an endless azure, sprinkled with feathery strands of light clouds. It was the soft blue of early spring, divested of the summer sky's harsh radiance. Soft fragrances and faint music wafted about with a mild breeze, and fresh green meadows rustled softly towards the far horizon, where distant mountains hovered like purple shadows.

"Do you two hear bells?" Dara withdrew completely from Rowan, making a slow swivel on her heels. "Like wind chimes, and something more...far away. Could that be pipe music?"

Tir Na n'Og...the Otherworld. Was she caught, somehow, in a surreal dream?

Even the squishy feeling of treading in mud was gone. Bemused, Dara lowered her eyes to the ground, only to find herself submerged up to her knees in rustling green. The tall grass blades were bejeweled with slow-melting dewdrops, trembling slightly in the soft breeze.

But wherever they were, something wasn't quite right about this beautiful land. Dara couldn't place her finger on it, but something vague was there, making the back of her neck prickle. She sneaked a glance at Rowan. If he felt something, he sure wasn't showing it. Maybe the odd feeling sprang from the wet t-shirt that clung to her every curve, clearly outlining her nipples and the roundness of her butt.

She shrugged with practiced ease into her dagger's shoulder rig, then tugged nervously at her soaked shirt.

Goddess, she could be a finalist in the local wet t-shirt competition!

Assuming they held one here, of course.

"How did we cross the Veil? I didn't feel us move, Brighid." Rowan filled his lungs with the cool, fresh air, hoping to chase away the erotic haze that Dara's rich flavor had impressed upon his senses. He drew in another lungful, his mind clearing somewhat.

Good.

He needed to stay sharp for this one.

"There are many more ways of moving, Rowan, than putting one leg in front of the other," Brighid replied. She walked through the grass, striding away from the mauve-shaded mountains, obviously expecting Dara and Rowan to follow. "The Veil between the Realms grows very thin on *Samhain*. It's easier to see the Gateways. The Portland Safe Grounds do have one, you know. So while you two were...*at it*...I just gave us all a little push—so we'd slip right through." She tossed them a satisfied grin over her shoulder, smoothing a hand through her wind-tousled locks.

"*Samhain*? You mean Halloween?" Dara was standing still, her eyes wide.

"*Samhain*, Dara—Summer's end, the first of the four Celtic fire festivals marking the turning of the seasons." Rowan shook his head. "Didn't your parents teach you anything, sweetheart?"

Well, actually no, they hadn't. She blushed profusely.

"I'm not your sweetheart," she mumbled vaguely, averting her gaze from his. "I was just thinking—uh—Halloween's Eve is celebrated on the thirty-first of October, and we ended up here, wherever here is, on the first of November. Does your nifty 'Veil Theory' also apply to All Saints Day?"

She knew she was babbling. *Big time.* She started to plow through the tall grass, the light wind failing to cool her heated cheeks.

"It doesn't really matter, Dara. The Celts measured the day sundown to sundown." Rowan joined Dara's side in two long strides. He reached out and gently brushed aside her mass of black curls, exposing a scalding cheek. "What's the matter?" he softly inquired.

Dara shook his hand away with an almost-violent head jolt. "Why are we following this banshee—Brighid—anyway?" She halted abruptly, forcing Rowan to wheel about in surprise. "*Where* are we following her?"

Brighid stopped and turned to face them with obvious annoyance. "'Tis my duty to escort you both to *Lia Fáil*. Traveling Below is safer than the Upper Realm's ocean and sky with its ships and airplanes. Imagine..." She bit her lower lip in thought. "Oh—imagine we're taking a shortcut, a side alley, instead of crossing the main road."

"Hmm." Rowan seemed less than satisfied with the explanation. He glanced Dara's way, troubled by her odd change of mood. What had he done wrong *this* time? Not counting kidnapping her, almost getting her killed, and forcing sex on her. There was something else his reluctant mate wasn't telling him, and he was determined to get to the bottom of her current sulking.

Meanwhile, he had a banshee to interrogate.

"Say, Brid. Not that I'm not grateful for your services, but why's a banshee playing tour guide instead of attending to her own Mortal family? And *which* Mortal family do you care for?"

Brighid rolled her eyes skyward, clearly unimpressed. "By the Morrigu, do you truly expect me to go over the ancient prophecy *now*?"

"Aye." Rowan cocked an incredulous brow. "Since I know not a bleedin' thing about this *prophecy*."

"What prophecy?" Dara exclaimed, utterly at a loss.

The redheaded banshee gathered her gray cloak tighter about her shoulders despite the temperate climate, her blasé attitude evaporating. Evidently she had blurted out much more than she had intended. She shifted from one foot to another, opened her mouth and closed it about three times, and still said nothing.

"Nice fish imitation." Rowan glowered at her. "Now, speak!"

Brighid lanced him with a sour glance.

"Aye, the prophecy, well," she grated out, "'tis said that some minor passages are missing from the formal texts of the *Lebor Gabála Érenn*. And 'tis said as well that if you feast your eyes on the original texts, the completed ones, you might find in there Queen Eriu's full prophecy."

She was staring at her own feet now with keen interest.

Rowan sensed that was all he could hope to worm out of her for the time being. His undivided attention focused on Dara as he prowled towards his mate with a predator's stealth.

She went stock-still as his gaze fell upon her, like a deer caught in the headlights.

"The *Lebor Gabála Érenn* means Book of Conquests in Gaelic," Rowan softly intoned. His sizzling gaze spanned her frozen outline as he slowly moved around her. She was still attempting to evade his eyes, her tongue flicking over her lower lip in a nervous gesture.

"The book was compiled during the twelfth century, maybe earlier," Rowan murmured at her back, dropping his mouth to her ear. "'Tis an ancient text, it tells of the six waves of invasion to Erin—Ireland—by races of gods and men. The earliest of recorded Irish history. Should I go on, Dara?"

He rolled her name on his tongue, soft and lilting.

Dara had never guessed her name could sound so... risqué.

"Go on," she urged, shifting with unease as he slowly circled her. The man's blatant virility kicked her aura into a high-voltage state.

Rowan halted, facing her. His fingers trapped a dark curl, smoothing it away from her face. His heat thrummed over her skin. Dara gazed at Rowan, unthinkingly molding into his touch.

It seemed their bodies were engaging in a nonverbal dialogue of their own.

Rowan spoke with a husky voice, his mate's closeness swirling sugary heat into his body. "Our distant ancestors, the *Tuatha dé Danann*, made the fifth wave of invasion to Erin," he continued. "They overthrew the former inhabitants—and reigned over the isle for almost two centuries. Then they were defeated by the last wave—the sons of King Miled of Spain—"

"Spain?" Her voice was breathy.

"Aye, sweetheart, Spain—the ancient Iberian peninsula. These new invaders were named the Milesians, after their king, Miled. They were Celt-Iberians—the first Celts to settle in Ireland. You probably know the rest of it..."

"No, actually I don't," Dara whispered. She expelled a shuddering breath she wasn't aware she'd been holding.

Rowan quirked a brow, evidently puzzled by her words. He smoothed gentle fingers down Dara's burning cheek, and made an effort to tie up his tale. "The *dé-Danann* retreated to the Otherworld, leaving the Upper Earth to the Milesian Celts," he said roughly. "But a few were chosen by the Goddess Danu to keep to the Upper Earth. These chosen few became the true founders of our bloodline, the Kanjali—the Bound-Ones. Is this all new to you, Dara?"

"Most of what you've just said, yeah." Her voice was tight. She briefly shut her eyes, trembling as Rowan's fingers brushed lower, feather-light, sketching the outline of her neck.

"I don't understand, Dara. 'Tis our history, our *blood*. Those that remained in Ireland know this story by heart, as should be." Rowan spoke quietly, nothing humorous about his tone now. His fingers halted their sensuous glide, lingering over the shallow hollow at the base of Dara's neck.

Dara stilled beneath his touch, her face heating even more. Her eyes popped open, wounded and dark. "You think I like it, then, Mackey?" she lashed out. "You think I *like* being this way?"

"What way, sweetheart?" He regarded her face, his gaze intent and wary.

"Ignorant," she said offhand, once more refusing to meet his eyes.

She caught a flurry of red and green out of the corner of her eye—Brighid, who was rather annoyed at being ignored for so long.

Quick, strong fingers captured Dara's chin, tilting her face up. She found herself staring straight into Rowan's solemn green eyes, this time unable to escape. One of his fingers stroked along the line of her jaw, a gentle back-and-forth. This small movement danced hot currents down her spine. She drew in a shaky breath, her captive gaze shackled to the Irishman's stormy one.

"What *do* you know, sweetheart?"

Rowan's voice dropped to that rough-soft blend that had earlier raised goose bumps all over Dara's bare skin. Her frenzied heartbeat suddenly leaped to her throat.

"I-I've always known my family was different, but I didn't know exactly *how*," she mumbled. "My parents used to make a big secret out of everything. I caught some bits here and there—I knew that there were others…"

Her words died away as Rowan lowered his mouth over hers, lips almost touching. His breath heated her skin, both his hands now draped about her nape. Her breath hitched. It felt just like back at that party, when she'd first seen him, when she'd been sure he was about to kiss her—

"Sweetheart," Rowan spoke roughly, scattering her thoughts. "I didn't know you'd never been *told*."

His mouth hovered so close, she could feel each softly voiced word breathed over her lips. His warm hands nestled against her neck. She yearned for his touch, his taste, his male-beast scent suffusing her breath. She longed for this man to close the hairsbreadth gap between their mouths and just kiss her.

"*Rowan, no. Don't.*" Dara heard her own pleading whisper, felt the slow, reluctant release of his hold on her.

He said nothing, only watched her with the same raw look in his eyes she'd seen when they'd kissed in the midst of the downpour.

She broke away from him, shaken at the thought that the soft male mouth sealing hers, the large, powerful yet gentle hands teasing her flesh, should have been someone else's.

Aidan, her spirit screamed soundlessly. *I shouldn't be doing this. Not when I can still feel you nearby...feel you right here.*

"What's missing from the Book of Conquests?" Rowan had turned towards Brighid.

"*That* you shall learn at a later time, Kanjali," the banshee sourly replied, frowning at him. "*Maybe.*"

Rowan squinted. Tearing his gaze — along with his mind — from Dara O'Shea–Neilan had cost him the better part of his famed willpower. He was in a desperate need of a cold shower, and 'twas likely he wouldn't have one anytime soon. He was in no mood for games. Not *this* kind of game, anyway. "Then tell me something else, Brid," he growled. "Which of the Mortal families is under your care?"

This time he got nothing more than the slightest of shrugs.

"Why should we follow you, then?" he offered quietly, a tiny muscle ticking in his jaw. "For all I know, you've been leading us straight to doom's gates."

"'Cause your other option would be finding your own way back Up, all by yourselves," the banshee tossed back at him.

Rowan mumbled something incoherent that sounded particularly tangled and spicy.

Dara gave a tight, humorless chuckle. "The only upside I can see here is *you* getting a spoonful of your own medicine, Mackey."

He shot her a quick look, about to answer, when the air filled with a rising howl. It breached their consciousness, making them realize the sound had already been there for the last few seconds—distant, swelling slowly, spilling down from the purple mountains. It also assumed an individuality as it grew louder, like features becoming readable on a face as it emerged from the darkness. The sound became a bloodcurdling blend of a human scream and a beastly howl.

A couple seconds passed before the three of them realized the sound had already died away, leaving only far-off echoes trailing behind it.

Chapter Seven

Rowan was the first to react. His hand shot out and he pulled Dara tightly against his chest, draping a protective arm about her. She made a futile attempt to elbow him loose, finding it very much like pounding against a rock.

"Let me go!" she whispered through her teeth.

Reluctantly, he did.

Dara swayed away from his body heat, her gait somewhat unsteady.

The man had a way of effectively clouding her mind whenever they shared the same breathing space. *She needed some fresh air, stat!*

Brighid's face went a shade paler. "It must have come through the Veil with us," she whispered.

"*It?*" Dara managed, shooting the banshee an inquiring glance.

"The Hound," Rowan said softly. "Back Up there, you made that extra push a little too hard, didn't you, Brid? You made it possible for others to breach the Veil along with us."

"But the Hound—it needs nighttime to change, and the moon, doesn't it? Same as our kind?" Dara's hand climbed unconsciously to her left shoulder, touching the spot where just hours ago an arrow wound had been. "Doesn't it?" she demanded again, her eyes darting from the redheaded Sidhe to the bare-chested Irishman by her side.

She couldn't help the shudder that racked her body.

Rowan noticed, but didn't reach out for her this time, though he ached to.

Dara had just made it clear she didn't want him touching her. She had a right to reject his touch. He'd almost got her killed. Had forced intimacy on her while she'd still been craving another. Had crashed into her life…

"The Hound might follow a different set of rules in the Otherworld," Brighid was telling Dara, her voice drawing Rowan away from his tormented thoughts. "It is a creature of magic, after all, so it will likely grow more powerful here…might be able to shapechange during the daylight as well. And 'tis always daylight here."

"Why can't we just go back Up, then?" Dara demanded. Her hands were balled into tight, sweaty fists.

"Up is no better," Brighid replied faintly. "Up is where you almost got yourself killed, Dara. I prefer taking our chances here, where we might get *some* help. Look, we'd better get moving."

"Don't *we* have any say in this?" Dara's voice was oozing sarcasm.

"We're wasting precious time standing here!" the Sidhe snapped back.

"*Hey*," Dara exclaimed, anger flashing in her eyes.

"Say, Brid," Rowan swiftly cut in. "If the Hound grows stronger here, does it also mean the other rules don't apply? That it might go for a kill not using arrows?"

"It probably will, you idiot!" the Sidhe snarled agitatedly. "If your mind went any slower, it would likely catch up with itself on the way back!"

Rowan's temper heated instantly, but then his searing gaze fell upon Brighid's fingers—clenched within the green woolen cloth of her gown.

"Wanna tell me what's biting your arse, Brid?" His voice was cool again, the heat pushed back from his gaze.

"We're in the wrong kingdom to have long, useless discussions, is all." The wee banshee swiped her arm at the purple shadows of the mountains. "See there, this is the seat of the Knockfierna Mound. 'Tis Prince Donn's dominion. He...doesn't like your kind."

"Our kind?" Dara murmured, confused.

"Kanjali," Rowan quietly told her. "Even if you have no knowledge of where you came from, Dara, there are always those who'd remember it for you."

"Aye." Brighid nodded. "The Gateway threw us in Princess Grian's dominion. It shares a border with Knockfierna. Grian herself won't attempt to harm you, but she's either too weak or too unwilling to stop Donn should he find out you're here."

"Look, I know nothing about all of this mounds and princes blather," Rowan spread his arms wide in a desperate gesture. "I want to bleedin' trust you, Brighid. Goddess knows I do. But you'll have to tell us a bit more than that!"

"You two *want* to die, is that it?" Brighid collapsed in the grass like a puppet whose strings had been cut. She sat miserably in the circle of crushed grass blades, her legs folded beneath her. "Aye, that's what it is, a death wish!"

Dara stared incredulously at Rowan. He was crouching beside Brighid now, gently clutching her slim arms in his large hands.

"Not asking for a long lecture here, lass," he told the reluctant banshee. "Just tell us where we're heading."

"To the kingdom of Midhe, city of Khree. 'Tis the Lower Realm's center, and holds a direct Gateway to *Lia Fáil*." Brighid's voice was dull, all the anger drained out. "We have three kingdoms to cross to get there. Mumha, Connachta, then Laighin."

"Then we'd better get moving, aye? I trust you to lead the way. This—" Rowan gestured wearily over the endless stretch of whispering grass. "'Tis all the same to me."

Dara had been watching the two of them in dumbfounded silence. She couldn't make heads or tails of this mess.

Rowan straightened up, then reached down and yanked Brighid to her feet. "When we're safely out of Mumha, then by Danu, I *will* ask you for that long lecture, Brid." He shook his head. "'Tis all unbelievable, this."

The light was back in Brighid's eyes. "If we all shapechange, we'll be able to travel faster," she said.

"I can't shapechange at will!" Dara's tone bordered on panicky. "I need the full moon for that kind of a trick. Besides, I'd never go full *mac'tir* if I had a choice. *Way* too dangerous." She shrugged. "Sorry."

"I have much better control than she, but I still need the moon's Power to draw on," Rowan sighed.

"So did the Hound, but it might be different for you all down here," Brighid reminded him. She was beating grass out of the green folds of her dress. "So maybe you two can try and do your thing anyway?"

"*No.*" Dara shook her head, her curls hopping with the sharp movement. "I will not 'do my thing'. I'd rather die human."

Rowan slanted a glance at the sky's soft-glowing blue. "When we transferred here, I felt something was strange about the way things looked. Now I know what it was. There's no sun up there," he pointed accusingly at the sky's blue dome. "I thought of drawing Power from the sun, instead of the moon."

"Rowan, you can't," Dara exclaimed. "That would be suicide!"

Hmmm…so she did mind his safety. That was good news. Rowan cast Dara a charged glance. "Goddess knows 'tis dangerous, Dara, unheard of. The moon's Power is like cool water, the sun's touch is burning, deadly—impossible to work with. But problem solved, isn't it, Brid? No sun in here. No moon. No Power to use."

"*No Power?*" Brighid slowly repeated, her lips twisting into an ironic smile. "Kanjali, this place *is* Power."

Rowan shot the Sidhe a stunned look. "By Danu, you may be right," he murmured. "In that case…" He began loosening his fly.

Dara gave Rowan a funny look. "What the hell are you up to now, Mackey?"

He arched a fiery brow at her, tugging at his zipper.

"I-I don't think you should do that," she mumbled, yet her eyes seemed glued to his hands' movements.

"What, *this*?" Rowan flashed Dara a lazy smile, slowly tugging his zipper down over his bulging erection. "You've already seen it all, sweetheart."

"And I don't wanna see it again," she snapped, still staring at his hands intently.

"So why do you keep watching?" Rowan's grin broadened as mild shock spread over Dara's face. Her entranced look was an immense turn-on. He tugged the zipper lower, his hard shaft straining against his fly.

"Oh—" Dara flushed.

His zipper undone, Rowan's massive erection forced its way out through his gaping fly. He slipped both his thumbs beneath the waistband. "'Tis just that I mean to shapechange," he said matter-of-factly. "'Twould be foolish if I tried that with my jeans on, eh?"

Dara looked mesmerized. "I guess 'twould— I mean, *it would*—"

Rowan grinned, slowly guiding the faded jeans down his hips, peeling them over his ass. His balls hung heavy and his cock was fully erect beneath Dara's heated gaze, its engorged head pointing to his abdominal muscles. He paused in mid-crouch, the waistband hugging his thighs. "Want a rear view, too?"

"Ye—*No!*" Dara crossed her arms over her breasts, her face burning. "Shut up and get it over with, Mackey!"

He chuckled, slipping completely out of his jeans, chucking them onto the dewy grass. "Now, where was I?" he murmured, completely at ease. "Aye. About to look for some bleedin' Power."

Closing his eyes, Rowan eased the tight hold controlling his own life force and let it uncoil, stretch out in a gentle search for another force to play with. Power eagerly answered his careful call. He gasped as tangling, vibrant energy snared his unprepared senses. Power simmered in the air he breathed, in the earth and the grass he trod upon. Sinking down to his knees, Rowan withdrew, tucking the battered shoots of his force back into their shields.

The world about him grew indistinct.

Chapter Eight

"Rowan!"

Dara gave him a third rough shake, and he still hadn't responded. He stayed crouched on his knees, his back hunched. Dara was starting to get worried.

"Dammit, Mackey, snap out of it!"

That was loud enough to wake up the dead.

Rowan finally cracked his eyes open. Dara leaned closer, scrutinizing his face with concern. He shook his head, still looking out of it.

"Rowan, are you okay?" She squeezed his arms tighter.

"Aye, I'm fine." He managed a smile, but his voice came out husky. "I wasn't prepared when I reached out for the Power. 'Tis a bit like putting your lips up for a chaste kiss, and instead getting a deep, full mouth workout."

"What?!"

Rowan's gaze dropped in response, and Dara's eyes followed. She took a nervous swallow. The man was wearing nothing but a smile, and he was *hard*. His cock head was nudging her shirt—*his* shirt—*Oh, dammit!* Suddenly her face felt dangerously close to his, her hands clasped *way* too tight on his arms. Dara's cheeks heated. She snatched her hands away from the impossible rogue and scrambled to her feet.

"Oh yeah, you're definitely okay," she muttered.

"Next time I'll do it right. More gentle." Rowan stayed kneeling, his eyes climbing from Dara's dew-covered bare feet to her face. His smoldering gaze told her he'd been just discussing more than his shapechanging.

She found herself sizzling beneath the intensity of the man's blatant, green gaze. He was looking at her as if she were the only thing that mattered in the world, both Above and Below. The impish twinkle in his eyes told her what he'd like to do to her right here, right now. His fully erect cock backed up that statement.

Dara drew back a step.

"Stop that," she whispered.

"Stop what, Dara?"

"Stop looking at me that way. Don't."

"In what way?"

"*That* way," she finally voiced. "Like I'm the most beautiful damn thing you've ever seen."

"I can't look at you any other way." Rowan's voice was soft, flavored with his rough brogue.

He continued staring up at her, kneeling naked in the grass beside his discarded jeans. *Goddess, but he looked delicious!* His sweat- and rain-soaked mane tumbled in wild tangles about his face, sweeping down his chiseled shoulders. A thin glaze of moisture sheened his well-defined muscles into gleaming masculine perfection. His huge erection jutted towards her. *Not fair!* Her fading logic screamed for mercy. Dara longed to touch Rowan again, to skim her hands over the velvet of his chest. To slide her fingers along the hard length of his shaft. No, scratch that. She wanted to try those things with her tongue.

She closed her eyes, drawing a quick, trembling breath. *This couldn't be!* He couldn't be talking to her this way, trying to convince her she was the most beautiful thing in the world.

She wasn't doing any better herself. Naked or not, the man only had to glance her way, and her tongue lolled out like some horny teenager's. *Goddess, but this couldn't be!* She'd had love and she'd lost it. She didn't believe in happily-ever-afters anymore.

Dara's eyes flew open with a yelp as unmistakable, powerful arms enveloped her from behind. A soft, male chuckle of pure mischief teased wisps of her hair, as a rough, square jaw fitted itself perfectly into the crook of her neck. Something else, long and hard, fitted itself nicely into the curve of her back.

Mackey was a fast healer — and a fast mover!

"Come off it, Mackey," she snapped, vainly attempting to break his hold.

"Come off what? You?" Rowan's low laugh brushed her skin, and Dara's body throbbed in response. "Mmmm, no, I don't think so." He started to nuzzle her neck in an extremely addictive way.

"You don't *think*, Mackey. *Period*," Dara ground out, twisting her head away from his. In her current position it only granted Rowan more access, which he liberally abused. One of his hands sneaked up and tangled in her hair, keeping her throat fully exposed to his mouth's mastery.

Dara moaned, against her better judgment.

"I love it when you go all *teacher* on me, sweetheart," Rowan murmured seductively, his trailing mouth now pressing beneath her jawline. He sent a nimble tongue out to explore.

"Mmmmggh," Dara eloquently replied, her knees turning to mush. Rowan's steely chest felt like smooth velvet behind her. His cock pressed shamelessly into her back, through her shirt. A sweet tingle started between her legs. Her nipples tightened, throbbing in unison with her cunt. She was hot all over, her pussy growing damp. *Damn that Irishman!* Helplessly she sagged against him, going pliant beneath his mouth, beneath his sure hands. Right now, she couldn't spell *judgment* if someone held a gun to her head.

Both of Rowan's hands were caressing the soft swell of her hips in a slow, inflaming rhythm. Dara sucked in her breath, shaken by a rough tremor. She was soaking wet.

"Where's the banshee?" he unexpectedly hummed against her cheek, his tongue hunting one angle of her mouth.

"Who?" Dara struggled to regain focus. "Oh, B-Brighid. It's odd, you know — I wasn't looking for barely a sec, and she disappeared."

"Banshees have their ways," Rowan drawled as he swirled his tongue around the delicate shell of her ear, setting it afire.

"You think she maybe shapech—? *Mmm*...Goddess, Rowan, what're you doing?"

His lips had just fastened on her earlobe, drawing it into the searing heat of his mouth. He gently tugged and let go, his tongue next tenderly penetrating her ear's sensitive, dark passage.

Dara gasped sharply, at a loss for words. Talk about tongue-tied! The man was sure taking his sweet time to reply.

"I want to show you how you look in my eyes, Dara." His answering whisper brushed her blazing ear, caressed her sensitized nerve endings. His hips gave a subtle forward thrust, teasingly bumping his cock against her derriere.

Dara didn't mind Rowan showing her whatever he damn wanted, as long as he didn't stop what he was doing. As his mouth captured her earlobe again, tugging with gentle teeth, she renounced all coherent thought. As his talented lips skimmed down the contour of her neck and sucked their fill, she all but melted into a boneless puddle.

Rowan bit back a smile, breathing heat over Dara's flushed cheek.

"Close your eyes, Dara. Let me show you what I see."

"Rowan—"

"Cream," he whispered against her contrary ear, sliding his hands from her hips to the curvaceous thrust of her thighs. His fingers crinkled her masculine t-shirt as he oh-so slowly dragged the cloth up. The fact that she was wearing nothing but his own oversized shirt aroused him fiercely.

He finally touched skin.

She was hot, smooth silk, just as he remembered.

"Sweet cream," he softly uttered in her ear.

Dara released a long-held breath. He felt her narrow rib cage heaving and falling within his embrace.

His hands drew up her thighs, nudging her shirt further up her body. His fingers converged over the dark, moist curls. Dara's head fell back against his shoulder, her eyes fluttering shut. Her taut fingers curled against his forearms.

"Rich, dark honey," Rowan breathed in her ear, gently stroking over the raven-black pelt above her mons. Again his hips gave a gentle forward thrust, trapping her sex between his hard cock and his hungry hands. Dara let out a half-sob, her sooty lashes trembling. The excited, quick pulse in her neck drummed against Rowan's pressed face.

"Mmmm...like the juiciest of apples." Rowan moved his hands around Dara's thighs, each finally cupping a lush ass cheek.

She seemed to be under a spell. With a soft sigh she leaned further into him, her back arching, her body now fully supported against his solid chest and his nestling hands. Her subtle change of posture beautifully arched her full breasts beneath the crumpled shirt.

Rowan's hands roved up the subtle swell of her tummy, and stroked sensual paths up her slim waist. His hands' movement rolled her shirt up 'til it was stopped by her dagger's leather harness. His fingers splayed against the underside of her breasts, teasing the supple flesh with feathery circular strokes.

"Even more sweet cream," he whispered against her throat as each of his hands supported a breast, his tone softly teasing.

"Oh please," she whimpered, and he understood perfectly.

A sultry, pleased grin quirked Rowan's lips as his hands moved from play mode to business.

Dara couldn't help but cry out as Rowan nestled her breasts with a firmer grip, his kneading hands giving her just the right amount of rough. Those long, devilish fingers of his stroked around her blushing areolas in tightening circles, caressing everywhere but *there*. His sizzling touch honed her nipples to aching peaks. She hissed like a cat and writhed against the man's front like there was no tomorrow. And what a hard front it was, too... Dara's wanton undulations seemed to have an effect. It was Rowan's turn to hiss in sweet agony.

He caught Dara's jaw, turning her face towards his. Their eyes clashed, two pairs of smoking embers. Rowan angled his head down to Dara's and covered her mouth with his, his tongue swiftly sinking between her unresisting lips. He growled, his tongue eagerly exploring the dark, sizzling hollow of her waiting mouth.

"By the Morrigu! But you two are *at it* again!"

Her two Kanjali tore their mouths from each other as she changed to her womanly form and shrilly announced her arrival. Brighid grinned impishly. She hadn't made her presence known immediately after landing—for a brief moment she'd simply enjoyed watching the two Upper Realm shifters.

Rowan Mackey, dressed in naught but his pelt, had Dara Neilan locked in his embrace, her back to his chest, her shirt riding high above her breasts. She didn't seem to mind. She was wearing nothing but Mackey's hand over one aroused breast, and his face on hers. Oh, and that mean-looking ritual dagger of hers.

Dara was staring speechless at the banshee, her eyes wide, pupils still dilated. She slowly ran her tongue over her misted, swollen lips.

Rowan was catching his own breath, giving Brighid a harsh once-over. He released Dara's shirt, allowing it to slide back down over her nudity. "*Nice* of you to have joined us again, Brid," he said pointedly, his "nice" emphasis clearly conveying his feelings regarding the rude interruption.

Brighid beamed with an elfin smile. "Later you can wear each other's faces for breakfast, lunch and dinner, for all I care! 'Tis not the right time now. We should start moving."

"Oh, should we?" Dara muttered, at last regaining the power of speech.

"Aye, Dara. We should be moving like our arses are on fire." Brighid glared at her. "I've been touring the land and spotted no trouble—yet. For now we have an open road all the way to the Connachta border."

"Hmmm." Rowan's deep-throated rumble vibrated against Dara's nape, where his mouth had come to rest. Gently, he released her from his passionate embrace, brushing his mouth against her mussed hair as he stepped away from her.

Her eyes shot his way, heated and anxious. What was he up to?

She understood quickly as he knelt once more amidst the fresh greenery, his handsome features assuming a look of intent concentration.

Damn the stubborn Irishman, he was trying transformation again!

Mists were swirling around Rowan's naked, crouched form, a product of the connection between his own life force and the Power he was drawing on.

He was manipulating the energies in silent concentration, slowing the shapechanging sequence down to a crawl. Haze shimmered and flowed, thickening to milky-white, blurring his features beyond visibility.

Dara's nails burrowed into her flesh as she watched. Why was he playing with the Powers again, and so soon? The first time had literally brought him to his knees. If she spoke now she might break his concentration, boosting the odds that things would again go wrong.

Dara held her breath as the fog slowly stripped away from Rowan, melting into the air. A mild slapping noise sounding from the still fog-solid core startled her into a yelp. Water splattered over her already wet shirt, legs, arms and face. She yelped again and leaped back. She attempted to drill through the cloudy essence, tracing a movement, something resembling a huge—dog?—vigorously shaking water out of its fur.

No, it was a huge *mac'tir*.

Brighid's silvery laughter rang close by. "Aye, Rowan, that's the way to handle the Powers!"

Rowan's beastly incarnation took a smooth, flowing step towards Dara, shedding the last bit of mist from its fur. He trampled over his shed jeans. Almond-shaped amber eyes shone with a familiar roguish glint. Dara gasped, tentatively extending fingertips to the rich flow of tawny, copper-streaked fur.

I won't bite.

She caught his golden gaze, dazzled, searching. Was that Rowan speaking to her? His voice had echoed clearly in her mind, even though she could swear her ears only heard a soft growl emerging from his throat.

I won't bite, unless you insist, his voice whispered in her mind, spiced with familiar mischief.

His maw held a smile, if a maw could ever hold one. Dara broke into laughter, ringing boundless and carefree in the open air. She was able to understand him! He truly remained himself inside that *mac'tir* beast! She sank her hands fully into the thick, warm silk of Rowan's neck fur. Her palms found the soft skin beneath and waded towards his flanks. His rib cage swelled and eased beneath her hands with the slow, steady rhythm of his breathing.

"Our first stop will be at a friend of mine's," Brighid announced. "He's a *Lúracán*."

"He's a what?" Dara blurted.

"A fairy shoemaker," Brighid supplied helpfully, "making his living on the border between Mumha and Connachta. We need help in the crossing, and he might know some ways."

Hop on, then, sweetheart.

Rowan's voice was an enticing whisper in Dara's mind. It was an offer she could hardly refuse.

Chapter Nine

"Stop."

The man gave a gentle tug to his horse's reins as he uttered the soft command. The massive white horse halted with a snort, its nostrils flaring. His escorts did the same a short distance behind him, the crunch of leaves dwindling into silence.

A dark, slender figure slid out from behind a curtain of shadows and leaves. The prowler went down on his knees in the forest's dark flora.

"Prince Donn."

"You may rise, *Adhamh.*"

Adam flowed back to his feet with a predatory grace.

"'Tis good to hear my true name spoken again."

Donn leaned slightly over the braided reins. Velvet clung in deep indigo waves to his olive-brown skin. His hair was pulled back from his sharp-angled face, woven into sepia braids. His saddle's high pommel gleamed silver between his thighs, the saddle's soft leather-covering heavily embroidered with silver knotwork and triskeles.

He crooked one dark brow.

"Is that what you came here for, Hound? To hear me speak your name?"

Laughter rose in a soft hum from the Prince's entourage. Leaves crackled again as horses rocked and huffed with unease beneath their shadowy riders.

Adam's gaze stayed on the prince, dark and impassive. "I am honored to be addressed by Donn of Truth, Prince of the Knockfierna Mound, son of King Miled. I came here, Highness, hoping you'd grant me your gracious help."

Donn straightened in his saddle. The hushed laughter behind his stiffened back abated almost at once.

"There is no need to summon my pedigree to your aid, *Cú*. I remember well who gave me a second life here...and who cost me the first one."

He hopped down from his horse and strode to Adam. Well-tanned deerskin boots hugged his calves and were tied at the knees with silk cords, each wound three times about his legs. A short, cruel-looking sword was secured against his left thigh. He halted a hairsbreadth from the motionless Hound, staring him in the eye.

"If you are here, so are *they*," the Prince said softly. "How many?"

"A couple of Upper Realm *dé-Danann* shifters," Adam answered. "Kanjali—a man and a woman. They have a *bean-sidhe* with them for a guide." The Hound's blank gaze dropped to Donn's sword. It was iron, double-edged, with a long tapering point. Weapon-wise, the Prince had obviously stuck to his old Celt-Iberian heritage.

Donn nodded thoughtfully. "You know the Sidhe's identity?"

"She goes by the name of Brighid."

"Brighid..." Donn paused. "Isn't she the solitary banshee? The one with no Mortal family attached?"

"The Prince remembers well." Adam held Donn's hot gaze, his own face blank of expression. "But I'd like to set straight a misguided assumption. There is no such thing as a 'solitary banshee'."

A hint of darker color tinted the Prince's olive cheeks. "This 'misguided assumption' is considered common knowledge. Brighid is the only one of the six guardian Sidhe with no Mortal family to tend."

"I believe this specific piece of knowledge has been spread around for a reason." Adam wore a thin smile. "To protect the mysterious Mortal family that is truly under Brighid's care. And such a family does exist, I vow it."

"An intriguing thought." Donn scrutinized Adam's face. "Is there any special reason for bringing this up now?" His mind tried to reach deeper into Adam's thoughts, but tumbled into an impermeable shield. Behind him he sensed his escorts soothing their horses with a blend of muted murmurs.

"Four thousand years is time enough for anyone to come up with intriguing thoughts," Adam said, giving Donn a slight nod. "Indeed, there is a reason. I think that even as we speak Brighid is doing her duty, loyally serving her Mortal family. I think…" He was purposefully drawing out the words, and Donn gritted his teeth. "That one of the two Kanjali shifters traveling with the banshee is a descendant of her Mortal family's lineage."

"One of the shifters is a mixed-breed, then," Donn said. "Mortal and *dé-Danann*?"

"I believe so."

"Which suits Eriu's prophecy well," Donn's voice darkened. "It mentions a mixed-breed, doesn't it?"

"If I recall the ancient prophecy correctly," Adam's voice slithered like a snake brushing velvet, "Eriu's exact words were, *'a seed from a union above and below'*."

"*Enough.*" Donn's whisper breathed fury. "If all your guesses so far have been accurate, then I can make another one. I think I can safely guess the identity of Brighid's Mortal family." His lips tightened into a crooked, wry smile. A name slipped from his mouth with a hiss, and his right hand brushed his sword's pommel as he uttered it. "*Amergin.* Brighid's Mortals carry Amergin's blood in their veins."

Adam nodded. "It appears that your younger brother didn't die heirless after all. Though someone went to great trouble erasing that fact, along with others, from the ancient texts. I do believe that the mixed-breed shifter traveling with the banshee can be traced straight back to your brother, Amergin."

"The mixed-breed, is it the man or the woman?"

"I don't have this knowledge, Prince."

"So," Donn's tone was acrid. "My pious little brother left a bastard behind, did he? I can't stand such inconsistencies." The Prince was still smiling. "The ancient texts should always mirror the actual truth, don't you think?"

"I would be glad to set it straight if the Prince would be kind enough to lend me his aid."

"Why do you need my help, *Cú*?" Donn's smile dissolved. "*Silence!*" he barked abruptly, half-turning his face towards his muttering escorts. Quiet spread beneath the dark-barked, gnarled trees of Kilduv, the Black Forest. Unappeased, the Prince turned his sizzling gaze back to Adam.

"Knockgreany's borders are guarded, Prince." Adam's tone was as stolid as his face. "When I followed the Sidhe through the Gateway she'd opened, I was sidetracked here by protective wards. Else—" he gave an unpleasant smile, tugging at the bow slung against his back, " —they all would've been dead by now, and we wouldn't be having this conversation."

"Knockgreany," Donn repeated. The Hound's smile caused a chill even in *his* bones. "I've been thinking for some time now to pay the sweet Grian a courtesy visit."

Adam waited silently for the Prince of the Knockfierna Mound to make his decision. Of course, hunting down the two Kanjali shifters and evening up an ancient score with a long-dead brother would make too-tempting a trophy for the Prince to refuse.

Adam's silence had been honed to perfection by nonstop tracking of endless prey in search for the right kill, followed by lonely stalking, then silent killing from afar. Always the same means, when it came to the Kanjali—his silver-tipped arrows, their tail etched with his name. He couldn't choose any other way Up there. The Law had been set by Her long ago, compelling him to use no other weapon but this one.

Kanjali. There had been so many of *them*, and so few such as *him.* But only a handful of *Others*, those born Guardians, had been able to kill *his* kind. Kanjali and *Cú*, Bound-Ones and Hounds, their deadly game had always had rules, an ancient Law carved in stone and water and trees, enacted by She who had borne the Kanjali, and He who had conjured Adam's kind. Their arena had always been Up there.

And now that he was the last of his kind, the game was about to end.

He could smell it, could feel it like an ache deep in his bones.

The arena had finally changed, and here they seemed to have no rules.

Chapter Ten

Dara squeezed her bare thighs on Rowan's hot flanks. His muscles flowed beneath her flesh as he tore through the meadow, making sky and grass swirl into a blur. She twisted her fingers within his tawny mane, clutching fistfuls of his fur. Having nothing on but a borrowed shirt, Dara was completely bare against Rowan's lithe body—nothing shielded her cunt from the feel of silky fur and velvety skin, the raw energy unleashed in the muscles rippling beneath her. Dara suspected that Rowan rather liked her riding style.

Well, *she* didn't exactly dislike it, either.

High above them circled and crowed an oversized raven with a blazing feathery tuft topping its head. It alternated between smooth soaring and deep dives that could put to shame a preying hawk.

Brighid makes an interesting bird, aye?

"You could say that again!" Dara yelled her reply against the wind and ate a mouthful of her own hair. Rowan's answering bark of laughter rippled beneath her, and she tightened her arms and legs on his undulating muscles. Those delicious ripples sent a white-hot frisson of pleasure right through her pussy.

Indeed, Brighid had changed into quite a unique raven. The banshee had been right to suggest they shapechange—in a short time they had covered an incredible distance.

"How long to the Mumha–Connachta border?" Dara dared another scream, her cheek pressed tight against Rowan's neck. His scent assailed her senses, tangy and bestial and male. His reply drifted almost immediately into her thoughts.

Brighid says not long now. I could use a short break. Toying with this place's Powers nearly squeezed me dry.

Dara still couldn't shake the odd feeling of hearing Rowan's voice within her head. Funny, it seemed as though Rowan in his *mac'tir* form could communicate with Brighid on some level Dara couldn't detect, somewhere way off her scale. She wondered if she could do the same if she shapechanged. Straining to see through the dark tresses tumbling over her face, she managed to trace a large black bird surfing the airstreams. Brighid was guiding them towards a group of white-clad trees.

Soon Brighid's raven form disappeared as Rowan slipped into the cool shadows of the blooming trees. He slowed down to a trot and then to a weary amble, wading deeper into the grove through the undergrowth. A babbling brook split the wood's lush earth. The *mac'tir* crouched beside it, letting Dara slide down from his back. He was panting heavily. A couple more minutes went by before he rose and lowered his muzzle to the stream, downing the cool water in big gulps.

"You okay?"

Rowan's beastly form turned away from the water to meet her gaze.

"You haven't changed back yet to your man-form. Is everything okay, Rowan?" Dara repeated, absently stretching his sweat-soaked shirt over her thighs.

Rowan's amber gaze scanned her face.

'Tis a place of strange Power, he whispered in her mind. *Playing with it has been far from easy. First times are always the hardest. I will change back soon.*

"Oh." Dara studied him as he drew near, dripping water all around him. He looked bright-eyed and bushy-tailed. His intense golden gaze made her blush. "Everything's fine with you, then."

Aye. Everything's fine.

Dara gasped as Rowan exhaled a soft, warm breath that stroked over her breasts. Her nipples instantly obeyed the gentle caress, tightening against her thin shirt. She froze, taken by surprise, and he inched yet closer. Dara sucked in another sharp breath as his tongue thoroughly laved one peaked nipple through the shirt's sodden cloth. Her hands rose with a will of their own and dipped into Rowan's silky mane, pulling his magnificent, large head closer by fistfuls of his fur. One wet nipple was teased to an aching hard knot as Rowan's tongue moved to tend her other breast. She gave a soft, lingering moan.

I really liked that ride, sweetheart, his voice teased in her mind.

"Rowan..."

Her other nipple grew pebble-hard, too. Rowan's large, tawny head butted gently against her tummy, a wet muzzle touching the shirt-covered juncture between her thighs.

"Oh Goddess, Rowan, we shouldn't... *Rowan!*"

His gentle shove sent Dara stumbling back. She landed on her butt in the cushioning grass, the oversized t-shirt riding high up her thighs. The large, exquisite beast lowered its head, breathing a gentle, hot line from Dara's neck down her quivering body. She shuddered as Rowan's breath hovered between her spread thighs, the shirt making a flimsy barrier between the rough tongue and her sodden cunt. Was he a wolf indeed, or was he more like a very big dog? Dara couldn't tell anymore, but she loved that recipe's winning result. *Goddess, she was wet for him. Wet and aching inside.*

Another moan escaped her mouth.

The large head rose from between her legs, golden gaze centering on her face. Rowan's seductive whisper, full of dark, sultry promise, penetrated her thoughts.

Would you like me to stop now, sweetheart?

Rowan scanned his mate's face. Dara's pupils were huge, making her brown eyes seem almost black. Her breath was coming in quick, shallow gasps. She didn't, or couldn't, answer.

He took in a whiff of her arousal, pungent and tantalizing. That was his undoing. Nothing, absolutely nothing could stop him now. He *had* to taste her, fully, deeply. He bent his head again and shoved a questing muzzle beneath her shirt.

Dara yelped. She sank to her back as the large, rough tongue swiped over her cunt. Her shoulder rig's straps etched into her flesh, the dagger beneath her left arm scraping the grass. She dug her fingers into the ground, looking for something to hold onto. Anything.

Rowan washed Dara's pussy with a long, leisurely lick, starting at the puckered tight ring of her anus. His limber tongue plowed up to the damp, dark fuzz of curls topping her mound. Her nether lips were swollen and glistening with her juices and his tongue's wet work. She wanted him just as badly as he lusted after her. His sensitive tongue found the slick nub of her clit and lingered there, circling and exploring. *By Danu, having a long, thick tongue was proving to be quite handy!*

"*Goddess…*" Dara's thighs squeezed hard on the large furry head.

She was in oral sex heaven! Her hips were rocking against Rowan's face, slow at first, then falling into a sharper, more desperate rhythm. She writhed against the crushed flora, both staggered at what she was allowing, yet unable to stop. The rough tongue left her clit and stabbed deep into her vagina's wet, hot tightness, thrusting into her pussy with long, slow movements.

Rowan's *mac'tir* tongue felt so big.

Dara screamed senselessly. Her legs squeezed tightly around Rowan's large copper-streaked head, the rocking of her hips growing erratic and jerky. And then her hips bucked, her body going rigid. She came on a loud moan, her cunt squeezing Rowan's tongue in short, quick spasms. She was shivering all over, thinking she'd never stop.

A while later, when the haze had cleared, she opened her eyes to the green-white dome of the blossoming trees. A man's large hands were supporting her outer thighs. Hard, warm flesh with not a hint of fur on it was pressed against her legs. She struggled up to her elbows with an anxious sob.

"That sure looked like fun," Rowan grinned up from between Dara's legs.

His shoulders were supporting her thighs. The hard flesh she'd been feeling against her calves had apparently been Rowan's naked back. He had shifted to a man and she hadn't even noticed.

She had never lost control the way she had just now.

"Rowan, I usually don't..." Dara started, her face burning. She tried again. "I mean, I've never..."

"Shhh, 'tis okay, sweetheart." Rowan released his hold on her thighs and with predatory grace slid up between her splayed legs. His muscle-bound body was burning against her sweat-sheened skin. Her shirt—*his* shirt—was still a crumpled barrier between their bodies. He propped his arms on the ground, careful not to saddle her slim body with his full weight.

"But, you can't love me." Dara's eyes were wide and close, her voice a husky whisper. "Because, I can't love you back, you see? Because Aidan is...was..."

Rowan pressed his mouth down on hers, silencing her with a hard, thorough kiss.

"Mmmm..." She twisted beneath him, pushing both her hands hard against his chest. *Goddess, this wasn't right.* She must be out of her mind, letting him do this. Letting herself moan and writhe on his tongue, and worse—letting herself love him while Aidan was—

Love?

She barely knew the man!

Dara groaned, pushing hard.

Rowan lifted his mouth from her kiss-bruised lips. "Why are you fighting me so hard, sweetheart? I can smell your want." He stared into Dara's baffled gaze, and his tone softened. "Relax, lass. Here you're protected from unwelcome desire. What do you see when you look up there, above us?"

"Trees?" she mumbled, hesitant. She was still pushing weakly against him, but the tension had partly eased from her muscles.

"Aye, but which trees?" Rowan chuckled.

"H-hawthorn."

"Aye. You know, some believe hawthorns are witches who have changed themselves into trees. And in Ireland some use hawthorn leaves to enforce chastity on lusty virgins, or celibacy on lusty wives. As long as they can stand the hawthorn smell." He gave another chuckle. "So, sweetheart, you are safe from my burning desire beneath so much hawthorn."

Dara rewarded him with a soft grin. "The hawthorn didn't seem to work on you earlier. Maybe in *mac'tir* form you are immune to its magic?"

"Maybe," Rowan smiled. "Or maybe this specific hawthorn is defective. There's only one way to find out."

He lowered his lips to her mouth again. Dara's hands had stopped pushing for the last few minutes. Her fingers now tentatively climbed up his body, stroking along his damp back. His hand moved beneath her shirt, cupping her left breast. He circled her nipple with his thumb, feeling the supple velvet knotting into a hard kernel. He was growing hard, too, so deliciously aching and hard. He went on kissing her, imploring, demanding, until her tongue began answering his play. Her legs loosely wrapped around his. His balls tightened. Rowan shifted slightly, nestling his cock against her inviting, hot opening. *Great Danu, he had to get himself inside her!* And she wanted him inside her, too. She was holding him tighter now, mumbling his name—*his* name!—into his mouth…

"Och stop, *stop*! What are you two at?"

Dara tore her mouth from Rowan's at the shrill sound of Brighid's voice.

"Go away, Brighid," Rowan groaned, shooting a quick glance in the alarmed voice's direction.

Aye, that voice had been Brighid's, all right.

Surprisingly the wee banshee still had all her clothes on, even after shifting back from raven to humanoid.

Gotta learn that trick, Rowan mused.

"Get off me!" Dara was pushing hard against his chest again. He rolled over with a muffled curse.

"They've just crossed into Knockgreany." Brighid ignored Dara's attempts at tugging down her misused shirt and Rowan's slow scrambling into a crouch. "Prince Donn and your Hound."

"Bleedin' what?!" Rowan was back on his feet, quick as lightning.

"When I was flying." Brighid struggled to breathe slower. "I saw them when I was flying. Prince Donn, the Hound and the Prince's escort have just crossed to Princess Grian's dominion. Rowan, take Dara and ride to the Connachta border, as fast as you can. By Manannan's beard, what is that *smell*?" Her gaze darted around in a frenzied search, lighting upon the white-flowering branches.

"Aye." Brighid's eyes shone with feverish hope. "Hawthorn. That's Princess Grian's summoner tree! I'll call on Grian for help. But before I do that, I want you two to take a look there, see? *That's* where you should go."

With wide gestures she urged them both to the low hill she was standing upon, a shallow prominence above the level grassland, mildly sloped. They squinted their eyes at the horizon, their gazes following Brighid's outstretched hand. There, fringing the farthest edge of the unfolding meadow, they saw a swirl of colors crowding about the shimmering bands of what looked to be three rivers.

"That's the border town of Commar," Brighid said. "*That's* where we were heading. Go now, try to find that *Lúracán* I told you about. Wait for me at his dwelling."

Dara gasped as Brighid vanished in a swirl of mist. An overly large raven flapped its wings and soared up from where she'd been standing, shaking scraps of fog from its shiny-black feathers. The red tuft crowning its dark head trembled with the bird's zeal.

"That's the way to do it," Rowan mumbled with unconcealed envy at Brighid's swift transformation. "Quick and painless. But what's she bleedin' doing now?"

The raven that was Brighid was wrestling with a nearby tree. The bird crowed and beat its wings, agitated. The tree rustled with similar annoyance. After a quick struggle the raven tore away a twig rich with white flowers, shook hawthorn leaves out of its feathers and launched itself back into the sky. In the blink of an eye, it vanished along with its loot.

"So." Dara was glad her voice sounded steady. "She just turned herself into a bird and ripped a branch off a tree in order to call some...princess. In Oregon we use phones for that."

* * * * *

"Sometimes I wish we used a simpler way of summoning." Princess Grian frowned at the twig of white flowers dropped into her lap from above. Its thick smell hammered at her senses and startled her away from the intricate Tarot spread on the garden's oak-wood table.

Her sister arched her brow. "Remind me to get you one of those...uh...chamber-phones on my next visit to the Upper Realm."

"Cell phones, you mean. That would be nice, except everybody else here uses the weed system." Grian wrinkled her dainty nose disapprovingly. "Not to mention, Aine, how I *hate* the smell of hawthorn. 'Tis like a flock of rotting sardines!"

"Now, now," Aine grinned. "'Tis one of my summoner-plants, too. If its odor is attractive enough for midges and butterflies, who am *I* to complain? Besides, I'd rather think of its smell as the people of Arabia do. The scent of an aroused woman."

"Midges and butterflies. Not to mention Arabian erotic literature. You've obviously been spending way too much time in the Upper Realm." Grian gave her sister a warm, sunny laugh. She plucked the hawthorn twig from her lap with a dainty thumb-forefinger pinch and tossed it aside. "You may come down now, Brighid," she informed the raven circling above.

The bird made an enthusiastic dive, almost crash-landing into the grass in the Knockgreany Royal Mound's garden.

"The Princess is very kind." Brighid stepped out from the rapidly dissolving scarves of fog and dropped to her knees at Grian's feet. "Oh, Princess Aine," she added quickly with breathless awe, bowing her head to the unexpected onlooker.

"You may rise now, Brighid." Grian shared a brief glance with her sister. "Rise, and tell me what's wrong with my cards."

"Princess?" The banshee climbed to her feet, confused, smoothing down ruffled hair and battered clothes.

"What deck are you using, Grian?" Aine tilted her head, golden-haired like her sister's, over the cards spread upon the table. The Tarot made a colorful tapestry over its darkly tanned face. "Oh. This deck is *unlike you*, Grian. Its cards are dark, twisted. It throws too many pasts and presents at your face, too many futures all warped together. Maybe you should try a—"

"I've exhausted every other trump existing, even had ones painted for me by a *Leanan-Sidhe*." Grian laced her lean ivory fingers in her lap. "Tried every spread, even made some up. Each time, 'tis the same."

"What is?" Brighid blurted and immediately flushed, embarrassed by her own discourtesy.

"I can't *see*, Brighid," Grian elaborated, giving her a soft smile. "The cards make no picture. Tell me no story. Like colors smeared on a canvas by a child's play. Like words strung randomly into senseless chains."

"Could it be the work of dark sorcery?" Aine suggested as she scrutinized the cards.

"Could be, but it doesn't...well, it doesn't have a dark magic *feel* to it." Grian sent Brighid a sudden sharp look. "I think 'tis an interference, maybe," she said. "A new Power woven into the Tapestry. Have you any knowledge of who, or what, that Power might be?"

"I have two Upper Realm shifters traveling with me," Brighid admitted, squirming beneath Grian's gaze. "But they have only just arrived, while you said there had been something wrong with your cards for a much longer time."

"Does it matter whether your travel companions arrived here just recently?" Grian arched golden brows. "If the new Power is residing within them, does it matter if they are traveling Above or Below? And keep in mind, time runs a different course in both Realms. The two Realms are *connected*, Brighid. 'Tis like *this*." She linked two bowed forefingers to demonstrate. "When one quakes, the other trembles with the aftershocks. So tell me, Sidhe, what is it that makes everything shudder all of a sudden? What Power have you introduced to my dominion?"

Aine crossed her arms over her breasts, listening with silent interest.

"The Princess has a keen eye." Brighid lifted her gaze to Grian's. "I'm escorting two Kanjali shifters to *Lia Fáil*. One is a man of pure Goddess blood, and the other is a woman with both *dé-Danann* and Mortal coursing in her veins." She paused, allowing the meaning of her words to sink in.

"The woman traveler is of mixed blood? She must have forefathers among your own Mortals then, Brighid."

"Aye, the woman's Mortal half is indeed under my protection. But since I find it hard to protect only half a person, she's all mine." The banshee grinned at her own feeble joke. She wasn't surprised that Grian knew she wasn't solitary, and indeed had her own Mortal family to minister to—just like her other five Sidhe sisters. The Princess of Knockgreany Mound had an odd habit of knowing things that others didn't.

"Mmm." Grian took in this new knowledge, then something flickered in her eyes. "And you're taking both your shifters to the Stone of Fal. '*Lia Fáil* will again utter a cry, the first and the last in one and a half-thousand years'," she cited. "You're throwing yourself right into an ancient *dé-Danann* quarrel, Brighid, and you're not even one of us."

"True, I am Sidhe, not *dé-Danann*," she responded. "Yet, as a guardian Sidhe, my duty lies with the Mortal family appointed to my guardianship. Amergin's descendants have been given to my care. The Kanjali woman is a daughter to Amergin's lineage, and her life is my responsibility. Therefore your quarrel has become mine, whether I want a piece of it or not."

Grian nodded. "Is your protégée aware of the prophecy?" she asked softly.

Aine's eyes widened. "The prophecy, Grian! You don't think that's truly—?"

"The woman I'm guarding is quite innocent of any kind of knowledge," Brighid assured Grian, smiling wryly. "And I do mean, *any* kind. 'Tis my understanding her parents withheld information from her, attempting to protect her." She went on hurriedly, completely abandoning the customary third-person address, "Prince Donn of Knockfierna and his entourage crossed to your dominion a short while ago, along with a *Cú* hunter. If they catch up with my shifters..." Brighid shuddered visibly, spreading her arms with a plea. "Please, please Princess, don't let *dé-Danann* blood spill on your soil!" Then, quickly, she added, "Your Highness," her face flushing again.

"I will not go against Donn—"

"Princess, *please!*"

"*Directly.* I'm much more the, er, 'passive-aggressive' type." Grian arched a golden brow at Brighid's bold interruption.

Brighid let out a long-held breath.

"Easy, Sidhe, I *will* help you and yours. 'Tis a disgrace if I let you fight a *dé-Danann* battle all by yourself. Fighting might be far better, after all, than—" the princess gave her a tight smile, "—staring for hours at meaningless Tarot strings."

Chapter Eleven

"Think that's the one Brighid told us about?"

Dara squeezed her words deep into Rowan's tawny mane so that the wind wouldn't snatch them straight out of her mouth.

The border town, aye, he replied.

Rowan's mental voice was so like his physical one. Low-pitched, husky around the edges, tinted with that damned sexy accent. The wind blew his musky scent in Dara's face, and the sultry image of his large head hugged by her thighs popped into her mind. His incredible *mac'tir* tongue, wedged deep inside her…

Her skin bloomed with sudden goose bumps. In reflex she tightened her legs hard on Rowan's hot flanks.

Miss me already, sweetheart?

Dara's wind-flushed face burned even hotter. He'd felt her hard squeeze on him. Had guessed her exact thoughts —

Mmm, don't stop now, Dara, it felt so good. Squeeze me hard again.

Oh, Goddess! Dara's skin felt teased all over by Rowan's voice. That husky male timbre made her nipples tighten beneath her clinging shirt, made her bare pussy tingle and grow damp.

Ride me, sweetheart, he went on, coaxing. *You're doing it so bleedin' good. I want to feel your thighs, sweaty and tight. Feel your feet pressing hard on me…*

"Rowan," Dara panted into the wind. Her fists clenched harder on his fur, so hard that it almost hurt.

You can feel me, too. My breath, slowly moving over your pussy. My tongue, playing around your clit. You're so wet. I want to taste you. I want to slowly lick around your sweet, juicy cunt, then go deep, deep inside…

Dara moaned, a delicious tremble coursing from her toes to the roots of her hair. Going *right* through her wet, teased pussy.

You feel my tongue entering you. Slowly going inside. 'Tis a long, big mac'tir tongue, big enough to fill your cunt. To stretch you tight around me. You taste so sharp and sweet that I can't get enough. I'm sliding out, then drive my tongue back in, all the way. You shudder. You scream. You squeeze your legs on my head, so hard…

Dara groaned. Her body responded to Rowan's titillating command, her thigh muscles bunching. Her legs squeezed so hard on his lithe, muscular body that her ass bunched, and her cunt tightened with it. A jolt of pleasure thrust up her passage. Dara shuddered, her eyes squeezing shut.

"Oh, Goddess," she breathed.

Ahh, yes, Dara… Ride me. Ride me hard. You feel my tongue move inside your cunt, in and out and around. I want to feel you move, too. Back and forth, sweetheart, I want to feel your sweet, wet pussy rubbin' me…

Dara was panting hard, her blood fizzing with the wild ride. Her hair blew wild about her face, the wind slashing through her throat. Drawing herself forth by fistfuls of Rowan's coppery mane, she groaned and pressed her cunt hard against his pelt. He was smooth silk beneath her, and flowing, rugged muscles. Dara's thighs bunched again, *hard*. She started to move against Rowan, a slow, tight undulation.

Yesss, Dara, don't stop… You feel so good around me. Up and down, sweetheart. Keep moving on me, love. Do it harder. Faster…

"*Rowan*," Dara gasped. Letting control go, she swayed above Rowan's muscled body, rocking her wet, throbbing pussy against his animated back. Her eyes tightly closed as she slowly, rhythmically, tightened and relaxed her inner muscles. Nothing else existed but the sensation of movement—of Rowan's feral, sweeping gallop, of her own body moving against his. Sweet, pulsating pressure built low in her tummy. Her blood gushed excitedly through her veins, engorging her clit, her nether lips, the hot, soaking flesh of her cunt. Goddess, she was so wet. She felt hot and teased, inside and out. A loud moan broke her lips. She couldn't take it much longer...yet she didn't want this to end. Her movements were wild now, rough. She was deaf and blind to the outside world. With a desperate cry, she crushed her clit against Rowan's back, tightening her inner muscles in concert—

Yes, Dara, let go...

She cried out as orgasm hit her, her empty cunt clenching so hard that she almost blanked out.

Dara! Sweetheart, keep grabbin' me tight, Rowan's voice cautioned, threaded with gentle humor. *I'd hate to lose such a fine rider.*

Dara's eyes finally popped open, her pupils still dilated with ecstasy. Her breath was coming in wheezes—she was beyond talking. Clinging to Rowan's body with all her remaining strength, she wasn't about to let him go any time soon.

As time went by, Rowan's mental answers transformed into single words and clipped sentences. His fur was drenched, the flesh beneath pulsing with heat. He was drawing on the last of his strength as he surged through *Máigh-Mór*, the Great Plain, struggling to keep the wrestling Powers in balance.

Dara knew that her weight must have been taking its toll on him.

The border town of Commar was perched on the verge of Mumha's Great Plain, at the confluence of two rivers. The River of Gold, named so because its shimmering water seemed gilded, wound its way with sensual nonchalance, southeast to northwest. Its mate, the Ruby Glen, gushed through Connachta with vibrant force, its turbulent flow halving the kingdom in the opposite direction. Like lovers, the two rivers entwined into one, the Luran, golden and calm at parts and tumultuous in others. Flowing west and away from its parents, the Luran made a natural border between the two kingdoms of Mumha and Connachta before spilling into the Ocean. Thus the city of Commar had been split into three, the Golden bank, the Ruby bank, and a triangular peninsula termed simply Inis, the Island. The *dé-Danann* city belonged to both kingdoms, and yet belonged to neither.

"How are we going to enter the city, huh, Mackey?" Dara queried. "You left your jeans way back. Are you planning to go into town as a beast, or as a naked man?"

Which of those two options do you like best, sweetheart?

"Oh, quit it!" she laughed, nudging his flank with the heel of one small foot. Truth was, she rather liked *both* of the above options. She bit her lower lip, recalling how it felt to squeeze her thighs on that big, furry head. To get off on Rowan's fluent, powerful body. To have his large, rough tongue moving inside of her...

I think they're more used to shapechangers than seeing naked men roaming the streets, Rowan teased in her head. *But the mac'tir form, I don't think we should flash it in their faces right now.*

"You'd rather flash something else in their faces?" Dara joked. She sighed, letting the sassy memory of his artful tongue go for now. Rowan did have a point. She consoled herself by clinging to his lithe, powerful body with a squeezing hug of both arms and legs.

Finally, he slowed his gallop, his weariness palpable. Dara slid off his back. Rolling her shoulders beneath her dagger's leather harness, she watched Rowan's *mac'tir* form as it crouched down heavily within the tall grass.

"Oh shit. I shouldn't have kicked you, Rowan, I'm sorry."

"'Tis fine, Dara. Tell you the truth, I enjoyed it."

Rowan rolled to his back with a groan in the clearing mist. His transformation was swifter this time, faster than it had been before. He sat up, not bothering to shake the grass out of his hair. She watched him as he climbed to his feet, stretching to his full height, and realized that she wasn't bothered anymore by his nakedness. Rather the opposite…

She wanted to see more of it.

"I hurt in muscles I didn't know I had." He grinned as he turned to face her, the familiar mischievous sparkle back in his eyes.

It hit her that she'd come to like *that* about him, as well. Damned if she hadn't actually been missing it.

"The way we both look right now, we should search that town for a fairy tailor, not a fairy shoemaker," she said. "Though we're barefoot, as well."

"He's a Leprechaun, actually," he answered.

"Huh?"

"Brighid's acquaintance, the fairy shoemaker—he's a Leprechaun. 'Tis the common name for his kind."

"Can't wait to meet the tiny bearded trickster," Dara admitted with a smile. "Brighid said he was living in the island part of the city, right? I wonder if he has a crock of gold stashed somewhere?"

"I thought you didn't believe in fairy tales," Rowan teased. "If he *does* have gold, Dara, I don't think he'll share it with us. You know the story about greedy Tom who caught himself a Leprechaun, don't you?"

"The one with the red garter." Her eyes shone. "Mom used to tell me that story over and over."

"A red garter would look really *nice* on you, Dara. But only if you wear nothing else."

"I think *you* need it more right now. To wrap it around your—"

"You insult me, sweetheart. Am I that small?"

"Around your *hair*, to keep it from falling into your eyes," Dara finished with a grin. "Goddess, *men!*"

They both halted, coming across the first squat houses fringing the Golden slice of Commar. Dwellings were scarcer here, some surrounded by small farms — no, not exactly farms, there were no crops to be seen, no plowed fields.

"Look there —" Dara pointed to a mixed herd of cattle and sheep grazing not too far ahead. Her voice was imbued with excitement, that of a little girl introduced for the first time to nature lurking just outside city limits.

Rowan grinned to himself. Funny, finding out she was in the legendary *Tír Na nÓg* hadn't drawn this kind of a joyous cry out of her like tumbling into these few lunching cows and sheep. *Women, go figure.* His mind conjured a steamy image of Dara, posing gloriously naked except for one sexy, red-hot garter slipped up her right thigh.

He considered that.

Mmmm, no, her left would be cuter.

Dara regarded the Irishman. "What's going on in your mind, Mackey?"

He arched both brows innocently. *Aye, definitely her left.*

Dara eyed him with mounting suspicion. Was his look getting smokier or was she imagining things? Sighing, she relinquished the matter for now. "I keep waiting for one of these cows to float," she told him.

"I don't think that would happen." Mackey's grin broadened. "These don't look like fairy animals to me. They seem more like stolen, very-much-Mortal cows and sheep. I bet there are very angry Mortal farmers looking for them right now."

"Well, how can you tell these are *not* fairy cows?" Dara demanded with some disappointment. Her eyes moved from the pasture to Rowan's roguish expression. *Oh my.* The man was definitely surveying her from her toes to the roots of her hair with that smoldering bedroom gaze. What lewd, X-rated film was he currently running in his head? She had a feeling that whatever it was, she'd been granted a starring role.

Dara was about to address the subject when something suddenly detached itself from the herd and made its way towards them, a smudge of gold and green.

That *thing*—whatever it was—was moving damn fast. Rowan reached and laid a cautioning hand over Dara's forearm, the heat in his eyes swiftly dissolving.

What looked like a tall, slender woman drifted closer to them among the grazing blotches of browns, grays, blacks and whites. Her hair, a pale gold, flowed down to her knees. A loose green robe billowed about her body, simply cut but elaborately embroidered, long enough to hide her feet. The ballooning shift made it look as if she were hovering just above the grass. She drifted to a halt, facing them, her smoky complexion apparent now, and studied them with large eyes of a deep blue-green.

Like still pools, Dara thought, *not stormy seas like Rowan's.*

"Name your weapon," the woman commanded Dara in a sweet silvery voice. Her stagnant eyes briefly lit with an odd hunger as she surveyed Rowan's nude physique.

"My weapon?" Dara inquired acerbically, shooting her an irate look. *She'd better start staring elsewhere!*

"Don't," Rowan swiftly whispered to Dara, slanting a wary glance towards her ritual *Scían*. "Don't *name* your weapon. Just describe it to her."

As if she could utter her dagger's Gaelic name without breaking her teeth on it. Dara shot Rowan a baffled look. "I have one mean dagger," she finally informed the audacious blonde. "Damascus steel, inlaid with silver."

"Forge-welded and folded by a master bladesmith," Rowan added helpfully. "See, you forge-weld alternating sheets of low and high-carbon steels, so that—"

"*Iron*," the woman growled. The delicate beauty of her high-cheekboned face was somewhat offset by the sharp fangs she'd just revealed.

The blonde was a vampire. And she seemed to *really* like Rowan. Dara's hand immediately shot to her dagger's bone hilt.

"Yeah, iron, lots of it," she hissed. "Really impressive. Want to have a real close look at it?" Odd, though—movie vampires usually avoided a wooden stake to the heart, not cold iron.

"What do you want, travelers?" The blonde vamp seemed deflated at the sight of iron. "I will do as you wish as long as you leave my herd in peace."

"Who are you?" Dara's fist was still tight on her dagger.

"I cannot tell you my name," the toothy blonde replied.

"Fairies are real touchy when it comes to a first name basis," Rowan intervened. "I can tell you *what* she is, though, Dara. A Glaistig, if I guess right."

"A *what*?"

The Glaistig stood motionless, watching them with her still-pool eyes.

"A Glaistig—a Water Imp," Rowan repeated. "In truth, I believed her kind to reside only in the Scottish Highlands. She's a water spirit, living close to rivers, streams, and lakes. The River of Gold is not too far from here, aye? When a Water Imp is good, she's kind to kiddies, grannies and grandpas. Loves herding cattle, blessing them with plenty of milk. A good shepherdess, she is."

"But?" Dara's dismayed gaze was fixated on the woman. "There's always a but, Rowan."

"But—" he grinned, "—when she is bad, she is *true evil*. See the sharp teeth on her? She likes grabbing a man for a wild dance, and then, like a vampire, she feeds on his blood. She also doesn't care much for travelers, has this habit of slaying—"

"*Slaying*?" Dara exclaimed. She drew out her dagger, completely removing it from its sheath.

The Imp reared back, snarling, her fangs glistening cruelly in the perpetual daylight.

"No, no, easy, sweetheart—as long as you don't tell her your weapon's name you're safe, and she will do as you ask."

Just to be on the safe side, Rowan took a step that put him halfway between Dara and the snarling woman. He was standing much closer to the Water Imp than he cared to be.

"Okay, then. In that case," Dara turned to the Water Imp, motioning with her dagger. "You. Give him your clothes."

Without a word the Imp slid her green robe over her head and handed it over to Rowan. He took it from her hands, noting her unsheathed silvery claws stroking over the cloth. The ornamented green fabric was sheer and almost weightless in his hands, like a piece of cloud, fluttering against his naked flesh in the soft wind. The Imp measured him with another hungry look, her lips curling slowly into a smile that bared her fangs again. Slowly, he withdrew from the smiling vampiric fairy.

"Rowan, but she's half a… Her legs are not…" Dara stammered in shock. She was gripping her dagger so hard, her knuckles went white.

"Oh, aye," Rowan grinned. "I forgot to mention *that* part. Her lower half is…not womanly."

The Imp growled, outraged. Willowy and smoke-skinned, she stood draped in nothing but her light gold hair. Strands of it fell against her small, firm breasts, like those of a young girl on the verge of womanhood. Her nipples peaked in a shade darker than her skin, almost bluish in color. The feminine curves of her narrow hips ended in a pair of tapering goat legs boasting white, silky fur.

"You *forgot* to mention," Dara mumbled. She stared hypnotized at the delicate silvered hooves bejeweled with tourmalines, red and black.

The Imp shifted slightly, stomping the grass with one hoof and then the other, obviously ill at ease with Dara's scrutiny.

Rowan meanwhile pulled the green gown over his head. It was long enough to reach his lower calves, its folds shifting around his body with each small movement. He made a face. Still no sassy comment from Dara, her eyes were glued to the Water Imp.

"Go, go back now," Dara ordered in her kiddie teacher tone. "Back to your herd. I'm sorry for doing this, it's just that I had no choice, and..."

That pretty much left her speechless. She obviously wasn't accustomed to robbing half-women-half-goats of their clothes.

The Imp gave Dara a dirty look, then gave Rowan an even dirtier one. "We'll be dancing yet, pretty one," she murmured in a husky voice much more suited to a cat than a half-goat.

"Hey!" Dara shouted angrily.

"I think I'll pass." Rowan grinned at the fairy, laying a restraining hand over Dara's lush backside. His mate jolted in surprise, her gaze whipping back to him.

The vampiric Imp gave Rowan a *"we'll see about that"* predatory smile, and then swirled within the gold cloud of her hair. Now that her gown wasn't conveying the illusion of a graceful walk, the Water Imp didn't bother to appear humanlike anymore. She took advantage of her powerful legs, launching herself back to her precious herd in a series of powerful, oddly graceful leaps.

"I'd be watching my back if I were you." Dara's gaze followed the creature's movement as she again sheathed her trusty dagger.

"Oh, lassie, I didn't know you cared." He gave her juicy buttock an appreciative squeeze.

Dara jumped with a yelp and swiveled to face him, then stared at him openmouthed. "Goddess," she started, then pressed both her hands against her quivering lips. It looked like she was wrestling with something huge swelling inside of her, her torso quivering and her face flushing scarlet. And then she gave in, and it spilled out through her slackening fingers — ringing peals of laughter, one chased by the other.

"Aye?" Rowan frowned. "Is something not right?"

"You," she gasped between giggles. "You look...like..."

"Go on. I look *like...*?" he demanded, crossing his arms over his chest in a gesture that only made Dara laugh harder, hugging herself and bending in half.

"Like Robin Hood in a dress!" she finally managed, squirming with giggles, her butt hitting the grass.

"Come now, lass, get up," Rowan groaned and leaned above her writhing form, extending one of his hands. "'Tis better than walking around naked, right?"

"Oh, I don't know." She grabbed his offered hand, and he yanked her back to her feet. She was still panting, but the worst of the laughter had subsided. "I never thought I would say it—" she shot him a grin, "—but after seeing you in this outfit, I think I prefer watching you prance around naked."

"I'll keep that in mind," he said, flashing her his roguish grin.

Before Dara managed to regain her breath Rowan gave her wrist a slight pull and gathered her into his body, swiftly trapping her face in his hands. His mouth came down over her stunned lips, brushing, teasing, demanding entrance. She opened her mouth wider for a quick breath, accepting his tongue with it. Her hands climbed up his shoulders, sought his tangled, wild hair. The man's devilish tongue took swift control of her mouth, swirling within its moist depths, sensually unraveling each of its dark secrets, playing a sizzling game of dominance.

Dara's moan slipped into Rowan's mouth, and he welcomed her tongue in with it. His commanding hands slipped to her waist, pressing her tighter against him. With luxurious leisure he guided her velvety exploration inside his mouth, then shamelessly sucked on her tongue, making her moan with building ecstasy.

And then he released her tongue with a soft "pop".

His green eyes twinkled as he studied her dazed expression.

Finally remembering to roll her tongue back in her mouth, Dara thought Rowan had made his point perfectly. Dress or no dress, Mackey was one hundred percent pure male.

Chapter Twelve

The river town of Commar thickened around the two Kanjali shifters as they ventured deeper in, towards the River of Gold that wound its way through the city's heart. The twining streets bore no hint of a name and no numbers, only colors. Maybe that was how their denizens recognized them, Dara mused, by hues and shades—or perhaps the townsfolk needed no obvious markers to navigate through their own avenues. She was ambling with Rowan along winding lilac, the pavestones gleaming a soft purple, same as the pudgy brick houses. Even the air they had been breathing felt lightly perfumed with lavender.

Though Kanjali and *dé-Danann* bloodlines had entwined in a distant past, this didn't feel like home. Now and then the two of them drew questioning glances from passersby, who recognized them for the outsiders they were. The town dwellers, typical *dé-Danann*, were a long, lithe breed, boasting fair complexions and hair ranging from golden to fiery. Men and women alike wore their hair long and intricately braided. They were clothed in various shades of green, ranging from deep emerald to pale celadon, with stirred-in hues of browns and grays, earth, sea and grass. The faces they glimpsed were all fine-featured and young, not one ridged with old age, but Rowan and Dara had noticed no children skimming through the streets, either.

"At least you blend in well," Dara teased. "A redhead in a green dress."

"That didn't sound like a compliment." Rowan gently squeezed her arm, and she rewarded him with hushed laughter. Her lips still deliciously tingled from his last, branding kiss.

"I think we're kind of lost," she said. "Maybe we should ask someone to point us to the river?"

"Mmm, how about those two?" He pointed to an entangled couple half-shaded by a low-hung arched balcony.

She glanced where he pointed and quickly averted her gaze. "Uh, *you* ask them."

Rowan's hand closed over Dara's wrist and he gently rolled her into him with a swift motion, yanking a surprised squeak out of her mouth. He enfolded her against his chest, each of her hands captured in one of his.

"What," he whispered, his voice low and husky, "is so terrible about watching these two, sweetheart?"

His voice breathed over the delicate shell of her ear, making a soft jolt shoot down Dara's spine. Though Rowan held her gently, he gave her no chance of escape.

"They don't seem to mind. Look."

Dara shook her head, straining against Rowan's grasp, when a breathless feminine moan sounded from the shadows, drawing her gaze to the tangled lovers.

The woman's back was pressed against the murky brick wall. Her hair spilled to her waist in a dark red cascade, and a generous side-split in her gown bared the long curve of one raised thigh. Her flesh was milky-white against the robe's forest green. She crooked her knee, squeezing her leg against the man's thighs, trapping his dark cloak beneath her.

He pressed his hands hard against the wall, framing the woman's face. His cloak fell away from his arms, baring bulging sinews gleaming with sweat.

She panted a small, excited laugh, her face partly blocked from Dara's view by her lover's broad shoulders.

His head bowed deeper, a shock of golden hair tumbling forward. The redhead's hands were working low on him, concealed from view, doing something to his body that made him groan and thrust his hips with mounting need. His hands tightened into fists against the bricks.

"Mmmmm," the redhead purred, working on him with a swifter tempo. She leaned her head back against the wall, watching his face.

"Enough," the man growled hoarsely.

Still swaying his hips, he jerked one hand from the sweat-dampened clay and captured the redhead's slim wrists. Dara could see her shifting against the wall behind him, face and torso mostly hidden.

He pinned her arms against the wall, and she responded with a tiny yelp.

"Leave 'em there," he breathed in soft command.

His fingers trailed a slow route up her trembling arm and back down again, then stroked up that never-ending, milk-white thigh. His lingering caress slipped into the gown's deep split, his back muscles bunching beneath his cloak. The redhead gasped sharply as he buried his hand deeper between her thighs, her back arching against the wall with a violent shudder.

Then, slowly, he pulled his hand out, wetness dousing his fingers, and Dara's breath caught in her burning throat as she watched.

Clutching the woman's waist, the man easily heaved her back against the wall, and thrust hard between her thighs. She screamed as he drove himself inside her, spearing his cloak with her fingers. Both her legs locked around his waist as he started to pump into her in a lazy, steady rhythm. He cupped her ass through the twin side splits in her gown, forcing her tighter against him as he fucked her.

Her short, snatched moans swirled into the air. She tightened her arms on his back, crushing his cloak. Her head fell against her lover's shoulder, mingling her fiery locks into his fair, lightly braided ones. Her eyes fluttered open for a brief second, staring directly into Dara's, then fluttered shut again.

Dara, stunned by the redhead's blunt stare, shifted at Rowan's soft chuckle in her ear.

"You're panting, sweetheart," he teased, and laid a sizzling kiss against the long line of her neck. And then, feeling her stiffening in response, "Aye, let you go, right?"

Rowan's grip loosened on Dara and she tore away from him, blushed to the core and struggling to calm her breathing. They resumed their walk along the winding pavestones, the couple's escalating moans fading behind their backs. Dara almost stumbled, so vicious was the sweet tingling between her legs.

A sharp gasp tore from her mouth as Rowan caught her slim waist from behind, pinning her against his front. He seemed to be fond of that particular position. His arms caged her slender form in an uncompromising hug, his large body draping hers.

"You looked like you were in pain, sweetheart." He dropped the soft words into her hair, his mouth teasing one cheek.

She writhed against his arms, her breath hissing out in a furious huff. "Rowan, dammit, let—"

"Do you truly wish me to let you go, Dara?" He eased one hand's grip.

"Yeah," she whispered, but her body quieted as his hand took a slow tour of her body. It lingered over one heaving breast, measuring its quickening rise and fall. A desperate moan breached Dara's lips—Rowan's gently pressed palm could surely feel the tautening nipple beneath it.

Her body always seemed to betray her, time and again.

"Come, sweetheart," Rowan uttered as he guided her towards the mauve mouth of a narrow alley. Entwined with her, he was walking her, bit by bit, away from the wide street's leisurely bustle.

Dara breathed out a sobbing protest as Rowan's hands captured hers, bracing them against the lilac wall. Behind her, he froze at the sound, his grip still fixing her against the tinted bricks. He let her trapped hands slip from his grasp, gently spinning her to face him.

"Dara…"

Her name tasted sweet and sharp, like the enticing scent wafting from her, like her vibrant, unique life force.

"Dara, sweetheart, relax."

She shot him a dark, mystified glance, one that told him her thoughts were again being tormented by the ghostly presence of her long-dead lover.

Rowan drew in a shaky breath.

His fingers gently tilted Dara's chin up, sliding to stroke along her satiny cheek. Finally, nestling her face in his hot palms, he bowed his head down to hers. He brushed his fiery lips against his mate's cool brow, aching to banish the wraithlike chill from her eyes, wanting to infuse her body with his own heat instead.

He thawed her face with searing kisses as she sagged back against the wall. She tipped her head more to meet him, and he captured her mouth with a slow, probing kiss. Her dewy lips slackened to admit his tongue deeper. She countered him, hot and velvety, her lean fingers trembling against his unshaven jaw.

"Dara," he finally whispered against her mouth, his tone raw. "Sweetheart, let me love you. Just a bit."

Her response was a low, lingering moan that wrenched his insides.

Rowan took that as a yes.

Dara arched her neck as Rowan slid down from her mouth, tasting the crazed pulse throbbing beneath her jawline. She tunneled shaky fingers through his hair as he licked the vulnerable skin and then sucked it into his mouth. She groaned, pulling his head down harder as he feasted on her flesh. His hands were everywhere—molding her back, palming her ass, crushing her t-shirt and kneading her flesh through the battered cloth. He released her well-kissed neck and licked his way down to the sweat-slicked curve at the base of her throat.

"*Rowan*," she panted, swaying against him, shivering uncontrollably.

He slid lower, his body tight against her deep curves. Her fingers twined deeper in his hair as he crouched down on his knees before her. His fiery gaze captured hers, unrelenting. His hands kept moving beneath her shirt. He watched her face as he stroked over her bare hips and made slow love to her belly button with his mouth.

She gasped, her fingers wreaking more havoc in the blazing mayhem of his hair.

His hands moved to cradle her breasts.

"Rowan. *Yes!*"

Dara's back arched sharply, her head pressing against the mauve bricks. Her nipples wrinkled and tightened beneath Rowan's circling, tugging fingers. A wave of heat washed over her writhing body. She called out as one of Rowan's hands sneaked between her parted thighs.

"You're so wet, sweetheart," he whispered against her navel, his head wrestling her shirt further up her rib cage.

She moaned, eyes shuttered, as one long finger eased its way inside her, another quickly joining it. Rowan braced her against him, kissing around her navel, as his fingers moved and kneaded inside her cunt.

She swayed against the wall, out of breath.

He granted her no mercy, kissing lower over the dark fuzz of curls shading her mound, 'til his lips finally hit the spot.

Dara hissed out a sharp gasp as his talented mouth trapped her clit's slick knob. Her eyes wrenched open, gazing upon the fiery head moving between her thighs.

Rowan gave her clit a vicious suck, then drummed his tongue against the hard, tiny bulge. His fingers kept fucking her, unrelenting. She closed her eyes again, shuddering all over. Breathing hard, she untangled her sweaty fingers from Rowan's hair, digging them into his bunching shoulders.

"*Rowan.*"

His tongue stroked a sure path down her swollen vulva and drove inside her cunt, replacing his fingers. He tasted her fully, lapping up her pouring juices, dining on her engorged inner flesh. She danced her hips above him, her buttocks bunching, her thigh muscles taut with the effort. One short moan after another broke from her lips, in rhythm with her undulating motion. Rowan's fingers dug into her ass cheeks, pulling her down hard on his face.

"*Oh Goddess, yes!*"

Dara jerked against Rowan's face as orgasm hit her, swift and sweeping, her pussy clenching on his tongue over and over. She screamed, sinking back against the clammy bricks. He kept his tongue inside her, his firm grasp on her buttocks forcing her against his face until the tight waves of rapture dwindled and subsided.

He pulled her down then, nestling her prostrate body against his chest.

"It's not fair," she mumbled, in between quick gasps of air.

"Not fair, sweetheart?" Rowan searched her face, slowly licking her taste off his glossy lips. His fingers skimmed over her damp brow, tenderly brushing aside sweat-plastered clumps of raven-black hair.

"Each time, I swear I won't do it," she whispered. "And each time, you win."

Rowan didn't answer, apparently finding no suitable retort to her breathless accusation.

Dara gazed up at his face. Something raw flickered in his eyes, something like…pain, and was quickly pushed back.

Unable to stop herself, Dara reached up for Rowan, stroking his rough jaw. His skin still felt hot, damp from her release.

She wanted to love him back.

"Dara—?" he asked, surprised, as she struggled up in his hold.

"Shhh...don't talk," she whispered, looping her arms around his neck, drawing herself up against him. Her lips hovered over his mouth, bathing in his warm breath.

"Sweetheart, you don't have t—"

"Shhh..." Her mouth sealed his lips, silencing him. She pressed against the softness, wanting entry, *needing* it. Her tongue tasted him, skimmed against the seam of his lips, hesitant, thirsty.

He froze against her. Suddenly his fingers threaded through her hair. Exhaling a soft breath, he let her in.

Dara let out a relieved moan, wrapping her arms tight around Rowan's neck. She stroked her tongue over his lips, dipping into the gap between. His hot mouth invited her deeper, his tongue sliding against hers with a velvety caress. She pressed heavily against his body, her breasts flattening against his hard muscles. His strong heartbeat drummed against her breasts— steady, virile. She opened her mouth wide over his, deepening her kiss, hearing him groan. She felt his fingers stroking her hair. Felt his hard cock pressing demandingly against her stomach beneath his thin, green robe.

Dara broke their kiss, pulling back from Rowan with effort, and he mumbled a plea, or a soft curse, unknowingly slipping into Gaelic. She kissed down his throat, tasting salt, tasting *him*. His fingers convulsed on her shoulders as she shifted against him, her mouth falling to his chest. Damn that robe, she needed to feel *skin*. She covered Rowan's hard muscles with kisses, dampening his robe's light fabric.

"*Dara.*"

Rowan was trying to gain control over his rough breathing. He kneaded her shoulders, spreading his legs wider to make more room for her.

Dara dropped her gaze to his cock, rearing against the stretched fabric. She glanced up at his face. "Lean back a bit," she whispered, gently pushing him to lean against the mauve bricks.

"Sweetheart—" he began roughly.

"Rowan. I—I want you." She licked her lips. "Please."

He slid his large hands from her shoulders in a slow caress, leaning back on his elbows. His eyes were afire, his body tense as if he was struggling to hold still.

Dara tugged at his robe's hem, dragging the cool fabric up his muscled thighs. His breath hissed in as she lifted the cloth over his rampant erection, revealing his fully erect cock. She lightly touched his shaft, and he curbed a shudder.

"Rowan. You're so hard." She shifted between his legs. Her fingertips left his cock, trailing down the long, steely muscles of his thighs. His flesh was hot, silky-smooth, gathering sweat. He clenched his fists against the bricks. Slowly, she stroked him higher, to his naked, slim hips, deliberately avoiding his cock. He sucked in his breath as her fingers touched his soft ginger curls.

His cock head looked swollen, its tip oozing moisture.

"I'll kiss it better," Dara whispered, leaning low. She ran a hungry tongue over Rowan's flat stomach, over his inner thighs, his heavy balls. She'd been wanting to do that to him since she'd seen him standing beside his motorcycle, raindrops slicking down his naked skin, trailing along his flat abdomen to disappear beneath the edge of his jeans.

Rowan threw back his head, his hips rocking slowly. "Dara," he groaned.

She steadied his cock against her lips, running her tongue up, licking along his shaft. She heard him hiss, felt him buck. Moistening her lips again, she took his smooth cock head into the wet heat of her mouth. He was big. There was no way she could take him all the way inside. Cupping his shaft, she swirled her tongue around his engorged tip, gathering his briny fluid. His hips gave a slight jerk as her mouth closed on him, he was breathing hard. She loved the feel of him against her tongue. His taste. Smell. The texture of his skin…

"Dara," Rowan heaved hoarsely, his hips picking speed. "Sweetheart, no, wait—"

She wasn't listening. She kept laving his cock, one cupped hand pumping along his shaft in wicked rhythm with her mouth. Goddess, she wanted Rowan to come in her mouth. Wanted to give him back as much as he'd given her. Wanted—

"*Dara*!" Rowan's hips gave a violent thrust and he exploded deep in her mouth, shuddering with the force of his climax. Her hands were still cupped around him as his hot semen washed down her throat. Slowly he sat up, sweeping her into his arms. He hugged her to his chest, stroked her hair, pressed his mouth hard over her salty lips.

She didn't respond.

He whispered her name, softly, urgently—

With a sudden moan, Dara struggled against Rowan's embrace.

He let her go, watching her in silence. Saying nothing.

She leaped to her feet, tugging her shirt down over her sweaty skin. Drawing away from Rowan, she lifted her trembling fingers to her mouth.

Aidan.

How could she have done this to him?

He'd been her first. Her only one. She'd never slept with another. After he'd died, she'd never wanted to take another man inside her—

"W-we should go and find that Leprechaun," she stammered, refusing to meet Rowan's gaze.

"Aye, I guess we should," Rowan whispered. Slowly, he climbed to his feet.

The mauve street opened to an ivory-white plaza, its air flavored with sweet pipe music and a salty-sea taste. Manannan the Ocean Lord had made his presence felt in the vicinity of each river joining his Ocean realm. Rowan plucked a plump green apple from a nearby tree, slipping it into Dara's hands. Famished, she burrowed her teeth into the fruit's flesh, sour-sweet juice bursting down her chin. Rowan laughed, wiping the dribble from her jaw with gentle fingers, then giving each finger a thorough, meaningful lick. Huddled close together, they wended their way through the slowly gathering throng, finding themselves carried towards the undulating melody. Slow and mellow, it sounded like an old tune, long forgotten. As they neared, the music picked up the pace.

"That one over there looks like some ancient version of Uilleann pipes," Rowan remarked. "The girl uses only one big bag instead of two, see it tucked beneath her arm? The way she squeezes it?"

Dara nodded, watching the trio of players. Dressed in sea-green, hair tucked into numerous flaming braids, the three women huddled in the small clearing made by their listeners. The girl Rowan had pointed to was seated with a spread of pipes spilling over her lowered right thigh, her left hugging a large inflated leather bag. Her agile fingers ran over a wooden chanter held lightly in both hands. Her two companions were standing to either side, half a step behind, one of them holding a panpipe and strapped with an assortment of slim whistles, the other carrying what looked like a Highland bagpipe. Neither woman was playing, allowing the seated one to play solo with her bewitching tune.

"Reminds me of music I heard once, spending a night on a fairy mound," Rowan whispered.

"What, all by yourself?" Dara quipped.

"Well, I actually had with me a —"

"They're mainly carved from the wood of an elder tree, their pipes." The admonishing voice made them both swivel around sharply to face an irritated banshee. Their ears tuned to the music, they had missed Brighid's flutter of wings as she descended into the crowd wearing her raven form.

"Took me a bit to find you," she said reprovingly. "Shouldn't you two be elsewhere, right now?"

"The river's bridge," Dara muttered sheepishly.

"Aye, the Third Bridge at the least, on your way to Inis's Leprechaun Alley." Brighid's thin eyebrows drew together in a frown. "But no time to look for bridges now, there's been a change in plans. Instead we've got ourselves a date with the Merrows."

She slipped her small hands into theirs, pulling them with surprising strength through the thinning back rows of the small crowd, and then further away over the cerulean cobblestones that snaked away from the Plaza.

"Merrows?" Dara panted as she scampered after the small Sidhe, struggling to wrest her hand free.

"Princess Grian agreed to help us, sort of," Brighid tossed over her shoulder. "Here, turn here, quick!" She waved them both into a cherry-themed alley. "The Princess made contact with her father."

"Her father?" Dara groaned. The combination of a crimson lane and the two fizzy redheads with her was overloading her senses. Otherwise she welcomed the sudden sprint, it was an acceptable alternative to her usual morning swim.

"Princess Grian's father is Manannan Mac Lir," Brighid blurted out in response. "Lord of *Tir-fo-Thoinn*. He'll send his Merrows to help us."

"The 'Land Beneath the Waves'," Rowan translated in Dara's ear, not sounding the least out of breath. "Manannan is the Ocean Lord."

"Why then—" Dara started. They twisted out of the narrow cherry lane into a sloping rosy one, and then the world unfolded before them with breathtaking abruptness. "Are we running?" she finished, her eyes widening in wonder. Abann-na-Óir, the River of Gold, suddenly filled the near horizon. Its rippling face mirrored the eternal daylight in mellow gold. For a second they all stood silently, drinking in the sight and rolling the salty air on their tongues.

"Because," said Brighid, "we're late." She broke into a short run, her cape billowing behind her, her gown miraculously avoiding tangling between her legs. She skidded to a stop halfway from the river and turned back to shout at them, her arms decorating her words with urgent gestures. "D'you two need a royal summons? Get your arses down here!"

Rowan cocked an amused brow.

"Well, Brighid, if you put it *that* way," Dara muttered and started towards the banshee, taking a deliberately calm pace. Rowan chuckled behind as he joined her.

Then *something* growled.

Dara spun around in a blur, gripping her dagger and drawing it in the same movement. The wrought metal flashed wickedly as it met daylight, throwing dancing glimmers over Dara's face. Rowan was growling beside her, too, low in his throat, molten amber flowing into the green of his eyes. Dara completed her movement to face what he did, her dagger slashing the adjacent air. Her eyes froze in a wide stare, a familiar icy finger touching her core.

A tall, slender figure was silhouetted against the rosy hues at the mouth of the alley they had just emerged from. The darkness of his hair and clothes contrasted sharply with his deathly pale skin. His head was raised as if he were sniffing the air. As Dara watched he lowered his gaze, settling his eyes on her. He greeted her with a slight smile and a mocking bow of his head.

Dara fought the sick feeling that was coursing through her body, weakening her knees. Even from afar, she had sensed the weight of the Hound's gaze. Her left shoulder began to throb as the memory of a recently healed wound flared into life.

"Dara, *run!*"

She hardly recognized Rowan's thickened voice. He grabbed her wrist and yanked her from where she'd been standing, propelling her into a frantic sprint. There were more shadowy figures spilling out of the rainbow-colored streets, some on horseback, others walking with their steeds by their sides. Hooves clattered with dissonance against the cobblestones.

"To the river. Jump!" Brighid was screaming and waving as they loped past her. "*Jump, now!*"

Brighid watched as the Hound began to change, still smiling behind the mists he had gathered. He shifted slower than he was able to, like he was enjoying every moment of it. The oncoming riders halted at the mouths of the streets opening to the river concourse. One of them, mounted on a massive white horse, advanced forward from the semicircle they made. Silver shone from his saddle's embroidery and high pommel.

Donn. Brighid tensed, her hands making a cup against her lips, nestling a single remaining white petal.

Donn lunged from his horse, a cloud of mist exploding around him as he transformed mid-leap. The rich indigo of the velvet hugging his skin darkened to a black leopard's silky-smooth fur. In the rosy alley behind him mists were slowly peeling away from the Hound, baring something dark and huge in their core.

"Grian, by this hawthorn I call on thee." Brighid exhaled softly over the shuddering petal, and a tongue of flame consumed the white. Calling the Princess by fire...she had never dared this way of summoning before.

The black leopard landed in a crouch and leaped forward. A golden flash suddenly slammed into its elongated dark shape, breaking its jump. The puma and the leopard rolled against the pavestones, gold and black flashing alternately. The two big cats suddenly tore free of each other, immediately becoming engulfed by twin swirls of fog. These quickly receded, revealing the shapechangers' human forms.

Donn gave Grian a dark smile. "You make a lovely cat, Princess."

"You should have informed me earlier of your plans to visit." Grian returned his smile. "Then I would've seen to you being greeted…properly."

"I owe you no answers." Donn kept smiling. "Last I heard, your Knockgreany was not Mumha's Ruling Mound."

"Last *I* heard, your Knockfierna was no more a Ruling Mound than my Knockgreany. Which makes you a Lesser, just as I. High Prince Bodb has command of the Kingdom's only Ruling Mound, hence he's the only one who outranks me in my own dominion. You are standing on *my* land, Donn. You're not to give any orders here."

They stared coldly at one another, bodies tight like bowstrings. Neither one moved.

Diving from the sky, Brighid tore furiously with beak and claws at the golden eye of the monstrous *mac'tir* that the Hound had changed into.

"Ready to jump?" Rowan shouted beside Dara, squeezing her hand.

The Hound's howl of agony and rage sounded frighteningly close behind their backs.

Neither dared turn and look. The riverbank was briefly touching their feet, and then they were both airborne, water and sky swirling into a nauseating blur. A black smear crossed their visual field.

Brighid? Dara thought hazily, and then, *I didn't get to sheathe my dagger.*

Just before the water slammed into her body she drew in one last deep breath and tightened her grip on her dagger. Another stray thought leaped into her mind…

I hope the water isn't really gold.

Chapter Thirteen

All sound was cut off sharply, and then there was nothing but stillness, aside from her own blood pounding in her ears. Dara tore her eyes open and twisted around with a few practiced movements. She had lost her grip on Rowan upon hitting the water, but her fist was still clasped tight around her dagger.

There he was, his long hair swirling in slow-motion about his face, like dancing flames. He jerked his eyes open, and they blazed an oddly fresher green beneath the water. He wrestled out of his ballooning robe before it drowned him, and the swelling garb floated to the water's surface like a huge, green jellyfish.

Dara slid the dagger back into its scabbard, struggling with her own billowing shirt. She easily swam the short distance to Rowan, her legs thrusting behind her with long, powerful strokes. Down here, in Manannan's water realm, *she* was the faster one. Trying hard not to stare below Rowan's waist, she lightly touched his arm.

He signaled to his mouth, then up.

Dara understood. They wouldn't be able to hold their breaths much longer, and would have to go up for air soon. And what might be awaiting them up there?

Dara's chest was already burning with the effort. She guessed that by now they'd been holding their breaths for over a minute, and she was no expert freediver. Somehow she doubted Rowan had more diving experience. It was either opening their mouths to take a deep, deadly breath of river water, or going up to face whatever was lurking there.

Where the hell was Brighid, gone when she was needed? And who, or what, had the whimsical Sidhe intended they would find here, in the river's dark depths?

Dara's eyes locked with Rowan's. Oddly, this time he'd entrusted their fate to her. Finally, Dara jerked her right thumb up. Rowan nodded, placing both his large hands on her hips, preparing to drive them both towards light and air.

Out of nowhere something snagged one of Dara's ankles with a steely grip, pulling her down with force. Down, to the river's darkness, and away from the capering golden shimmers above their heads. Rowan threw a wild downward glance. Dara's mouth tore open against her will. Her breasts heaved as her rib cage expanded with a futile breath, about to pump her lungs full of algid water, and a few unfortunate minute fish...

Only instead, she was inhaling chill, mossy *air*.

Cool, succulent lips were sealing Dara's mouth. Long fingers enfolded the back of her head, like an eager lover's hands, but they weren't Rowan's. As precious oxygen again saturated her lungs, the red veil blurring her vision gradually dissipated, revealing an extremely close pair of large, luminous eyes. Hard nipples, grazing Dara's flesh through her sopping shirt, told her that whatever was holding her captive was likely female.

A low protesting moan caught deep in Dara's throat. Her muscles strained in reflex as she struggled to break free of her captor's forceful grasp. Her mind wrestled as well, trying to unearth Brighid's recent words. What had she told them exactly, before?

We've got ourselves a date with the Merrows...

Manannan Mac Lir...

He'll send his Merrows to help us...

The Merrow kept her firm grip on Dara, their lips locked together in a forced kiss. Unperturbed, she exhaled more air into Dara's reluctant mouth.

And that *shameless* ocean fairy was giving Dara some tongue, too!

Dara moaned her protest, putting up a good fight. Finally, the Merrow withdrew, replacing her lips with a long, lean finger over Dara's mouth.

A warning.

Don't breathe now, that sinewy finger hinted.

Dara curbed an urge to jerk herself away, instead daring a bolder peek at her lecherous savior. The Merrow's triangular, high-cheekboned face was delicately featured, tapering to a narrow chin. Huge slanting eyes of variegated green took up most of her face, their gaze unreadable and oddly penetrating. Her skin was pale and had a slight sheen, as if dusted with finely crushed pearls, and her hands were slender and fine-boned. She had finely webbed fingers, and…

Goddess!

Her waist tapered, and then flared into an iridescent, hazel fishtail!

A mermaid, Dara thought with shock.

The mermaid removed her finger completely from Dara's lips.

Damn, it seemed she was about to kiss her again!

Rowan was just parting lips with his own mermaid.

So, this was what Brighid had meant back on shore.

Manannan, the Ocean Lord, had sent his mermaids to help. The servants would probably get the two of them across to Inis, leaving them there to find Brighid's contact, the Leprechaun.

Rowan drew back a little to take a better look. His gaze fell from the dappled green eyes and lush, cool lips. The twin swells of his rescuer's breasts were bejeweled with small hard nipples, like a pair of rare pearls. His fingers itched to touch them, just to see how they *felt*. A red cap of feathers was fitted tightly over the mermaid's scalp, and beneath it long strands of silvery hair fanned about her body. The red cap was called a *cohullen-druith*, Rowan recalled from old legends, the enchantment allowing a mermaid to travel between dry land and her undersea world.

Rowan turned to look for Dara. A soft grin lit up his face as he watched her wrestling with her own mermaid, while she was kissing life into her mouth.

Truthfully, Dara's mermaid seemed way too pleased with her task.

Lean fingers flickered over Rowan's chin, diverting his attention back from his mate. A sleek tail wound between his legs. His own mermaid's face hovered close, her strange eyes on the same level as his. She swayed into him with a soft flick of her tail, and her lips again claimed his mouth.

His mermaid's lips were soft and chilly, her breath seasoned with the ocean's salty tang. 'Twas an odd feeling, and not exactly an unpleasant one. The mermaid's quick, sinuous tongue stroked over the gap in his lips, but to Rowan's utter relief, didn't attempt to invade deeper into his mouth. Seemed like their mermaids liked girls.

Rowan moved curious fingers through the silky cloud of silver hair. The mermaid's long cap feathers teased his face and shoulders. He tentatively touched her face—her shiny skin felt as smooth as a seal's beneath his fingertips.

The fairy broke their kiss and tilted her head. She slinked her arm about his waist and her tail beat forcefully, propelling them both forward. Dara and her mermaid were already spiraling through the darkening water just ahead of them. Rowan tightened his hold around his mermaid's slim waist. She advanced like an eel through the shadowy underwater world, her body flowing in sinuous undulations. Like well-aimed torpedoes, the two odd pairs shot stealthily through the water. Their speed slowed each time the mermaids joined their mouths with those of the Kanjali shifters, breathing air into their lungs.

Suddenly, with an elusive flick of a tail, the mermaids were gone with the same abruptness with which they had appeared.

Dara swung wildly about. Rowan hovered close, a few feet away. Daylight trickled into the water in glitters and jittery currents. She drove herself up with a forceful thrust, her head finally breaking the water's surface. Eyes shut tightly against the light, she opened her mouth wide and gasped loudly for air.

"Oh, Goddess," she mumbled and drew another breath, a slower one.

"Strange." Rowan's voice was so sudden within the intimacy of the water and the sky that she startled and jerked her eyes open.

"What's strange?" she asked.

"You." He spoke low and soft, his voice rough, as he swam closer. The gentle waves stirred by his movements lapped at her breasts and shoulders, sending shuddering chills through her body. "You told me you didn't believe in 'the primitive mumbo jumbo'. Yet, I've heard you calling for the Goddess more than once."

"It's just a figure of speech."

She spoke breathlessly, sounding like she'd just had sex. She looked like she'd just had sex... The slow, sweaty kind. Rowan extended his arm and caught her waist, pulling her close against him.

"Are you trying to drown us again?" Dara's arms swung furiously in the water as she strained to keep herself afloat. "You—"

Taking advantage of Dara's brief lack of resistance, he cradled her head in his other hand and sealed her mouth with his. His legs kept beating in a strong, relaxed rhythm. She gave a surprised moan, her arms slashing the water in steadying arcs. Her legs whipped the water, almost tangling with his. He took advantage of her moaning, sending his tongue deep inside her mouth. She kept making small sounds that threatened to drive him out of his mind. He groaned with the frustration of wanting her, of wishing she'd just wrap her legs around his waist and let him bury his cock deep inside her sweet cunt.

She bit his lower lip, brief and hard, driving herself away from him with a few quick strokes.

"Don't try that again," she said shakily, looking dizzy.

"What? Kiss you?" he said. He touched two fingers to where she'd bitten him, his tongue gathering up a budding blood droplet.

"Kiss me *like that*. Like I've got no real choice in the matter."

"I thought you liked it."

"Oh, you're so sure of that?" she snapped, tiny water gems trembling on her eyelashes. She batted her limbs in livid arcs, raising a froth. "And *I* thought you liked kissing that...that...*sea creature!*"

"You're jealous," Rowan proclaimed, a hint of a disbelieving smile tugging one angle of his mouth. "Look, Dara, the mermaids were just doing our breathing for us, is all."

"I'm *not* jealous." Dara made a fuming turn in the water and started towards the white sandy shore. "And next time, *I'll* decide if I want to be kissed or not!" she tossed tartly behind her back.

"Aye, and don't you bleedin' forget it!" Rowan shouted after her receding form. "*You* bleedin' *decide.*"

He knew she'd heard him well enough, though she gave no sign of it. A soft frustrated groan built deep in Rowan's throat. *By Danu, his body wanted her to decide quicker!* Beneath the hawthorn she'd let him kiss her in the most intimate of ways, and now a simple mouth-to-mouth threw her into a murderous fit. What...

He almost slapped himself.

The chase by the river, and then their underwater escapade—it all must have been too much for her. He should just let her go right now. Give the lass her sweet time. Rowan gritted his teeth as he watched her dark head and pale shoulders bobbing up and down in the water.

Aye, that he would do.

Give Dara plenty of time. Time to decide. To let her mind understand what her body had already known...that she wanted him.

Slash. Slash. Slash.

Dara sliced through the water like a hot knife sliding through butter. Before she realized it her toes were burrowing into sand and she was wading in waist-deep water.

Dammit, she wasn't jealous!

She swiped angrily at a dripping tangle of hair that dangled over her face.

Earlier she'd let Rowan kiss her lower and deeper than what he'd just done. And Goddess, every inch of her body was craving his touch. His large hands all over her. It was just that...

She hugged herself against the sudden chill, the water now lapping at mid-thigh.

It was all happening way too fast. She was out of control here. She hadn't even figured out yet where *here* was!

Her wet feet kissed shallow grooves against the water's silver edge. The long shirt's hem slapped wetly against her low thighs, and she paused to inspect herself with an acid glance.

Wet t-shirt contest finalist, again.

Chapter Fourteen

"Hey, wait. Dara!"

Rowan cursed as he leaped along the already fading trail of her footprints. She didn't slow down, keeping up a steady-as-hell tempo.

"Mind telling me where you're heading?" he inquired softly as he reached her, searching her face for answers.

"I wasn't really thinking about that."

Thump, thump, thump.

Her small feet kept thrashing the muddy sand with a ruthless, silent rhythm. Rowan ached to seize her arm and stop this senseless march, make her look at him. He didn't dare.

"We'd better figure it out quickly then, sweetheart, because I don't think we're anywhere near Inis."

Dara stopped and turned, giving him a long, assessing look. It seemed as though she was finally contemplating the gravity of their situation.

"Funny," she said, "how you're *always* ending up naked, Mackey!"

She resumed her brisk stride, leaving him behind.

His eyebrows drew together in a fiery red line.

"Fine," Rowan muttered behind her back. "I guess you *think* you can handle a *dragún* all by yourself, then. Gutsy lass."

She stopped dead in her tracks. "I can handle *what*?"

"A *dragún*. A Water Dragon. I truly admire your nerve."

"You're bluffing."

"A full-grown Water Dragon is a matter too serious to be bluffing about, Dara."

She did a full one-eighty so she could scrutinize his face. "You're *serious*, aren't you?"

He gave her a grave stare in response. *She was about to fall for it.*

"Fine." Dara glared at him, placing both her hands over her hips. "So, you have any bright idea as to where we should go?"

"I know this place no better than you." One angle of Rowan's mouth quirked in a soft grin. "However, I believe the mermaids have taken us further than intended, through the River of Gold and down the Luran. And I remember Brighid speaking earlier of kingdoms and border crossings. I think right now we're in the kingdom she named Connachta."

"And that's a big help, how?"

He shrugged. "It's a start, at least."

Dara's hand shaded her eyes as her gaze toured the sky, searching for a familiar black speck marring the blue. "Well, I don't see a raven rushing in to help," she sighed. "I hope Brighid is okay."

"She better be," Rowan growled. "The brat still owes me quite a bit of explanation!"

"Not to mention, we're hopelessly lost here without her." Dara frowned. "Look, I don't know about you, but I'm back to Plan A."

"What's Plan A?"

She spun around, water beads glittering in her knotted hair. "Walking," she tossed behind her back.

Rowan watched her go *thump, thump, thump* along the shore again, a muscle twitching in his lower jaw. He turned a wary gaze to the new shore they'd been just cast upon. To his left shimmered the Luran, a river so wide that no land could be traced across its farthest waters. Only now could he fathom how far the mermaids had led them. To his right, wet white sand gradually dried and stretched until gnawed by shallow rocks and patches of grass, and these were quickly dissolved into the shadows of a huge pine forest. The deep scent of sweet and bitter pine took over the air, chasing away Manannan's salty tang. The woods climbed the ribs of shallow hills, cladding them in dark green. Far away, something glistened like a diamond within the coronet of hills, but Rowan couldn't make out what it was.

His face darkened as he looked back to the edge of the wood.

"Problem taken care of, Dara," he called, his tone controlled. "Seems like someone else has already decided a Plan B for us."

He glanced at her, finding her staring in the same direction as he. He started towards her in long, deliberately unhurried strides.

Riders spilled from the woods, steering their steeds to cross their path. For a frightening split-second he thought these were the same ones who had earlier chased them to the River of Gold. His nostrils flared as he sniffed the air. No blood-tinged Hound scent haunted his senses, and these riders looked different in clothing and manner. Moreover, unlike before, their chieftain was a woman.

She rode her dark stallion bareback and bridleless, her long hair streaming behind her in loose red curls. A slim golden coronet glittered within the red. Rowan laid his hand over the small of Dara's damp back as the horse neighed above them, rearing on its hind legs and settling back down. The large beast's display of power sprayed them both with muddy sand.

"Who are you? Who disturbed my wards?" The woman's voice was the same silver-sweet that they had grown accustomed to hearing by now. She bent slightly over her horse's long arched neck, her pale fists full of its black mane. She had an elongated, fine-boned face, but her blue eyes were sharp and impatient.

"These *wards* are worse than a silent alarm," Dara muttered.

"You are not from these lands." The woman shifted on her horse, scrutinizing them both curiously. Her gaze, unabashed, centered on Rowan in particular, sliding down his bare skin and missing nothing. Her next words were meant for him. "Your woman is dark-haired and speaks with an odd inflection, and your skin is the color of honey, like folks of the Upper Realm. Where are you two from?"

"I'm not his wo—" Dara started in protest. She gave a small yelp as Rowan squeezed her arm none too gently.

"Please, not now, sweetheart," he whispered, his mouth tight against her ear. "'Tis important that you stake your claim on me here."

Dara glanced up at the woman, eyes squinted against the unfocused daylight. She looked like a warrior-princess taken straight out of history. Her ample breasts were barely packed into a tight corset of leather and brass. Two generous side-splits in her scarcely there leather skirt revealed muscular thighs. Calf-high boots of dark leather and glistening brass buckles completed the picture, and…was that the protruding hilt of a long sword strapped against her back?

"I understand not, isn't he your man?" The question had been aimed at Dara. The warrior's ravenous blue gaze roved over Rowan's body, lingering low and long enough to make him squirm uneasily.

"Yes, he is…*my man*," Dara responded so swiftly she even surprised herself.

Rowan chuckled beside her.

"Oh, shut up," Dara whispered, "before I give you back to the bad lady to play with!"

About five riders were now circling the warrior princess. One of them ordered his stallion forward to her side, both the horse and his rider of massive proportions. The man looked like a giant—wild chestnut locks wrestled about his face and were tied against his nape into a long, untamed ponytail. A vest of loose chain mail glistened against his enormous, sculpted upper torso. It left his muscle-bound arms bare but for a set of twin silver arm-bracelets and a snaking blue tattoo in a language unknown to Dara. His soft leather slacks were molded against his flesh in a way that left no detail to the imagination.

"Highness." The giant touched the haft of the sword secured beneath his knee, and flashed a lopsided smile. "I thought that whenever I dropped by for a visit, *I* would be enough to satisfy your appetite."

"Oh aye, you are more than enough, Fergus." The warrior woman gave him a sultry smile. Her seething attention focused back on her unexpected guests. "'Tis rude of me, leaving you not knowing who you're speaking with," she said. "I'm Medb of Rath Cruachan. Grant me similar grace and tell me who you are."

"Highness," Rowan answered warily. "We're only travelers from the neighboring Kingdom, who're making their way up north."

"For now, 'tis enough." Medb patted the sweat-glistening neck of her steed. "You'll tell me the rest in my palace, at the banquet held for *Imbolc*."

"Sounds like an offer we can hardly refuse," Dara mumbled. She gave another small yelp as Rowan squeezed her arm again.

"*Not* a bright idea, making the bad lady angry with us," he hissed in her ear.

Fergus motioned to one of the riders hovering in the back. In response, a heavy roll of brocaded plush landed at Rowan's and Dara's feet.

"Put this on," Fergus advised them both, a smile curling beneath his matter-of-fact tone. "A couple of mantles we didn't make use of."

"Why should I wear this?" Dara demanded.

Rowan muttered a silent plea for the Goddess's help as he knelt beside his obstinate mate, untying the small bundle.

"Because you're riding with us to the Ruling Mound's palace as Her Highness's personal guests."

"Ruling Mound?" Rowan, crouched above the spread of velvet robes, raised squinted eyes to the mounted huge warrior.

"Oh, aye," Fergus grinned. "'Tis Medb you've just happened upon, High Princess of Connachta, and her word is law around these parts." He maneuvered his huge stallion with ease, pointing to what glimmered in the distance within the dark green garland of hills. "There is the palace of Rath Cruachan," he said.

"It'll take us *forever* to get there, it's too damn far!" Dara insisted.

"Your wee woman holds enough spirit to bring thirty able warriors down to their knees." Fergus grinned sympathetically at Rowan. Ignoring Dara's glare, he added, "We'll be taking the Woods Gateway. Time and distance play different there. We'll be in the palace before a single *cipín* burns fully."

"Before *what* burns out?" Dara frowned. She was still refusing to change into her new attire, leaving the embroidered gown in Rowan's hands. A sharp gasp squeezed out of her mouth as Fergus leaned down from his horse and plucked her easily from the ground, planting her on the saddle in front of him.

"You ride with Her Highness," he rumbled at Rowan from above, one eyebrow cocked with amusement. "So she wishes, and her wishes are my commands."

Dara's breath hitched.

Goddess, but Fergus *was* huge! Every aspect of him. His cock, pressed against her back through his leather slacks, was the size of several grown men's fists.

Dara sucked her lower lip into her mouth. She didn't want to imagine this *erect*. Unfortunately, Fergus had been watching her face, rather liking her unintended lip manipulation. She stifled a whimper as she felt his instant reaction pressing harder and longer against her back. Watching her frightened expression, Fergus threw his head back, his hearty laughter thundering above her head.

"Worry not, wee one," he finally managed. "My duties lie with my consort, Her Highness. Sharing her bed is enough to drain the essence of thirty regular-sized men!"

Dara glimpsed Rowan mounting the black steed, his arms wrapping around Her Highness's waist in a loose embrace. The front of his thighs pressed against the royal back of hers. Against her will, Dara's lips and fists tightened in protest.

A low chuckle roared and vibrated against her back. Fergus was sniggering, lowering his mouth all the way down to her ear.

"Haven't bedded your lad yet, have you?" he whispered. "Let me advise you this. Take him to your bed. Soon."

Chapter Fifteen

Passing through the Gateway, though Dara had initially feared it, had been hardly felt at all. One moment they were riding into the shadows of a pine forest, hooves crushing needles among its sharply scented trees, the next moment the horses were clattering against marble, and the pine forests were left far behind, adorning the ring of surrounding hills. They were now standing in front of enormous gates, an intricate mesh of bows and spines gleaming in ivory-white.

"The palace gates," Fergus growled from above.

"Where…where are all the guards? Up on the walls?" Dara was awestruck, gazing up to the full height of the gates, painfully craning her neck.

"At their rightful posts, they are," Fergus replied, a smile in his voice. "But Her Highness's palace is also guarded by protection wards. Those you can't see, no more than you were able to trace the Woods Gateway…unless trained in magic and sorcery."

The palace gates' sheen rapidly deepened before her eyes and the solid structure trembled, fogged. The bows and spines now appeared close to transparent.

"On we go," Fergus rumbled.

Honoring his consort and chieftain, he waited for Medb's black steed to sashay through the gates first, then followed. The rest of their small troop tagged along close behind. Dara couldn't help but squeeze her eyes shut as they ambled through what had been, less than a minute ago, a solid mass.

She yelped as Fergus's massive hands caught her just beneath her arms and swung her down from the saddle. She wrenched her eyes open, her feet slipping and staggering against the solid ground. Another pair of strong arms captured her, their touch startlingly familiar.

"Got you," Rowan breathed against her cheek. She half-turned in his hold and caught his neck in a loose hug, steadying herself against his hard chest.

Fergus's laughter thundered from above again. "I'm leaving you in most able hands." He grinned at Dara. "Remember my advice, wee one. You have ample time 'til the *Imbolc* banquet, many *cipín* yet to burn. Use this time well."

"What advice did he give you?" Rowan's fiery eyebrows drew together in suspicion.

"N-nothing." Dara's face took on the color of a ripe tomato. "Uh, what's this Ki-Peen thing he keeps mentioning?" she asked in a desperate attempt to change the subject.

"*Cipín* is a stick," Rowan replied, "but I've never heard the expression he uses. Maybe burning one *cipín* is a way to measure time here, in a place with no sun and no moon, no true day and no night." His arms tightened about her waist. He inclined his head lower as he spoke to her, his voice dropping. Dara let out an involuntary moan, her pulse speeding up.

"You'll be shown to your chambers now," Medb's voice sang sweetly beside them.

Rowan and Dara both started as if jerked out of a spell, turning their gazes to the High Princess. She had already dismounted her black steed, and was now standing with Fergus's arm resting lightly over one lusciously curved hip.

"Bathe and lie down. We shall speak again at a later time." She flashed her dazzling hot smile again.

"Bathe? Lie down? Hey, you don't think I'm simply going to—" Dara's protest was drowned in the buzz and bustle of servants, sweeping her and Rowan towards a gaping arched hall.

Medb of Rath Cruachan pressed lightly against Fergus Mac Roich as they both watched the Kanjali couple being swept away.

"What are your thoughts, Fergus?" she inquired softly. Her red-painted nails teased a tattooed, brawny arm.

"These two are the ones," he replied shortly, "that Queen Eriu has spoken of."

"Meaning Donn must be at their throats."

"Aye, Highness, most likely so."

"I dislike that conniving bastard. He's not a true *dé-Danann*, and his mind is warped with revenge." She sighed, and her consort nodded. "'Tis all Bilé's doing, having a Milesian residing *here*, in the Lower Realm—and as a Prince no less, ruling his own Mound. Conjuring his own magic. By Danu, the bastard wields an *iron* sword! He should have been left to drown at sea, I swear to it."

"Shhh, Highness, you don't wish to wake Bilé, the sleeping God of Life and Death, Ruler of the Otherworld, Guardian of the Sacred Oak. He's jealous for his scions' sake and honor."

Fergus Mac Roich strived to quench his mistress's burning wrath, though he wholeheartedly shared her views when it came to the rogue prince. Prince Eber Donn, none other than King Miled's eldest son, should have indeed drowned at sea near Erin's shores in the magical storm conjured by the *Tuatha dé Danann*, thousands of years before. The God Bilé, however, intervened and placed Donn at Knockfierna, as one of the Otherworld's Princes. Besides giving him his life and a dominion of his own, he'd also granted him magic.

"No, I don't wish to wake Bilé. I'm not sure I will have the Goddess Danu's protection if I stir her ancient rival out of his long sleep." Medb had left Fergus's side and was now pacing back and forth. "Though I *would* love to wring Donn's neck with my own bare hands!"

"If I may make you an offer, Highness," Fergus spoke quietly. "If you wish to help these two out of Donn's way without stirring earth and sky, there's a certain Gateway you can point them to, which requires no magic or sorcery, and leads straight back to the Upper Realm."

* * * * *

"No, you perv, take your damn hands off me!" Dara swiped at an overly eager servant girl who made an unrelenting effort to rub something scented into her bare skin. Dara had resented this maid from the moment she'd managed to rip her shirt away, leaving her naked, but for her shoulder rig. The girl now fled from her, only to try a fresh attack from the rear.

"*Hey, you!*" Dara spun around heatedly, swinging a well-aimed fist. It hit home. This time the girl crawled away, wailing, and didn't come back for more. Dara snorted with odd satisfaction. "Anyone else?" she growled at the group of huddled servants. "I'm tired, hungry, naked and I *hate* public baths!"

"I'd take care if I were you," Rowan sniggered at the knot of servants. A couple of giggling maids were busy peeling the plush mantle from his shoulders, and he didn't put up too much of a fight. "She's got one mean right hook, I tell you. Felt it myself."

"'Tis the Infinity Hall, one of Her Highness's most luxurious bathing halls," one daring male servant protested. "I know not this 'public bath' your woman is speaking of." Quite daringly, he paced closer to Dara.

Rowan groaned at the servant's careless use of "*your woman*". The poor bastard had it coming, and didn't even know it yet. Rowan watched Dara's cheeks ignite with an even angrier red.

"Not. Another. Step," Dara yelled at the servant, highly irritated. "Or you're going to lose a few inches. And I'm not talking height here!" Her fist closed on her dagger's hilt. Goddess, she *wanted* to use it. Badly. At the edge of her visual field Rowan was standing naked—*again*—his laughter a warm hum in the background.

She threw a miserable glance at the odd-shaped pool occupying most of the hall. It was shaped in a series of connected water channels, designed to look like a Celtic knot. That's probably why it had been named Infinity Hall. The channels' rims had been gilded, their glitter softened and blurred by milky steam. The water looked hot and inviting. Every muscle in her body was screaming. She wanted more than anything to sink herself into a hot tub, but Goddess, she wasn't prepared to put on a show for this bunch. Come to think of it, she'd been doing exactly that for the last few minutes. Making a spectacle out of herself. She couldn't help it—she'd been treated like she had no will of her own. This specific scene, however, was getting ridiculous. Her mind dug for an excuse that might appeal to the servants.

"Look," Rowan spoke softly to the servants, suddenly standing by her shoulder. "Our faith forbids us to, uh, be bathed."

"At all?" A gaping maid wrinkled her nose in disapproval.

"No, no. I mean we can't be bathed by strangers. The Goddess will punish us."

"Oh," the daring male considered it. "I've never heard of such. Her Highness's orders were—"

"That we take a bath to prepare for the *Imbolc* feast, and *that* we will do," Rowan cut him short. "Gladly, even. No orders and no faith get broken, and everybody walks away unpunished. You can leave someone to keep watch, if you wish."

Within the muddled buzz rising from the group of debating attendants, Dara turned fully to Rowan.

"Thank you," she mouthed silently.

"Sure, sweetheart." He smiled down at her. "You can let go of the knife now," he added softly, carefully covering her fist with one large hand. Her eyes lingered on Rowan's face as he gently unclasped her fist and entwined his fingers with her own, replacing the cold, bony hilt with the feel of his warm hand.

"I can't believe we're both naked again," she whispered. The tip of her tongue absently licked over her dry bottom lip.

"Almost naked," he corrected, his hand still laced with hers. "You're still wearing your harness. Turn around," his voice urged her, dropping low, meant for her ears alone.

Dara slowly turned, almost too giddy to stay on her feet. Rowan's arms wrapped about her, warm, hard-muscled, steadying. His body fitted itself against hers from behind. She felt his cock pressing against her ass and nudging the small of her back. His agile fingers trailed over the leather straps that circled her shoulders, lightly touching her skin. She trembled at this gentle butterfly touch, imagining how his hands would feel on her breasts right now. Harder. Squeezing. Her body still carried the memory of his touch on her flesh, had memorized it on that feverish night in the Portland warehouse.

Rowan's fingers tampered with the buckle fastening Dara's harness, then coaxed the leather straps down her shoulders. He let the whole rig slide heavily down her body to lie curled against her ankles. Her gaze followed the plummeting weapon. It was already blurred by the soft mist rising from the pool. Her eyes rose to see Rowan's hands, resting lightly above the soft roundness of her hipbones.

Honey on white. Hard against soft.

"Now," his rough whisper tickled her ear from behind, "*now* you're naked."

"*I* will stay with you," the daring one called from within the disbanding batch of servants. "And make certain that Her Highness's orders are properly fulfilled." He strolled closer through the vaporous tongues of mist snaking from the pool. Clearing his throat, he assumed a dignified pose within a safe distance.

"Want to try the water, sweetheart?" Rowan's lips breathed over Dara's hair, traced the side of her face. He ignored their chaperon.

"Yes," she murmured, barely hearing her own voice.

"Hmmm," he hummed, a raspy male sound that shot hot flashes down her body. He gently withdrew from her, and her abandoned back suddenly felt cold without him there. A soft protesting moan broke her lips before she managed to catch it. Rowan laughed, sliding his arm around her waist. He led her down the wide marble stairs that vanished beneath the slow, swirling steam.

She shivered as the water bathed her ankles, hot and delicious just like she'd known it would be. Weariness loaded her muscles like lead as she waded deeper. She was content for once to be guided, to empty her mind from thought.

"Here," Rowan said softly. "Place your hands here. Both of them."

She did as he bade her, pressing her palms against the gilded rims' surface. It felt startlingly chilly, a sharp contrast to the hot water lapping at her breasts. She heard the water softly slapping Rowan's flesh as he moved behind her, felt the gentle waves undulating between them both.

He placed his hands over the small of her back beneath the water, thumbs edging her spine. His fingers kneaded their way up, pressing, smoothing, patiently unknotting taut muscles. He daubed her exposed shoulders with the hot water, molding and soothing sore flesh.

"By Danu, lass, you're all knots," he spoke softly, his fingers easily tracing her shoulder blades. "Just...relax," his voice implored her.

She moaned and arched back as his hands rubbed deep into her skin, wanting more of his touch. He responded, moving even closer, shaping their bodies tightly together again. His hands slid up her rib cage and cupped her breasts.

"Oh...Rowan..." Dara gasped, jerking her hands from the gilded platform.

"No...leave your hands exactly where they are." He started kissing slowly down her neck.

She drew a quick, shuddering breath, flattening her palms once more against the hard, gleaming surface. Rowan's words conjured a steamy image in her mind, of the mating couple they'd watched back in Commar. Rowan gently hefted Dara's breasts, massaging the supple, ripe globes. Harder. Squeezing. Just like she wanted him to. His thumbs pressed her tightening nipples, testing her, rolling them between the roughened pads of his fingers.

"Mmmm...Goddess..." She squirmed and panted, not daring to remove her hands from the pool's edge. Her nipples peaked against his palms, blushed and tingling.

He kept his left hand on one plump breast, pampering her hungry flesh with gentle strokes. His right slid tightly against her skin, resting low on her tummy. Dara trembled, her hands squeezing into wet fists against the platform.

"Have you decided yet?" he inquired softly, his hand hot and still above the wet triangle of curls.

"W-what?" she stammered, dazed.

"Back in the Luran, when we were swimming, you said that next time you decide."

"Yes..." The word squeezed out, trembling. "*Yes.*"

"Yes what, sweetheart?" his voice demanded. He wasn't about to let her off so easy this time.

"Yes. I want...I want *this*. I want *you*." She was drawing shallow, quick breaths, her heart pounding.

"Spread your legs for me," he whispered hoarsely against her cheek.

Dara's breath hitched and she sank her teeth into her lower lip. Tentatively, she parted her thighs against the water's resistance.

"More," Rowan coaxed. "More."

She spread wider. Before she managed another breath, his hand stroked over her and slipped between her thighs. Quick fingers parted her nether lips, centering on her clit. He brushed over the small nub with the rough pad of his finger, slowly rubbing the sleek button, pressing it in a slow tormenting circle.

"Aaahh…no…wait!" She gave a soft yell, her hips jerking sharply towards his touch. Her hands stayed tight against the pool's gilded edge.

"Want me to stop?" He leaned his head above her shoulder, inhaling the familiar fresh scent of her hair, her skin's intoxicating aroma. The tang of her arousal mixed into it all like a hot flavor. His kiss traced the soft outline of her lower jaw, just above the pulse beating wildly in her neck. His hand kept moving between her thighs, immersed in the water, sinuously circling her engorged clit. She moved in his tight embrace, making small sounds, the same ones she'd made when he'd kissed her back in the Luran.

"Mmm…*Rowan*…" She moaned low in her throat, her short nails etching crescents into her palms. Rowan's hand abandoned her left breast, and was now gently spreading the cheeks of her ass. He eased a finger into her tight pussy from behind.

"*Rowan!*"

He slipped another finger inside her with ease. Crouching slightly and hooking his buried fingers, he pressed circles into her hot, puffy flesh. His bowed body enveloped hers, the tiniest of trembles conveyed straight from her flesh to his.

"Let go, sweetheart," he whispered against a cloud of dark, soaking locks. "I have you. Let go…"

His fingers moved inside her, tuned to her moans, the soft quakes traversing her flesh, the smallest sway of her hips. His other hand kept circling her clit, unrelenting, deliberately slow. He found that spot within her tight pussy that made her jerk and shiver the most, moan the loudest. His hooked fingers kept kneading that exact spot, sweetly torturing her.

"*Aaaaahhh*…Goddess. I can't…" She sobbed and moaned, writhing in his firm hold, her hands fisted. "Can't t-take it…"

He used his other hand, the one massaging her clit, to finally drive her over the edge. Dara bucked her hips, screaming, her cunt blossoming with violent ripples, sucking and squeezing Rowan's fingers inside her. He kept holding her, his fingers captured inside, riding her climax.

"Aye, Dara. Like this, let go," he mumbled softly, kissing her hot cheek, embracing her slim, shuddering form, both his hands nestled within her thighs' searing embrace. Slowly the trembling faded, her breathing eased.

"I want you," he said gruffly. "*Now.*" Random, faint waves still squeezed her sodden flesh around his fingers. His cock was throbbing with a painful erection, tight against her back.

Dara sucked in a shaky breath.

"Yes," she whispered.

Rowan let out a slow breath against her neck, as if he'd expected her to refuse. Gently, he rescued his two fingers from her tight embrace. She let out a lingering moan as he pulled out of her, water licking at her pussy lips again. Turning her head to the side, she saw him bring his wet fingers to his mouth, sucking them slowly. He buried his face in her hair, breathing her in. His damp hands shifted to her arms, slowly teasing their length.

He felt so good against her —

Yet she couldn't stop trembling. Her hands remained fisted on the golden ledge. Her breath kept coming in quick gasps, her heart struggling wildly against her rib cage. Maybe it was because she had waited for so long. Had refused to let anyone in, until she couldn't remember how a man should feel inside her. But, Goddess, she *wanted* Rowan inside her. Wanted him so damn bad that her pussy was hurting for him. So damn bad, that it was hard to breathe —

"Rowan," she gasped. "Please..."

His hands slipped down her wet back, seizing her hips beneath the water. He pulled her back slightly, his sure grip tuning her position to his own. Dara leaned forward against the platform, dizzy with excitement. Rowan's hard thighs pressed against the soft back of her own.

She couldn't take the wait much longer.

"Make love to me, Mackey."

Rowan breathed out a soft, hoarse chuckle. "I am."

He shifted behind her, crouching slightly. She felt his hands on her ass, parting her cheeks. His cock pushing between the soft globes. His cock head, nudging her pussy…

She gasped aloud as he penetrated her, his broad cock probing her wet heat, pushing against the initial resistance of her inner muscles. Unwillingly, she tensed.

"Sweetheart, you're too tight," he murmured. "Relax. You're trembling…"

Dara dragged in a shuddering breath. Forced her lungs to fill slowly, pressing her palms flat against the gilded surface of the pool. Rowan's fiery hands stroked slow circles over her hipbones, climbed tightly up her rib cage, cradled the underside of her breasts. Holding her against him, he drove his cock deeper inside her.

"Oh!"

He stilled, his cock half-buried in her cunt. "Did I hurt you?"

"Rowan," she moaned, squirming, straining to press herself down on him. "It feels… You feel incredible. Don't stop."

With a growl he thrust all the way inside her, driving his cock to the hilt. Dara cried out, her back arching. Rowan's hands squeezed and kneaded her breasts, pulling her hard against his muscled chest. Her fingers were yanked away from the platform and entwined with Rowan's. Before she managed another gasp he pulled back from her cunt completely and thrust hard again, impaling her on his massive erection.

Dara was sharply filled. Stretched. Her shocked pussy reacted with swift contractions, rippling with a soft orgasm around Rowan's wedged cock.

His breath hissed in, and he held still.

"That was bloody quick," he teased softly. His hands slipped down her stomach, his fingers still linked with hers.

Pressing his hands — her hands — over her mons, he steered them both, inch-by-inch, deeper into the water.

Dara closed her eyes with a moan, leaning back against Rowan's slick, hot chest. His rock-hard cock was inside her to the hilt, his large body wrapped around her. He gently rescued one hand from her grasp, sliding it up her stomach, splaying his fingers right beneath her breasts. His hand was so large, it almost spanned her rib cage. He bowed his head to kiss her shoulder, dug his face into her neck. She trembled sweetly as his hot mouth licked and sucked on her flesh, as his teeth grazed her skin.

He started to move within her, his hips rocking behind her with slow, soft thrusts.

"*Rowan*," she groaned.

Her inner flesh was already swollen and sensitized with Rowan's earlier handiwork, and his cock kept stroking and kneading her teased walls. She squirmed in his embrace, suddenly afraid she that couldn't handle so much pleasure.

"I can't—"

"Shhh... Aye, you can." He pinned her against his body, one large hand atop her mons, the other edging the underside of her breasts. There was no escape from his hold. His breath washed over her neck, hot, ragged. He kept pumping into her — soft, slow, steady. Mumbling her name. Coaxing. Kissing her neck, her hair, the side of her face. His hand on her mons shifted and pressed deeper between her thighs, his long, sensitive fingers touching her clit. Stroking. Circling. Kneading...

"Ahhh...*Rowan*..." Dara groaned, panted, pleaded.

Rowan kept her pressed against his body with a gentle, uncompromising hold as he fucked her. He drove into her with a swifter cadence, his thrusts growing longer, sharper. Water swirled and slapped at their sweaty skin, steam curling around their entwined bodies.

"Dara. Give me your mouth."

She turned her face to Rowan's, meeting his stormy green eyes. Hot. Intent. His mouth immediately came down on hers, bruising her lips with the force of his kiss.

His cock shoved inside her one more time, hard.

Dara's scream of release was stifled by Rowan's mouth. She fell apart, coming so hard that the surrounding world went dark. Her knees buckled. Through a cotton candy fog she felt Rowan's steely arms bracing her, felt him shudder and buck against her as he came with a throaty groan. His seed filled her with hot, intense gushes.

"Dara."

She opened her eyes, drew in a deep breath. Couldn't speak. Trembling, she pressed her hands hard over Rowan's.

"I'm not done with you, sweetheart." Rowan spoke gruffly, nuzzling her cheek. "I'm taking you to our chambers. They have to give us some bleedin' chambers, don't they?"

"Yeah, I-I guess."

Gently moving his hands back to her hips, he slipped out of her cunt.

Dara swiveled and her knees gave out beneath her. Rowan stooped quickly and caught her, scooping her up into his arms. He gave her a soft grin, the one she had come to know so well. Her arms looped around his neck. He squeezed her, brief and teasing, and waded through the water and steam, climbing up the marble staircase and out of the Celtic knot pool. His feet made growing puddles on the Infinity Hall's colorful terrazzo.

"Oy, lad!" he growled at the servant. "Enjoying the show?"

"Uh…" The servant squirmed beneath Rowan's gaze, his eyes moving again to Dara's fallen dagger. His arms were loaded with their brocade mantles.

Rowan flashed him a toothy smile above Dara's tangled mane. "We'd like to be shown to our chambers now. Our religion demands that we rest after bathing."

In his arms Dara stirred and mumbled weakly, "Mind if we put these mantles on *before* hopping out into the hallway?"

Chapter Sixteen

Dara gasped as Rowan tumbled them into the enormous bed, tossing her against satin and silk. She sank into the plush mattress among mounds of soft pillows, embroidered, beaded and tasseled. He crawled above her, twisting out of his mantle. His naked skin burned against the brocade cloth still shielding her. Dara's trembling fingers entwined in the upper laces cinching her robe.

"Goddess," she groaned with impatience.

"Let me help you," he said. He seized the robe's edges and tore them apart, laces snapping, exposing her breasts to his smoldering gaze. "Sweet," he whispered, leaning low.

She yelped as the wet heat of his mouth suddenly engulfed one jutting nipple, sucking her flesh with abandon, rolling the rosy bud hard against his tongue. He tasted her with a sudden soft bite, and her back arched sharply against the mattress. She wrung fistfuls of his flaming hair, breathing out a half-sob, pulling his head even tighter against her chest. His hand cradled the plump swell of the breast that his fervent mouth was sucking, licking and kissing.

"*Rowan.*"

Dara twisted and moaned, shoving pillows aside with elbows and feet, rumpling satin and silk. Rowan released her nipple with a loud pop. He gripped the still-laced lower fringes of her robe. She gave a soft scream as he ripped them open as well, baring all of her to his eyes.

"Should've done that straight away." He flashed a small grin.

His hands closed easily around her slim ankles, lifting her legs, moving them apart. Her pussy lips looked swollen, glistening. She yelped as he dragged her closer across the bedsheets, maneuvering her legs around him. He chuckled and sank between her thighs, his eyes ablaze with green fire. Their skin, damp and hot from the pool, was finally touching, with no barriers in between.

"I've wanted to feel you like this from the first moment I saw you." He bent his head, pressing his mouth against the curve of one shoulder. That same one he'd pulled an arrow from. His teeth grazed her flesh, swapping the older memory of penetrating pain with the new one of a pleasure bite. He licked over the reddened mark, soothing the small pain it had caused, and his hands gathered her thighs tighter around his waist.

He felt her shivering beneath him, digging her nails into his arms as his fingers slipped inside her again. "Still soaking wet," he said softly, twirling his fingers inside her. Her breath hissed out and she thrust her hips forward and up, pressing her sensitized flesh harder against his moving hand.

"Rowan," she moaned. "Rowan. *Rowan.*"

Her hips rocked and gyrated, her feet burrowing holes into the thick mattress. He felt her feverish hands slipping from his arms to his damp back, kneading his flesh over and over. Rowan groaned low in his throat, withdrawing his fingers from Dara's hot pussy.

She felt his nakedness sliding above, felt him moving along her body until their eyes locked. The head of his cock slid against her wet lips, nudging her entrance.

He watched her face displaying a rainbow of emotions. Propped on his elbows he bowed his head to hers, pressing his lips down. She opened her mouth wide for him, welcoming his tongue, answering his deep explorations with untamed want.

Still cradling her head in his hands, he entered her with a single, swift thrust, driving all of his length inside her. She felt hot and tight around him, her drenched cunt sucking his cock inside, coaxing a soft growl out of him.

His mouth stifled her scream when he drove himself all the way inside. Sharp, powerful, filling her all at once. He was big, and the move that had put him inside her wasn't a gentle one.

It felt breathtakingly, achingly...wonderful.

Her legs wrapped and locked around his waist. She managed to tear her mouth from his, turning her face sideways to take a quick, hissing breath, so she could cry out all over again. Her head's vigorous movement made his mouth slide wetly from her lips to her cheek. He kept himself still inside her as the second cry broke from her lips. She was shaking like a leaf in his arms, her eyes squeezed shut.

"Look at me," he mumbled roughly against her damp cheek. "Open your eyes for me, sweetheart."

Dara turned her face to his again, her breathing uneven and shallow. Their eyes locked once more. His gaze was rapt, intent, hard to decipher. He started to move inside her, a soft, slow rocking, so different from that almost violent first thrust that had driven him inside her. Her hips answered, undulating with him. Easy. Gentle. The small in-out movements of his cock slowly massaged her puffy, drenched walls, cajoling more of her juices out to lube him.

He dipped his head to nibble and suck on an earlobe, sliding his hands along the sides of her body, down lush curves and deep vales, until he cupped the full cheeks of her ass. His kiss slipped lower, sucking the hot pulse beating in her throat. Her neck arched and she dug a hand into his hair with a breathless moan, pressing his head tighter against her neck.

His thrusts grew longer, sharper. His fingers dimpled and squeezed her ass, pulling her harder on his cock each time. He groaned, his mouth full of her flesh, wanting to have more of her, to devour her whole. To melt their joined flesh together. To brand her as his, forever.

"Aaah, *Rowan. Aaaahhh!*" She answered each thrust with a short moan, a clipped scream, a single word. Just his name, whispered, moaned, yelled, over and over again. *His* name, not the one she had called that night, back in the storehouse.

"*Dara.*" Her sweat-beaded skin muffled his answering groan. He managed to capture her slender wrists, wrestle them with gentle firmness high above her head, force them against the mattress. She gave a broken howl, arching sharply against the crushed bedcovers. Her bowed body was sweetly trapped between his buried cock and his hands on her wrists. His rhythm peaked and he started pounding into her, breathing hard, flesh slapping wetly against flesh. Her pussy was sucking him in, massaging his sensitive cock head, ruthlessly pulsing against his throbbing shaft.

Dara cried out, squeezing her thighs harder around him, struggling to match him thrust for thrust. Rowan's powerful strokes were grinding her clit, pinning her body against the bed. Her trapped hands clenched into tight fists, her nails carving half-moons in her own flesh. And then she sharply angled her hips and shuddered violently, her pussy exploding with a burst of tight, successive spasms.

He followed close behind, coming on a throaty groan, his cock squeezing bursts of hot semen into her rippling flesh. Her wrists slipped from his loosened hold. She wrapped her arms around his back and kept clinging to him, hot and trembling beneath him. And then Rowan was finally spent, sinking against her like a drowned man. His weight pressed her body against the mass of pillows, the satin and silk of the linens drenched and twisted beyond recognition.

Rowan held her for a while, and then gently tried to roll sideways, trying not to smother her with his full weight.

"No, not yet," she pleaded and tightened her hug, arms and legs squeezing around him. "Stay here."

"I'll crush you, sweetheart." His laugh hummed against her cheek.

"I won't break that easily, you know."

"I know." His body remembered well the steely grip her thighs had kept on his waist just mere minutes ago. He brushed his lips over her skin, fingertips combing sweaty hair away from her face. His tongue snaked out to sample her taste again, that tangy mix of sweat and sex and Dara. Moving his hands around her waist, he rolled to his back, easily swinging her on top of him.

She grinned at him from above, shifting to straddle his waist.

"Don't we have a bleedin' feast to attend?" He flashed that teasing grin of his. His hands ran in long, lazy caresses from her ass to her shoulders, and back down again.

"Yeah. I think the Warrior Princess called it the—" she frowned in concentration, " —*Imbolc* banquet."

"Aye," he nodded, suddenly grave. "And now I'm reminded of something that troubled me before."

"What's that?" She leaned down and licked a sliding drop of sweat from his face, tracing it backwards from his strong, unshaven jawline to his left temple.

"Uh, see, *Imbolc* is celebrated on the first of February," he said, distracted by her devilish tongue. "While we left Portland in the morning following Halloween."

That brought about the reaction Rowan had expected. Dara sat up sharply as if she'd just spotted a hissing rattlesnake.

"*We lost three damn months?*" she yelled, eyes wide. Dara's thighs were still straddling Rowan, and he groaned as she unintentionally squeezed him. "But, Rowan, we haven't been here a full day!"

Chapter Seventeen

"A few hours, a few months — is there truly such a big difference?" Fergus rumbled over a speared, golden brown pork chop. He smacked his lips, leisurely licking the juicy glaze. His massive hand closed on his impressive, newly filled goblet.

"I bet you wouldn't have asked that if *you* had had three months stolen out of *your* life!" Dara punched the dining table with her fist. It *hurt*. Deep red wine trembled in her own bejeweled goblet. She sighed miserably. Having her wine spilled would have made a greater dramatic impact, but the cup had been too heavy to be toppled over by a small thump.

Rowan muffled his snigger with a long swig of wine from his own ornamented cup.

"Nothing has been stolen from your lives," Medb intervened. "Time Down *here* and Up *there* simply do not match."

The banquet hall was huge, more vast than anything Dara had ever imagined in her childhood daydreams. Multihued light was seeping from above, filtered through the colorful ceiling mosaic. It tinted the marble floor in the hall's hub with a softer version of the mosaic's pattern, an armored redheaded woman, a raven perched on one of her shoulders, and a squirrel on the other. *Most likely Medb's emblem*, Dara mused. She flattened her palms against the marble table, its face as milky-white as the flagstones, and latticed with fine, rosy veins. She let its coolness ooze into her flesh, easing her exasperation a bit.

Soon after the feast had started, it had become clear that the High Princess of Connachta and her consort knew their guests to be more than mere travelers heading north. This fact had been hard to deny when Fergus had inquired whether the Upper

Realm's grilled veal chops were still as juicy as he remembered. Having nothing left to hide, Dara had demanded to know where three months of their lives had gone.

Medb was currently scrutinizing them both, her sharp eyes seeming amused rather than irritated. "So clothes do fit you both," she grinned, diverting the conversation to different tracks.

Dara's face caught fire. Back in the bedchamber that she'd shared with Rowan, she remembered him soothing her confusion with hot, long caresses. Coaxing her to ride him as she straddled his lap. Cajoling her to turn her ass on him, face and fists pressed against the mattress as he slipped into her from behind.

After a long while the two of them had finally gotten dressed, tumbling into each other with hushed laughs. Their ankles were drowning in the thick fur covering the floor tiles. Clothes had been left for them, all rich greens and brocades and leathers, stretched against a mahogany-framed settee. Two pairs of boots had been displayed there as well, made with too many buckles for both their tastes. Rowan had tightened Dara's brocade corset laces over her ample breasts, then helped her secure her beloved dagger against the glimmering silk. She had pulled a tight, silken vest down his chest with a lingering motion. Slipping into their lower garments—his tight buckskin breeches, hers a side lace patent leather skirt—turned out to be a lengthier procedure, involving more mutual touches, both shallow and deep.

"Aye," Medb's grin broadened, interrupting Dara's reminiscing. She was addressing Fergus. "I told you a bit of enchantment would only do them good."

"Enchantment?" Dara's eyebrows arched. "As in, *open sesame? Presto? Shazam?*"

"I'm not familiar with the incantations you've just mentioned." Medb leaned closer against the marble, shoving plates and goblets aside with a careless sweep of her arm. "I only used a simple, harmless charm on you two, a wee thing involving my herb."

"Your herb, Highness?" Rowan sneaked a wary glance at Dara. "You mean, like, Princess Grian's plant, hawthorn?"

"Aye." Medb wrinkled her nose. "Hers is hawthorn. Poor lass, the *smell*! Mine is *cnáib*."

Rowan choked on his wine, putting his cup down with tearing eyes and a bout of coughs. Fergus gave a thundering, hearty laugh. Medb was still leaning against the table, watching her baffled guests with growing amusement.

"Rowan, you okay?" Dara gave his back a healthy pound. "What's this...Knau-b, anyway?"

"Aye, I'm...fine," he squeezed the words in between coughs, shielding his mouth with his hand. "It's just that...*cnáib* is Gaelic for cannabis. Hemp."

"What? You *drugged* us?" Dara let Rowan go and leaped to her feet, her massive chair screeching back against the tiles. Her eyes were shooting daggers at the High Princess.

"Well, not exactly." The High Princess studied her with a serene smile. "I just made sure the candles in your bedchamber were bearing the right kind of incense."

Dara sank back into her seat, her face drained of blood. Rowan quickly slid the chair beneath her backside, saving her from an embarrassing plunge to the floor. He leaned into her, his arm gently embracing her shoulders.

"What happened between us in there was *real*, Dara," he whispered.

"Was it?" she mumbled. "Maybe it was just a combination of a good spell and a little pot."

"A spell was cast on you, truthfully," Fergus softly interrupted. "Only, you two are the ones who originally conjured it, not the High Princess. She just added a wee bit of spice." He rose from his chair, swift and spry despite his size. "Now, for matters of no less importance. Knowing you're being persecuted in this Realm, Her Highness wishes to help you go back Up to yours."

"A way back Up?" Rowan's eyes darted back to Fergus. "Is that possible? Up where?"

"There is a cave, with one of its mouths in the Otherworld, and the other in Erin, in a place the folk there call Roscommon," Medb replied. "The cave's name is Oweynagat."

"You mean we'll enter the cave here and emerge in the county of Roscommon, Ireland?" Rowan echoed. "Back home," he added with a warm whisper. "I know of this place from old legends. Oweynagat, the Cave of the Cats. The Gateway to the Otherworld. They tell in Roscommon that each *Samhain* many ferocious beasts emerge from the mouth of that cave, and wreak havoc all over the countryside! Haven't seen one mean beast come out of there yet, I tell you," he chuckled. "But 'tis dangerous to trust old tales. Some even tell of Her Highness's and her consort Mac Roich's demise, if I may speak so boldly."

"And those tales were indeed highly exaggerated, as your eyes can see for themselves." Fergus grinned down at him. "However, lad, by Carabolg here—" he touched his sword's hilt, " —Oweynagat is a true Gateway."

* * * * *

Dara and Rowan followed Fergus Mac Roich on horseback out of the palace gates and down the hillside, gradually slipping into the woods again. They rode leisurely, a sharp pine scent again tantalizing their senses. Dara draped herself in silence, her thoughts unclear. Rowan concealed his disquiet, using the time to try and get the information that Brighid had promised him long ago. Fergus obliged, willingly granting him lengthy answers to each of his questions.

"Long ago," Fergus told Rowan, "We—the *Tuatha dé Danann*, that is—escaped to the Otherworld, or *Tír Na n'Og*, if you prefer the old name. Now we like 'Lower Realm' better. But this you already know." He raised one hand from his horse's reins, counting on his fingers. "So, back when it all began, the

Lower Realm was sliced into five kingdoms—Mumha, Connachta, Laighin, Ulaid, and Midhe."

"The names sound very much alike to Ireland's four provinces," Rowan said. "Munster, Connaught, Leinster, and Ulster. I guess your fifth kingdom—Midhe—is parallel to our Tara in county Meath."

"Aye, the names of Ireland's provinces are derived from this ancient split Down here—" Fergus nodded, "—which, by itself, had been originally modeled after the oldest split of all, that made in old Erin when the *Tuatha dé Danann* were still ruling the isle." He gave Rowan a brief glance before proceeding. "Each of our five kingdoms is further divided into a number of Mounds. Some call them dominions, but these titles mean the same, truly. Each kingdom holds one Ruling Mound and a few more Lesser Mounds."

"That I figured out by myself," Rowan responded. "And each Mound is governed by a Prince, or a Princess, aye? The one who has control over a Ruling Mound is called High Prince, or High Princess."

"'Tis indeed so. My chieftain makes a fine example." Fergus chuckled. "High Princess Medb has control of Rath Cruachan, the Ruling Mound of Connachta." He gently yanked his horse's reins, hopping down from its broad back in the same swift motion. "We'll be going by foot from here," he said, fondly patting his steed's flank.

"Is there a single ruler of the entire Lower Realm, then?" Rowan slid down from his horse and turned to help Dara, finding her already standing on solid ground. She flashed him a brief glance, quickly averting her gaze and turning away from him.

"There's no single king or queen here." Fergus was watching them, his expression guarded. "The title is taboo. Realm leadership shifts between the five Ruling Mounds. Current leadership is with High Prince Bodb, in Mumha. This *Beltaine*, control will finally transfer to Midhe. We'd better move on a wee bit faster now," he suggested.

He walked them in a meandering route through thick brushwood, where tree trunks were packed so closely together it was hard for a man to pass through. When Dara finally gave in and spoke, asking Fergus how he'd managed the narrow path, the massive warrior laughed and told her, "Just a bit of Glamour, lass. Just a wee bit of Glamour."

"What about the Ocean, Fergus?" Rowan panted, his brogue growing more obvious. It seemed that trees kept blocking his way, and low bushes kept tangling about his ankles. He stifled a curse, wondering how the bleedin' hell the massive warrior moved so swiftly among the trees. Magic was involved, for sure. *Glamour*—Fergus had said so himself. This was turning out to be one of the rare occasions Rowan wished the Kanjali shifters hadn't neglected the fine art of magic thousands of years ago.

"*Tir-fo-Thoinn*—the 'Land Beneath The Waves'—makes a sixth territory, outside the five-way split of the Lower Realm," Fergus raised his voice over the short distance between them. He kept a fast, steady pace, his image flickering in between the trees. "Its lord is Manannan Mac Lir."

Finally, both of them caught up with Fergus and stood still. The warrior bent down and lifted a curtain of branches and leaves, exposing a cave's black mouth. "In you go," he smiled. "And I shall be free to return to my mistress. You need not worry, no one will follow you up this cave."

"Fergus," Dara said, her voice unsteady. She took a few hesitant steps closer to him, gazing up at his face. "Before we leave, can I ask you what '*Garn*' means? This word, lately it keeps pushing into my mind, like some vague memory, and I don't..."

"*Garn*," Fergus placed a gentle, massive hand on her shoulder. "It means winter. It lasts half a year from *Samhain* to *Beltaine*, and then it's the end of the cold, dark winter, aye?"

"Yes," she nodded, wrapping her arms about his waist in a sudden hug. Of course, she was far from circling the full span of him. "Yes. Thank you."

"'Tis nothing," he replied softly. "Now go with your lad. You and him, you were foretold long ago."

"What?" she mumbled, but the giant warrior had already vanished with the faintest rustle of leaves. Her shoulder still felt warm with his touch.

"I hate it when they do that," she told no one in particular.

"Dara, you coming?" Rowan was crouched by the cave's mouth, staring inside with eager eyes. "Do you want to go back to civilization, or don't you?"

"Yeah," she called back, closing the short distance between them. "If you count Ireland as 'civilization'."

"Americans…" There was an obvious grin in his voice.

She squatted beside Rowan, staring into the cave's darkness, and then swiveled to look at his face. She found him watching her. His stormy green eyes held a sudden, striking clarity.

Like an invisible sun had lit up everything from the inside, she thought.

When he leaned down and tangled a hand into her hair, sweeping her head closer, she opened up for him with unreserved hunger. His tongue stroked in and out of her mouth, emulating the intimacy they had shared in Medb's bedchambers. Finally, winded, they detached their swollen lips.

"What we had in there — that was real," Rowan said gruffly. "That was no drug, Dara, that made me take you as mine. That made you have me."

"I know that now." She lightly touched his arm. "What about Brighid? Think she's okay?"

"Well…" He smiled. "I think banshees have their own ways of getting by."

Chapter Eighteen

They had to crawl on their hands and knees against the rock-studded earth floor, rough stone slabs pressing low above their heads. Rowan had insisted on going in first, relying on Fergus Mac Roich's promise that they wouldn't be followed from this end. He didn't like it. Trusting others, anyone not kinfolk, went against his nature. True, Mac Roich was *dé-Danann*, thus sharing a common, deep-seated link with the Kanjali. But still...

Soon the ground became mostly rock. Dara was close behind, finding it easier to move within the narrow confines. Her breath came soft and uneven behind him, interspersed with small sighs and half-moans that made his blood seethe even within this viscous blackness.

The light designating their entry point had gradually shrunk to a white dot and had soon been swallowed by the dark. As they moved deeper into the cave they were both able to walk upright, compressed between the narrow walls. The stone was coarse and clammy against their palms and cheeks, nearly the only solid sensation to hold on to. Rowan felt for jagged edges, alerting Dara with soft, terse whispers. They seemed to be advancing endlessly, losing the feel of time, their pace excruciatingly slow. Rowan found himself frequently reaching behind him, making sure Dara was still there. He needed the fleeting brush of warm skin against his fingers—the curve of a shoulder, the silken smoothness of a cheek.

Little by little they realized that their eyes could separate black from blacker. Soon they were actually *seeing* the play of shadows against the uneven, serrated stone.

"Getting near," Rowan said.

"Must be day outside," Dara whispered back.

To her surprise, Rowan halted and turned from the feeble evidence of daylight ahead. She bumped into him within the slowly fading darkness, and he caught her in a firm embrace. Puzzled, she squeezed him back, skimming her fingers from the small of his back up the mild bow of his spine. Their mouths fumbled in the dark and found each other, lips clinging. Dara's low moan slipped into Rowan's mouth, and he answered with a stifled groan from deep in his throat. His hands pressed her against his solid chest, against his rampant cock. Their shared breaths and tongues entangled until it was no longer clear in whose mouth each moved, licked and sucked. At some point, they both went up for air.

"Will you be mine in this Realm as well, sweetheart?" Rowan's raspy, warm whisper breathed over Dara's mouth.

"Do you still need to ask?" she mumbled back, and her tongue flicked across his lips, a gentle tease.

Still, that wasn't a yes. Rowan squeezed her one last time and released her, letting the question go for now.

They had to crouch as they went through the final passage, and soon there was an earth floor beneath their feet. Scanty daylight illumined slabs and blocks of pale limestone. The passageway abruptly opened to a low chamber, and bright sunlight burst in through the opening ahead. The entrance had been framed with massive blocks of limestone, creating a stone lintel. Wild grass thrived close to the sunlight, lapping the stones' base with green tongues.

"See those shallow, vertical grooves carved in the horizontal slab?" Rowan pointed to the low-hung stone lintel.

"Up there, close to the stone's lower edge?" She huddled close, daylight warming her face.

"Aye, there. It's an Ogham inscription."

"What does it say?" She crouched closer to the opening.

"'Tis just a name, one of Medb's sons," he replied. "She has many of those. Many husbands, too, not counting her lover,

Fergus Mac Roich. Stories say she used to bed thirty men each day, or go with Fergus once."

"You've made a narrow escape, then." Dara giggled and turned, now granting him a generous view of the soft rounded mounds packed tightly in her corset. The creamy breasts jiggled with her laughter. "The way Her Highness was ogling you back by the river."

She yelled as Rowan grabbed one of her ankles, exerting a soft, firm pull.

"Wait, Dara, let *me* go out first." He grinned. "Who knows what might be lurking out there, patiently waiting to ambush a luscious lass such as you."

"Go knock yourself out then," she retorted with a sweet smile. "Don't complain later that a certain luscious lass and her faithful, *very* sharp dagger weren't there for you just when you needed them most."

"Point taken," he nodded as he watched her, his stirring cock stealing the blood supply needed for his brain. He had to get himself out of there, fast, if he wanted anything done soon.

Rowan brushed past her a bit closer than necessary as he climbed out of the cave's mouth. Even the fleeting rub of their bodies made Dara's skin feel charged. She watched Rowan's receding back, thinking his ass looked good enough to eat in the tight buckskin breeches. She gripped her dagger's hilt, just in case something nasty was indeed waiting to ambush them.

Shouts from outside the cave made Dara curse and leap towards the entrance, dagger in hand. "*Dammit*, Rowan, what did I just tell you?"

She pressed hard against the chilly stone, partly hidden behind it, an assortment of terrifying visions playing in her mind. Her heart pounded like a caged bird. She strained to listen, to make something meaningful out of the jumble of sound.

Come on, Dara, while you're standing here wondering, something horrible might be happening to him!

She tensed, getting ready to throw herself into whatever was going on out there.

A head dipped into the cave, and she screamed.

"Just me, lassie. Get yourself up here, come meet a friend of mine." Rowan's laugh echoed and bounced against the small chamber's walls. "And put that knife of yours away, he might get the wrong idea!"

"Oh, yeah?" She shoved the dagger back into its sheath and climbed out of the cave, ignoring Rowan's offered hand. Her eyes squinted against the bright sunlight. "Goddess, I feel like I'm in a trashy vampire movie!" Her eyes widened at the sound of a soft, appreciative whistle. Slowly, she turned to face its source.

"A fine thing, she is!" The whistler watched her with a devilishly charming smile. He was about Rowan's height, his tangled hair a honey-colored havoc lightly streaked by the sun.

"Oh, it talks!" Dara crossed her arms, her gaze spearing the impertinent blond.

"Dara—" Rowan grinned, "—this is Teague, Teague O'Rourke. Teague, this 'fine thing' here is Dara." His voice softened as he added, "The one I went away looking for."

Dara's breath caught at Rowan's words. Teague's sky-blue eyes darted between the two of them. Finally he shook his head and lowered his amused gaze, hiding a broadening grin.

"Uh, I was sent here by the Bantiarna." Teague finally broke the stretching silence.

"Bantiarna?" Dara arched a questioning brow.

"The Bantiarna Niamh," Teague replied, his gaze flicking briefly back to her. "Bantiarna means Lady, Dara. She's the one giving the orders around here." His blue eyes went to Rowan again. "Since you disappeared, bud, many of us have been positioned at certain points, ones assumed to be…Gateways." He squirmed uneasily, adding, "Not that all through these bleedin' hundreds of years we've ever managed to go through one."

"How long, Teague?" Rowan demanded. "How long have I been away?"

"We're celebrating *Beltaine* in three sundowns." Teague's tone was cautious.

"*Six months.*" Rowan's lips twitched in a soft, bitter laugh. "Six bleedin' months!"

"But it felt like a few hours, just a little more than a day." Dara paled and turned to look at the cave again, as if its black mouth was holding back a secret. "A couple of days, maybe!"

"Time trickery. It's been known to happen before," Teague told her softly. "You know the legend of Oisin, Dara? The bard who traveled to *Tír Na nÓg*?"

"Better take us to the Bantiarna now, Teague, there'll be time enough for stories later," Rowan intervened. "I need a word with her, and there's a bleedin' Hound out there, very keen on biting our arses!"

"A Hound?" Teague shot a quick glance in Dara's direction. "That's what we figured when we found the bike you rented, along with her monster truck, deserted by that Portland warehouse. Not to mention the blood on the rug."

"Hey watch it, pal, that's my Silverado you're badmouthing." Dara glowered at Teague, suddenly missing her big, trusty Chevy. "What have you done with my truck, anyway?"

"*O'Rourke.*" Rowan scanned his old pal with a sinister look. "By now you should be walking us to Bantiarna Niamh fairly lively."

"Aye. Care if we drive over there instead of walking, though, boyo?" Teague appeared unruffled by his friend's harsh demeanor. "'Tis a bit hard to go by foot from Roscommon to Meath."

"You still driving that oul' Bronco?" Rowan teased as the three of them ambled away from the narrow cave's opening. "I think that oul' banger is the only car in Ireland with a left-hand drive."

"You off your nut, bud? My Bronco looks much hotter than that outfit you're sportin'."

Dara grinned to herself, eavesdropping on the prickly exchange. She wondered if the two of them had known Aidan. He'd grown up in these green hills, they had to have known him. Had the three of them been buddies? She lifted her eyes from the grass and took a sweeping, hungry look around, curious to see bits and pieces of this land Rowan called home.

Aidan's home.

They were strolling through a broad, grassy plain, with three large, green mounds rising from the fields. The wide-open landscape was studded with rounded hillocks, ring forts and ring-shaped barrows. Distant, shallow mountains with mist-shrouded tops crowned the far-reaching grassland. She paused in her walk, taking a slow, deep breath. The two Irishmen halted and watched her, similar looks on their faces.

"A beauty, isn't she?" Teague grinned softly, his smile very much like Rowan's. "The land. All of these acres are *Cruachan Aí*, the Plain of the Mounds." He swung an arm towards the highest of the three mounds jutting from the plain. "There is Rath Cruachan. Legends tell that's where Queen Maeve's palace once stood."

"He means our High Princess Medb," Rowan told Dara. "The folktales transformed her into Queen Maeve. Her palace is still standing, Teague, only not Up here."

"Yeah, it stands where it has for thousands of years—Rath Cruachan of Lower Realm's Connachta," Dara's gaze stroked over the sights. "Strange, Rowan, many place-names here seem to be identical to Lower Realm ones, or at least they're sounding very close. Like there's a 'Rath Cruachan' both Up here and Down there."

"Aye," he nodded. "There are many overlaps between the Realms. Mainly around Gateway points, I think."

"By Great Danu," Teague muttered. "I'm still trying to convince myself you two *did* show up from the bleedin' Otherworld!" He shook his head, exhaling a morose sigh. His expression brightened as they finally stopped by a pampered Ford Bronco gleaming in deep maroon and chrome, its side striping a blazing tricolored orange. The fiberglass hardtop was off, and there was no rear seat installed.

Someone obviously loved this car, Dara thought. "Hey, *nice* Bronco!" She ran appreciative fingertips over the truck's frame. She'd picked up her own love of trucks from Aidan. "It's a seventy-eight, seventy-nine?"

"A seventy-nine, all original, except for the tires," Teague eyed her curiously. "You like a good ride, lass?"

"Watch it, bucko!" Rowan growled.

Teague threw his head back with a warm, rolling laugh.

Rowan clamped his hands on Dara's waist. "We'll be riding in the back," he announced. He lifted her with ease into the Bronco's open trunk before she managed a protest, then leaped in after her.

"Suit yourself." Teague's laughter rang clear as he shuffled his car keys in his hand.

"What was that all about?" Dara demanded of Rowan, her face flushed.

Goddess, could Rowan be jealous?

Turning the thought over in her mind, she missed Teague hopping into the driver's seat and shutting the door behind him with a gentle slam. She also tuned out the Bronco stirring to life with a healthy roar. The truck's forward surge and immediate side-swerve took her completely by surprise, throwing her straight into Rowan's arms. They both fell onto the trunk's platform in a heap of arms and legs.

"I swear he did that on purpose!" Dara panted, squirming above Rowan. Another light bounce of the truck threw them both off-balance again, sending them rolling against the bumpy platform.

"You bleedin' mule!" Rowan bellowed, veins cording in his neck. He pounded with his fist against the truck's wall. "Teague! You want your teeth in a bag?"

"He can't hear you," Dara groaned beneath him. "Mackey, move your hand off of my ass!"

The ride had seemed calmer for the last minute or so. Rowan managed to climb to a crouch above Dara, just enough for her to roll over to her tummy. She propped herself against the platform, trying to crawl out from beneath him. She made it to a squat before the Bronco bounced gleefully over some obstacle, throwing them into a wild bundle again.

"Let's just...lie down for a bit..." Dara begged over the Bronco's roar. Once more she'd found herself lying on top of Rowan.

"That's Teague for you," he growled from beneath her, locking his hands over her ass. "You just wait 'til I get my hands on him."

The truck slowed down again. This time they didn't dare climb to their feet. Dara lifted her eyes to Rowan, wringing his soft vest in her fists for support.

"Nice pal you have there," she told him.

He grinned down at her, shaking his head. "He's truly a harmless bastard," he said. And then they both burst into a fit of laughter, gasping and panting with tearing eyes.

"This is going to be a long ride," Dara giggled.

"No, sweetheart," Rowan laughed. "He's going to have to take the N-5 soon, and then it's almost a straight, smooth road from here to Meath."

"Where are we heading?" she mumbled, her breath hot against his neck. She was heavy in his arms, swaying between wakefulness and sleep, with the sun warming her back.

"To a Lady," he answered softly, his enfolding arms roaming up and down her back. "A Lady living in a wood castle on the river Boyne." Nodding slowly, Dara curled up like a cat in his embrace. Rowan saw her eyes grow hooded, narrowing to slits, as she sank more heavily in his hold and fell into a carefree slumber.

Chapter Nineteen

"Tonight's all taken care of, then?" Niamh inquired without turning away from the broad window. Her gaze surveyed the endless stretch of intense blue and green, the river Boyne winding its way through the lush, sun-bright foliage. Small doll-like figures dotted the riverbank, mostly fishermen after wild brown trout.

"Aye, Bantiarna," Aislinn replied, taking another cautious step among the hall's shadows. "The Speakers have all been informed of tonight's Gathering."

"Good," Niamh gave a small sigh, finally turning to look at her protegee. "You did good, Aislinn."

The young woman returned a hesitant smile. She looked the picture of bottled-up tension. Niamh smiled inwardly, appreciating the girl's excitement. Her two foundlings, Rowan and, a while later, Aislinn, had been raised like true brother and sister. While red-haired Rowan Mackey had grown to be a big, sturdy man, with an energetic, confident manner, Aislinn had remained a petite, fragile brunette, tending to keep to herself. An air of insecurity seemed to cling to her every action even as she matured, leaving the past behind.

However, the difference between the two ranged further than appearance and demeanor. Aislinn was a mere human...a Mortal. Rowan was Kanjali, and further than that, he was the last of the Guardians born. The most powerful shifters among the Kanjali, Guardians were the first to hold back Hound attacks, and their slow disappearance along the centuries was a true loss.

Years back, chiding voices had been raised among the shifters, ill at ease with Niamh's decision to rear a Mortal amongst them. Niamh would have none of that, firmly hushing them all. She'd taken both children, Rowan and Aislinn, to her estate—a manor overlooking the river Boyne and fringing the small market town of Trim.

"The Castle", as Rowan had fondly named the estate, though it was built out of wood, not rock, held no turrets or trenches, and was enclosed by tall, clipped hedges of beech and yew instead of a high stone wall. Anyone keen on the dark gothic look could find it in the true Castle of Trim, built on the Boyne's opposite bank.

"Is there anything else?" Niamh quirked a sandy brow, seeing Aislinn hesitate.

"Well," Aislinn mumbled, and then the words poured out in a flood. "Has Rowan found his Chosen One? Is he bringing her over? Will she come?" she asked, eyes eager. "Is he all right?"

"Rowan is grand." Niamh bit back a grin. "Now, don't you have something better to do than stand there?"

Aislinn gave her a brief, hasty nod, retreating back to the hallway among the room's shadows. Niamh turned back to the window, her eyes readjusting to the day's brightness. She was no less keyed up than the girl, only far better skilled at concealing it.

Teague had finally made contact that morning, alerting her that he'd found Rowan and his Chosen at Oweynagat, The Cave of Cats. After six months, bless the Goddess! His *Chosen*, Teague had stressed. So, Rowan had truly found her... Little Dara O'Shea, Aidan Neilan's wife. Dara, who'd been both orphaned and widowed in just a couple of months, almost three and a half years ago.

Niamh squeezed her fists against the wooden window frame. Six months ago she'd been informed of Rowan and Dara's disappearance, the deserted vehicles by the Portland Safe Grounds' warehouse, the blood-soaked rug. She had feared the worst then. Feared that she had lost them both—the boy she'd taken as her own and watched grow to a man, and the girl she'd sent away from Ireland and had barely known since. She had feared that she had been mistaken in deciphering the ancient texts, that what she had seen within the time-yellowed scrolls had been no truer than a wishful mind's fancy. That *their kind* had lost its last flickering hope. But Rowan Mackey and Dara Neilan had turned out to be very much alive, and were making their way here this very minute.

And *Beltaine* was to be celebrated in just three nights...

Niamh forced her fists to relax and leaned against the cedar frame. Soon she would talk to Rowan and Dara. The Speakers circle had been called for an urgent Gathering, as well. All had been taken care of, there was nothing else she could do now but wait. Might as well enjoy the pleasantly sunny day as long as Erin's fickle weather allowed it.

* * * * *

They'd driven west 'til the day dimmed, through the grassy plains of Roscommon and Longford, and the bogs and lakes of Westmeath. The countryside was rich with multiple shades of green. *The Route of the Táin*, Rowan had called it.

"*The Táin*," he'd added, "is Ireland's most famous epic."

He'd then whispered in Dara's ear the old tale of Medb and the Cattle Raid of Cooley, and she'd listened, ancient names resurfacing in her memory, her mother's voice uttering them.

Rowan had told her other things as well, his lips hot on her skin. What he'd like to do to her, with her, right then and there. He'd been very imaginative, and quite elaborate, his roaming hands helping to explain some of the more complex details.

At some point she'd squeaked, hot all over, "Rowan, *that* is not anatomically possible!"

He'd promised to prove her wrong later.

In Meath they'd deviated from the legendary trail, their destination being the Bantiarna's estate.

"That's the Boyne, there. We're close, sweetheart." Rowan pointed to a shimmering band of water engulfed by the flourishing green landscape.

"Slowly," Dara begged of Teague as he lowered her from the Bronco's trunk. "I'm not sure I can stand up right now." The ground swayed beneath her feet. She clutched her stomach. Maybe it was a good thing she'd had nothing to eat for the last few hours.

"The Castle—" Rowan's hands had already replaced Teague's on Dara's waist, steadying her, " —of the Lady on the river Boyne."

"Home?" she asked, lifting her eyes to his. The warmth in his voice made her ask.

"'Tis the closest to home I've ever had," Rowan admitted softly. "Can you walk?"

"Yeah, sure," she replied, not sure at all. The alternative was being carried to the doorstep. Goddess, not as long as she was breathing and conscious!

Rowan nodded, a hint of a smile hovering on his lips, and steered her with a gentle touch towards a gray-white lane of pebbles. Dara took her first true look around and froze, gasping in surprise. Their path wound through a vast carpet of roses in pinks and reds and whites, their brightness dimmed by the looming dusk. Her gaze moved over vigorous and timid shrubs, trellises and arches covered by wild-spreading ramblers, a climber cloaking a wood pergola.

Dara's astounded gaze finally darted up.

Towering above all that splendor was a massive two-story manor, perched in the garden's hub like a sleeping Briar Rose.

"I guess she really likes roses, your Lady." Dara drew a slow, deep breath, taking in the intense fragrance. Something made her squirm with unease. "Funny, I feel like I've been here before, Rowan." She chafed her hands against her arms.

"Maybe you have," he answered cautiously, guiding her along the trail. He watched Teague strolling past them and up the garden path, whistling a soft tune, deliberately leaving them to themselves.

A few minutes later Dara wondered, exhausted, *when* exactly Rowan had managed to scoop her up into his arms. She gave in and pressed her face into his shoulder, his aroma briefly taking dominance over the roses' fragrance. He squeezed his arms around her in a wordless response. She swiveled her head, her gaze straying to one of the wide second-story windows—she could swear she saw a figure up there, watching them. *Rowan's Lady of the Boyne?*

"Let me down," Dara bade Rowan in a sleep-blurred voice as they reached the doorstep.

"What, already?" Rowan lowered her carefully to the paved lane, his hands reluctant to let go of her.

Together they climbed the two shallow steps onto the shaded front porch. The ornamented door swung open before Rowan could use the brass knocker. Dara met dark eyes at the same level as hers. A young woman was staring at her, openmouthed, from the threshold. She was probably around the same age as her, and yet the bare uncertainty in her face made her seem younger. Or maybe it was the light floral dress, nimbly clinging to her breasts and falling below her knees, that made her look young.

"Aislinn." Rowan spoke softly, saying the single word carefully as if it were something fragile.

The girl's eyes darted from Dara to Rowan. She threw herself past the doorstep as if it were a tangible barrier, her slim arms closing on Rowan's waist. She buried her face in his chest and her small body heaved with muffled sobs. He stroked her hair gently, sliding his hands over her shoulders.

"Now, now, lass," he muttered. "No need for that... I'm all in one piece, see?"

Aislinn nodded against his chest, still sobbing. "Oh, Rowan, I thought—I thought you were—"

"Ash...you know I'm not good with crying women!" Rowan gave his adopted sister a tight hug. Then, cupping her shoulders in a gentle hold, he managed to tilt her back from him and study her tear-streaked face. "So, tell me... How is the Bantiarna?" He gave Aislinn a warm smile. The weight of his gaze on his sister's flushed face convinced Dara that he'd wanted to ask her much more than he had.

"Niamh is fine," Aislinn returned a tear-saturated smile. "She wants to see you both. As soon as you're here, she said." Her eyes strayed to Dara again, then quickly returned to her brother's face.

"Had nightmares again?" Rowan inquired softly. "Is that why you were crying?"

Aislinn hesitated.

He studied her expression, then smoothed two long fingers down her chin. "Ash, I'd like you to meet Dara," he finally said, changing the subject.

"It's great to meet you," Dara smiled.

"'Tis grand finally meeting you, too!" A sudden smile brightened Aislinn's face, like a cloud swiftly dissolving to reveal the sun behind it. "I've heard about you, Dara. Not much. How your parents took you away from Ireland when you were just four years old. And then again, this morning..." she hesitated, "when Teague informed the Bantiarna that Rowan had found you, and was bringing you over."

Dara nodded. Her legs felt heavy, and she propped herself against the doorframe. Aislinn noticed and blushed harder, retreating away from the door and back into the hall's shadows.

"I'm sorry, Dara, please come inside," she mumbled. "Rowan, how could you let me be such an *amadán*!"

Rowan laughed in response, ruffling her hair. "I wouldn't call you an idiot." He stepped inside, sweeping Dara along with him. "Is Niamh in the study?" he asked.

Aislinn nodded as she scuttled along the hallway's wide-planked oak floor, her flimsy dress brushing her skin with a faint rustle. The short corridor opened to an airy, arched foyer with two broad staircases spiraling up from its opposing corners. Dusky light seeped in through the chiffon-draped French doors, which opened to the vast back gardens. Dara could envision the large hall flooded with sunlight during the day. It was softly lit now by candles carefully positioned in wall sconces, and one delicate, two-tiered crystal chandelier.

"The Bantiarna has a soft spot for dramatic lighting." Rowan flashed Dara an apologetic grin.

He captured Dara's hand in his and drew her up the right staircase, following his sister's quick, soft footsteps. Behind them, Teague's laughter drifted from the dining room adjoining the foyer.

Dara inhaled deeply as Rowan pulled her gently through the soft shadows. The vast house felt somehow alive around them, its wooden floors creaking faintly beneath their feet, and its dark walls exhaling cool, fresh-scented air. They'd passed a few wooden doors delicately engraved with flowering sprigs and embossed with hummingbirds, until Aislinn finally halted before one of them.

"I'll go in then, Aislinn." Rowan dropped a loving pat on his sister's back. "I need to talk to Niamh alone."

"I know that, Rowan." Aislinn nodded slowly. "Dara, 'twas grand meeting you." She gave a timid smile and silently turned to make her way back down the corridor.

"Is there something wrong with Aislinn?" Dara whispered. "She was crying earlier—"

"Aye, there's something wrong," Rowan stiffly replied. "When she was very young, she witnessed her family being slain. She's been this way since I first met her—frightened, always on edge." He gave the gleaming door handle a gentle tug and shove.

Rowan cracked the door open before Dara managed to grasp the full meaning of his words. Her mind numb, she followed him, finding herself standing in the midst of a spacious, softly shadowed room, its walls hidden behind heavily burdened bookshelves of solid wood. A soft summer breeze breathed in through the open window.

A woman turned away from the view to face them. Her short hair was very bright against the darkness, and her eyes were very blue.

"Hello, Dara," she said in a matter-of-fact tone, as if Dara had been ambling through the mansion's corridors each and every day of her life.

Chapter Twenty

"We've met before," Dara said.

"Yes, we have. You were almost four years old then." Niamh was motionless by the window, her calm voice easily filling the large study. There was no tension in her, but no ease, either. Her eyes were alight and observant, disclosing no emotion.

"It was you who sent my family away from Ireland," Dara said, surprise budding in her voice.

"I assumed at the time I was protecting you. Maybe I was wrong."

Niamh moved deeper into the room, her tread smooth and silent. She halted, facing them. Dara was standing oddly erect, her eyes too wide and too dark, her face pale, lined with tiredness. Rowan stood close beside her, wanting to hold her but not daring to, his mouth shaped into a straight, tight line.

"You both should get some food and sleep," Niamh said softly.

"Oh, *no*." Dara shook her head sharply, her curls bouncing. "Not before you tell me why you sent my family away."

"Because you were special, Dara," Niamh replied. "Your birth was special. With long-lived beings such as us, a newly born child is always a rare, treasured gift."

"Was that the only reason?" Dara demanded.

"You'll learn much more at tonight's Gathering of the Speakers," Niamh said. "Now go get at least a couple hours of sleep, child. I'll have dinner sent up to you. You, however—" she turned to Rowan, "—I'll need a word with first. Will you show Dara to the Summer Room and come back here as soon as you can?"

Rowan opened his mouth to answer when Dara raised her head.

"No," she snapped. "I won't be treated as a mindless child anymore, Niamh. If you don't wish to share information with me *now*, after all we've been through, I have no business staying here. I *will* take the first flight out to Portland's International Airport."

The room grew very quiet for one stretching second. The two women studied each other across a gap of almost a thousand years, icy blue eyes meeting heated dark ones. Rowan's fists tightened by his sides, but he kept silent.

Then, unbelievably, Niamh nodded.

"I'll arrange for some light refreshments to be brought up here while we speak," she said. "Please, Dara, sit down." She gestured to a pair of generously proportioned rosewood chairs, upholstered in deep burgundy leather.

Dara slipped into one with a thankful sigh, her hands absently stroking the lion's heads masterfully carved on the end of each arm. She briefly shut her eyes, shifting and stretching within the chair's snug embrace. A soft sound made her jerk, eyes flying open. Niamh was watching her, nestled in the other chair.

"These are English," Niamh said. "They are almost one hundred and fifty years old."

Dara stared at her uncertainly. She sneaked a quick glance around, spotting Rowan browsing through a leather-bound book by one of the shelves. Or, more likely, pretending to browse.

"I was referring to these chairs," Niamh repeated with a hint of a smile, patting her chair's carved arm. "But how about me, Dara? What, or who, am I? How old am I?"

"You're Irish," Dara replied, her voice hesitant. "As for your age, well..."

"My age is the simpler question. I am nine hundred and thirty-eight years old. But am I Irish, truly?" Niamh gently interrupted, arching a sandy brow. "Answering this question, Dara, demands that I choose between *tradition* and *blood*. If I choose tradition, then maybe indeed, living hundreds of years among the Irish folk has made me Irish, a Celt. However, if I choose blood, then no, I am Kanjali. Or, seeking my earliest roots, I am *dé-Danann*."

"Is there a point to this?" Dara frowned slightly. "I mean, besides telling me that defining a person's origins is far more complicated than defining a chair's?"

Niamh's smile broadened somewhat. "And so we come to you, Dara," she went on. "Knowing how tired you must be right now, let's leave *tradition* aside. Let's make a leap and go straight to *blood*. Whose blood is running in your veins, child?"

"I don't understand," Dara said. Somewhere behind her, the sound of rustling paper stopped.

"I don't wish to distress you with any more guessing games, Dara. So pay close attention." Niamh's cobalt-blue eyes were sharp and pointed. "You are of mixed birth, Dara. There is Kanjali in you and there is Mortal. Your Mortal essence was passed on to you by your father, and it was passed on to him along the generations starting with the bard Amergin, King Miled's younger son."

Dara lifted her numb gaze to Niamh's calm face.

"I will remind you of a story you should know," Niamh said softly. "I told this story to your mother when she was but a child herself." Her voice grew distant as she spoke, enchanting the outside world to utter silence. "Over four thousand years ago, the *Tuatha dé Danann* still ruled the beautiful land of Erin. Their charmed reign over the isle lasted for one hundred and ninety-seven years. However, since even a magical race can't stay invincible forever, and maybe because it was time to give the earth back to Mankind, the *Tuatha dé Danann* themselves were defeated in a great, desperate battle. 'Twas mere humans who beat them, invaders who had sailed from Spain to claim for themselves the green isle that lay in the track of the setting sun. The invaders were—"

"The sons of King Miled, the Milesians," Rowan broke in, casting his book aside. He took a step towards the two women. "They were the first Celts to settle in Erin, the true human ancestors of the Irish race that we know today. That's how you told it to me, Bantiarna, word for word."

"Aye, Rowan." The Bantiarna's smile warmed. "King Miled of Spain had eight sons, Amergin and Eber Donn among them. They led the Gaelic invasion to Ireland. Many of them found their deaths before Erin was conquered."

Niamh rose lithely from her chair and approached one of the surrounding bookshelves, selecting an enormous leather-bound volume. She carried her find back to her seat, allowing the book to rest dormant and heavy against her knees.

"At that time," she went on, "the island was ruled by three *dé-Danann* kings, all scions to the great Dagda. Their names are not important. Their queens, however, were called Banba, Fodla and Eriu."

"Eriu." Dara nodded. "Her name I've heard before."

"The entire story of how Erin was taken from the *Tuatha dé Danann* is a long and twisted one, and we are short of time." Niamh opened the book against her thighs, fingering the yellowed pages with a gentle touch. "Dara, I'd like you to read to us now a very small part of it."

She rose and laid the heavy book over Dara's thighs, split open at the page she had chosen.

"This volume, translated from Irish Gaelic, holds the *Lebor Gabála Érenn*, the Book of Conquests. Now, Dara, try to *see* it in your mind… The sons of Miled have just lost another brother to the sea, they've circled the island of Erin three times, but fail to see the land due to the *Tuatha dé Danann*'s magic trickery. They are not in the best of moods, to say the least." Niamh shot Dara a brief smile. "Finally, Miled's sons manage to climb ashore, led by the oldest of brothers, Donn, and the younger Amergin, himself a bard and a druid."

"Amergin," Dara echoed.

"To make a very long story short, the sons of Miled met on their way across the isle the *dé-Danann* queens Banba and Fodla, and each in her turn asked the brothers to name the island after her. To each of them Amergin promised to grant her wish. And then Donn and Amergin hit upon the third and the last queen, Eriu. Now, Dara, please read aloud."

Dara sighed, straining over the time-gilded page. Her eyes were hurting, and the large study didn't have enough light. The slender black lines danced beneath her struggling gaze and the crowding letters stumbled one over the other.

"*They held converse with Eriu in…Usnech of Mide.*" She started to read, her voice small and unsure. Her tongue stumbled over the strange names.

"*She said to them, 'Warriors,' said she, 'welcome to you. It is long since your coming was prophesied. Yours will be the island forever. There is not a better island in the world. No race will be more perfect than your race.'*

"*'Good is that,' said Amergin.*

"*'Not to her do we give thanks for it,' said Donn, 'but to our gods and to our power.'*

"*'It is naught to thee,' said Eriu. 'Thou shall have no gain of this island nor will thy children. A gift to me, O sons of Mil and the children of Bregan, that my name may be upon this island!'*

"*'It will be its chief name for ever,' said Amergin, 'namely Eriu.'*"

Dara lifted her eyes from the page. They felt as if sand grains had been pushed and rubbed into them. "The paragraph stops here," she said.

"Aye, so it does," Niamh was back in her seat, watching her. "So, Donn and Amergin meet Eriu. She welcomes the two

Milesian brothers, sharing her prophecy with them. The island shall belong to the sons of Miled and their children, she says, and their children's children. Young Amergin accepts Eriu's words with thankfulness. The older brother Donn, however, angrily rejects Eriu's prediction, insulting her.

"'We will win anyway', he growls at his younger brother, 'and it has nothing to do with her words!'

"Eriu retaliates by vowing he'll never enjoy the isle himself, and neither will his seed. So, Dara, the story seemingly ends with Amergin's promise to Eriu, to name the land after her. And thus Ireland — Erin — gains its true name."

"Seemingly?" Dara smoothed her hand gently over the pages. "Are you saying there is another ending to this?"

"Your weariness hasn't drowned your curiosity." Niamh gave a small chuckle.

Rowan cocked a brow. This display of emotion was unusual in the Bantiarna he'd known.

"The volume you're holding in your hands, Dara, is a collection of some of the widespread versions of the ancient texts," Niamh went on. "The ones every scholar of the Celtic Studies will swear by. The original scrolls, however, the ones holding the true and complete texts, are concealed elsewhere, not within the bounds of this modest library."

"For years I've suspected that," Rowan remarked, stepping closer. "That there were other texts, secret ones, hidden."

"Only a few possess the knowledge, Rowan, even among the Speakers themselves," Niamh replied. "And within these scrolls, among other things, there exists Eriu's complete Prophecy. These are the story's missing last lines…"

And Niamh closed her eyes and quoted from her heart.

"'My thanks to thee, good Amergin,' said Eriu. 'Long it will be before your brood reigns o'er the island, a seed from a union above and below. Lia Fáil will again utter a cry, the first and the last in one and a half-thousand years'."

"Brighid mentioned this Prophecy," Rowan's voice was soft, his expression bemused. "That's what she was speaking of when she claimed that some minor passages were missing from the Book of Conquests."

"What did Eriu mean, Rowan?" Dara lifted her eyes, finding him standing above her. The intensity of his gaze made her heart skip a beat and then hammer wildly in her chest.

"I think she meant, well..." he started, then shook his head and knelt by her side. He captured her cold, unresisting hand in his large one. "I think that we both are the 'union above and below' that Eriu spoke of. A union between *dé-Danann* and Mortal. I think that when we both rest against *Lia Fáil* in the eve of *Beltaine*, two eves from tonight, the stone will roar beneath us."

Chapter Twenty-One

"*No*," Dara jerked her hand out of Rowan's and leaped from her chair. The book slid heavily from her knees and landed with a dull thud against the soft rug. "No, Rowan, this can't be the truth!"

He sprang to his feet as well, facing her. "I thought you decided already," he spoke quietly, "about us. Back in that bed in Medb's palace, you decided."

"I'm not even sure *that* was real," she snapped. Her face was flushed, but she returned a blatant stare. "Maybe it was just the cannabis working."

"Don't you dare go there again." He clutched her arms tightly. "Don't pretend it meant nothing to you!"

She ground her teeth together, his steely grip imprisoning her, yet not bruising. "Just because we had great sex, you can't expect me to throw everything else away," she bit out.

"Throw everything else away?" he repeated, confused.

"I left a life back in Oregon. A home. My job. Friends," she whispered. "Rowan, I'm sorry. I refuse to let it all go up in smoke because of a thousand-plus-year-old prophecy. I won't have it. And then there's Aidan—"

"Dead, for over three years now," he lashed back at her, regretting it the instant the words left his mouth.

Dara stared up at him in silence, her lips parted as if she was about to say something. Her eyes were suddenly too shiny.

"Dara, I'm sorry…" he started, but she twisted against his hold with a desperate moan, and he dropped his hands. He watched her as she bolted towards the heavy door, tearing it open and escaping the room.

"Let her go." Niamh's voice was soft, but Rowan swiveled wildly about to face her, having forgotten she'd been witness to the bitter exchange.

"I'll lose her," he said, his hand skimming through his untamed hair. "I need to—"

"Sit down," Niamh commanded, gesturing to the newly vacant chair. "You won't lose her, she just needs more time."

Rowan sat down stiffly, as if he would jump out of the seat at any moment. He absently reached down for Dara's fallen book and pulled it into his lap, smoothing the ruffled pages back to order.

"She has learnt too much, too fast." Niamh watched him, motionless in her chair. "She *will* come to understand. Now, who is this Brighid you mentioned?"

"She's a banshee," he replied, his tone flat. "She was the one who transferred us from the Portland Safe Grounds to the Lower Realm." Seeing Niamh's arched brows, he added, "The Lower Realm is the name preferred by the denizens themselves, instead of what we call the Otherworld. *Tír Na nÓg.*"

"A banshee..." Niamh appeared thoughtful. "The Mortal family she cares for must be Amergin's descendants. Most likely, your Brighid was accompanying you both so she could watch over Dara."

"'Tis hard to believe that Dara is descended from the bard Amergin. Looking at the formal texts, Amergin was slain by his brother Heremon, dying childless." Rowan shook his head. "The O'Lalor clan—of the Mortal families—claims to have descended from Amergin through the legendary hero Connal Cernach, yet it was never proven..."

"Truthfully, Rowan, Amergin did leave a son behind after his wife's death," Niamh softly intervened. "There was enough detail in the ancient scrolls for the Speakers to track Amergin's descendants as far as Dara's father, Cuinn O'Shea." Niamh paused. "'Tis not clear when, exactly, Amergin's blood mixed with the *dé-Danann*'s. Some assume his son himself was the first of mixed origin."

Rowan nodded, his mind elsewhere.

"The Speakers will gather tonight. I need you to tell me all that you went through since leaving here six months ago," Niamh bade him. "Are you fit to do that, Rowan?"

He lifted his troubled gaze to meet hers, but gave her another swift nod. "I'll try my best to answer," he said.

With some effort he formulated images, sounds and emotions into short, bare sentences, and Niamh wrestled out the rest with carefully aimed questions. Finally, having entrusted to Niamh's quick mind all the knowledge he'd held, Rowan rose from his chair. "I should go find her," he said.

"Go," she agreed. "But I want you both at tonight's Gathering, Rowan. You remember where."

"Aye." He paused briefly by the door, his hand wrapped around the handle, before slipping outside.

Niamh collected the abandoned book, returning it to its spot on the proper shelf.

"So, what do *you* think," she asked it, lightly stroking its thick, gilded spine. "Have I been wrong all along?"

* * * * *

Finding Dara had been easier than Rowan had feared. Fiona, the housekeeper, had sent him through one of the French doors that opened to the back gardens. He followed the soft sound of hushed conversation to a stone bench aglow in the light of a plump, flawed moon. The pale orb lacked only a slim slice to be whole—the night of *Beltaine* would be graced with a full moon this year.

Rowan halted on a narrow lane rimmed with a splash of white petunias and night-stunned daylilies—the moonlight had frozen all colors to a silvery gray. Two dark figures huddled close upon the bench.

"How long have you been having the nightmares?" came Dara's hushed voice.

"I think, since what happened to my family," Aislinn whispered back. "I know that I was there when it happened—I was found hiding in a kitchen closet—but I can't remember a thing, see? I've just been having the dreams since then."

"Rowan is the only one who knows about them?"

"Aye, Dara, he's the only one."

"And your Lady Niamh?"

"No!" Aislinn sounded frightened at the thought. "I've never dared talk to her about this."

"So why are you telling *me*?" Dara placed a tentative hand on Aislinn's shoulder. "Don't get me wrong, Aislinn, I'm happy you trust me this way, but we've only just met."

Aislinn turned to Dara. "In a way, you're very much like Rowan," she spoke softly. "I feel it's all right to tell you. And besides, this last dream I had—this dream was different, nothing like my usual nightmares. If I don't tell *someone* about it, I'll…" She broke off, caught by a sudden shudder.

"So, tell me your dream," Dara coaxed. "I'm listening."

Rowan stood utterly still as he shamelessly eavesdropped, veiled in darkness. He'd suspected that Aislinn had been troubled by her old nightmares again. Rowan's adopted sister was purely human, a Mortal, not of Kanjali blood. She'd been the sole survivor of a slaughter that had wiped out her entire family. The murderer, or murderers, had never been caught. After a while, Aislinn had begun to suffer from recurrent nightmares—Rowan had been the only one who'd known. Maybe she'd chosen *him* to confide in since he'd lost his parents in a chillingly similar fashion.

"I've had the same dream a few times the last couple of weeks." Aislinn's muffled voice sounded again. "I see a bonfire burning upon a hill and a white, round moon filling the sky. Atop the hill a gray-white stone is standing erect, illumined by the fire, and as I watch, dark blood is splattered across it in a long, slanting line."

"Is there more?" Dara whispered.

"Aye. As I watch, I grow numb with dread," Aislinn mumbled. "Like something terrible has just happened, which cannot be turned back."

"And you thought to hide this from me, Aislinn?" Rowan stepped from the shadows into the moonlight. His whispered words had startled the two women. Dara and Aislinn both spun as one to face him. Aislinn had her hand clamped over her mouth, her eyes shadowed and unfathomable.

"Since you've obviously heard everything we've said," Dara spoke after a brief pause, "maybe you have some bright idea as to what her dream might mean."

"The only idea I have right now is that you should have told me right away, Aislinn." Rowan's voice was laden with concern. "How else can I make you feel better?"

Aislinn gathered her thin dress tighter about her and rose shakily to her feet. "You two should go now," she pleaded. "The Gathering is about to convene."

"You're not coming?" Dara asked, surprised.

"She's not allowed," Rowan answered for his sister. "No one should witness a Gathering but the Speakers themselves. Tonight we've been privileged—we've been *asked* to join. Come, sweetheart." He held out his hand to Dara. She took it, and he released a long-held breath, relieved. Aislinn picked that particular moment to slip back into the house, as insubstantial as a passing breeze.

"Where to?" Dara demanded of Rowan. "I haven't heard any commotion rising from the house, so I guess the party isn't here, right?"

"The Gathering is taking place elsewhere," he agreed. "The Speakers will gather tonight upon the Hill of Tara." He gently propelled Dara back towards the soft light spilling from the mansion's French doors. "Teague will drive us the few miles to Tara, and then we'll continue on foot."

"I hope no Speaker has a coronary seeing my outfit," Dara said a few minutes later, as she squeezed herself between Teague and Rowan on the bench seat. After their earlier experience with Teague's driving, both Rowan and Dara refused to ride in the back of the Bronco again.

Teague kept the car headlights low, and as they neared Tara he cut them completely.

"How can you tell where you're driving?" Dara whispered, frowning.

"Easy, lass, I know this path as I know the lines of my own palm," Teague responded with a chuckle.

The Bronco seemed to be taking them up a gentle slope. Dara closed her eyes and slumped against the seat, determined to relax. It only made her more acutely aware of the two men framing her, the hard muscles of their arms and thighs pressed against her flesh. Their aroma wafted about her, male and beast intermingled, as she remembered from her night at the Portland warehouse, and from many nights with Aidan. The waxing moon accentuated the tangy scent, and a fine tremble traversed her flesh. They were so alike in a way, these men—and again she found herself wondering whether they'd all been close once—Rowan and Teague...and Aidan.

She felt the mild deceleration as the Bronco slowed and stopped. Teague made a small movement beside her as he stilled the engine. Dara opened her eyes just as he half-turned to her. She caught the gleam of his eyes, and the edge of his warm breath touching her face. His fingers brushed over her cheek, rough and gentle like Rowan's.

"Teague," Rowan warned from the opposite side, his voice a soft growl.

"'Tis nothing but a wee touch," Teague protested, swiftly withdrawing his fingers.

"Aye, I've seen your wee touches," Rowan retorted. He pushed the Bronco's door open and slid out, pausing for Dara.

She followed him, feeling Teague's gaze hot on her back. Somehow she knew he would never attempt anything deeper than a fleeting touch, his friendship with Rowan too solid and deep-rooted to betray his friend's trust.

Rowan palmed Dara's hand in his, leading her along a path invisible to her eyes, leaving Teague standing beside his Bronco.

"Careful." He paused to shove open a small iron gate. "We're cutting through St. Patrick's churchyard to the Hill."

An odd couple of Standing Stones crowded together, and Celtic crosses loomed atop silent graves. Dara shuddered. Rowan seemed immune to the sight. As they left the church behind them Dara drew in a deep breath, casting a look at the sky's black dome. The air felt chilly, suiting an Irish spring night. A hint of the almost-full moon shone feebly beneath a dark gray layer of clouds, and the silver dots of a few stars gave scanty, useless light. The night thickened around the both of them, sheets of darkness heavily layered, like oil paint on canvas. The trail was slow and tortuous, and Dara twisted her sweaty hand within Rowan's, finally whispering his name with unease.

"Dara?" He briefly stopped and whispered, "Walk as close to me as you can, sweetheart. Tara is full of earthworks."

To her surprise, he turned amber eyes on her, and she froze, pulling back against his grasp.

"What's wrong?" Rowan whispered, the soft gold of his eyes oddly spellbinding.

"Your eyes," Dara mumbled. "H-how? It's not a full moon yet. How did you manage to...?"

"I told you, sweetheart, shapechanging is a knack of mine." Rowan's words breathed heat over her lips. "I am more sensitive to Power than most shifters, able to change also during the nights fringing a full moon."

His words didn't calm Dara. A fine tremble rushed up her spine. Rowan cradled her face in his hands, touching her lips with his. She briefly shut her eyes, succumbing to his familiar touch, and the fear subsided.

"Have you ever heard of Guardians, sweetheart?" Rowan spoke softly. "I *am* one. If there were no Guardians among the Kanjali, who could battle against the Hounds?"

Dara nodded, her fingers and toes as numb as her mind. She let Rowan draw her forward until she could see a shallow, rounded hillock framed by a soft orangey glow.

"The Mound of Hostages," Rowan said softly, sparing Dara the Gaelic term. "'Tis a many thousands-year-old tomb. Are you ready to face the Speakers, sweetheart?"

Dara suppressed another shiver. "Yes," she finally told Rowan, forcing herself to smile into the enigmatic gold of his eyes. "I simply can't wait to tell your Speakers my opinion of their dick-shaped stone."

Chapter Twenty-Two

Rowan tugged Dara towards the blaze-delineated hillock, as soft whispers fanned towards them on a gentle breeze. As they circled the shallow mound they finally saw the fire blazing at its foot, close to the large, square hole gaping at its side.

This mound is really a tomb, Dara recalled.

Together the two of them breached the circle of firelight, and suddenly dark shadows were shifting all about them, touching the light's edge. There were no more than six, maybe seven of them at a first glance, although the jittery glow made it difficult for Dara to tell their exact number. Their shadowy hosts clung mostly to the darkness, and their faces were distorted beyond recognition by the illusory play of light and dark.

Determinedly, Dara jerked her hand out of Rowan's.

"So, what's the big melodrama for?" she demanded, her tone defiant. The blunt words had been enough to crack the silence. It made her feel oddly better.

"Dara," Rowan whispered, cautioning.

"No, Guardian, let her talk," a raspy voice spoke, sounding amused. It had drifted from the dark figure standing at the farthest edge of the circle's unsure glow. Dara hadn't noticed him until he had spoken.

There are seven of them, then, she silently concluded.

"'Tis a bit of a mix of reasons, see?" the Speaker volunteered, a smile threaded in his rough voice. His brogue was a solid, vibrant one. "The first being, as usual, timing. *Beltaine* night is only two sundowns from now, and the Veil between the worlds grows thin again. 'Tis a time of great magic and nasty surprises. And, same as your American boy scouts, Dara, we like being well-prepared for the nasty bit."

Raspy didn't sound like he was about to introduce himself.

Dara frowned.

"What are the other reasons for summoning us up here?"

"*You*, of course," said a melodious contralto from the opposite rim. "And, naturally, *him*."

Dara swiveled sharply to face the feminine voice, blinking against the dark.

"Not to mention the prophecy," caressed a new, luxuriant male voice, only slightly tinged with an accent. He sounded like a famous radio DJ.

Dara swung wildly from *Contralto* to *Radio DJ*, feeling Rowan's hand clamping on her arm with a steadying, gentle grasp.

"Easy, sweetheart," he hummed in her ear.

The warmth of his palm against her skin managed to soothe her a bit. Dara drew a quick, nervous breath. She hadn't been able to discern any facial features, but the Speakers' voices sounded vibrant and young. She felt her cheeks grow hot with embarrassment, recalling the conversation she'd had with Rowan back in Oregon. What had she told him then? Something about a "circle of demented elders"?

"What is it that you want so damn bad?" she finally said, her voice edgy with anger and apprehension. "Why did you send Rowan Mackey to track me down in Portland, six months ago?"

"Dara, daughter of Cuinn O'Shea, a scion to the bard Amergin."

Dara gasped aloud, recognizing Niamh's voice.

Rowan struggled to suppress a smile. Though a leader of the Speakers circle, Niamh had been standing as an equal among the rest of them. And, he noted, she hadn't lost her flair for a bit of melodrama.

"Rowan Mackey is your Chosen mate, child," Niamh spoke softly. "All *I* want is for you to look into your soul, and tell this Gathering if we have chosen incorrectly."

"No. You can't play me like that." Dara shook her head, eyes ablaze.

"You're right, Dara, what I'm asking of you now is uncalled for," Niamh replied, venturing further into the light. "Unfortunately, we can't afford the luxury of subtlety, nor that of time. There are forces wishing the both of you dead, and 'tis only thanks to the Goddess that you two are yet alive."

"No!" Dara gave her head a more violent jerk.

"Why are your parents dead, Dara?" Niamh strode closer, merciless. "Was it truly an unfortunate road accident that claimed their lives? And why isn't Aidan Neilan sharing your bed anymore? Was the Hound arrow that took him truly meant for *him*?"

Dara made a strangled sound, her hands instinctively climbing to her throat. She hadn't withdrawn, though, studying Niamh's smooth face with wide, wounded eyes.

"And why was Aislinn's family slaughtered, Dara? You should know, perhaps, that Aislinn's family moved to *your* parents' farm shortly after they left Ireland with you. I think we can safely chalk *those* murders up to a case of mistaken identity." Niamh's tone softened, but her eyes stayed cold and uncompromising. "Were Rowan's parents truly killed by bandits? I think not. In each of these cases, Dara, the killers have never been found. But most important of all, how is it possible that the three of you have all lived? Who has been guarding your lives — Aislinn's, Rowan's and *yours*, Dara?"

"Bantiarna, enough of this," Rowan intervened, his voice strained. Speaking to Niamh so was against any Law he'd known, but he couldn't bear Dara's trembling by his side.

"The girl is stronger than you might think, Guardian," Niamh retorted coolly. "Now hear me out, the both of you. Only the Goddess Danu's hand has guarded your lives to this day.

Her sacred will is the only reason you are still standing here, breathing. But there is Dark working against Her, and there are still many desiring your death."

"Even if half of what you're saying is true, I can't possibly change any of it," Dara said bitterly. "I still can't figure out what the hell it is that you want of me."

"Aye, you can." *Raspy* cracked a laugh. "You're bright enough to figure it out by yourself, lass."

"Do you love your Chosen mate?" *Contralto* sang from the dark.

"If you do love him, then prove it," whispered *Radio DJ*.

"By joining with him against *Lia Fáil* on the night of *Beltaine*," concluded a new voice dryly, flat and devoid of emotion.

"Joining?" Dara repeated. "What do you mean, 'joining'?" She turned to look at Rowan suspiciously.

He evaded her gaze, pretending to clear his throat.

Dara's brows drew together in suspicion, her voice dropping. "Rowan, you'd better tell me I'm *not* expected to have sex with you against that dick-shaped stone, with everybody cheering in the background! You'd better tell me that *now*, Rowan Mackey!"

"Uh, didn't Aidan talk to you about the Stone, sweetheart?" he managed hoarsely.

"No," she replied using the chilliest of tones. "He meant to take me there, but obviously, we didn't make it. And I'm *not* your sweetheart, Mackey." She spun around furiously. "I won't do it," she screamed. "Do you hear me? I *won't*!"

Only silence echoed her. Dara held her breath. Her own blood was hammering in her ears, driven by her madly beating heart. The dying fire shivered and hissed against the hummock's gaping black mouth, casting a shriveled ring of light. The Speakers weren't surrounding the circle anymore.

"I think this meeting is over," Rowan remarked softly behind Dara's back.

"Not fair," she muttered. "Where have they all gone to?"

"They have their own ways," he said. "Some say there's a network of passages worming through these grounds, unknown to anyone else but them."

"I'll ask Niamh directly, then, when we meet face to face."

"She won't be at the house for the next couple of days."

"Goddess, but what am I supposed to *do*?" Dara's limbs felt as if they were loaded with lead again. Her knees gave out, and she sank to the dark earth. "What am I supposed to do," she repeated miserably.

She felt Rowan's hand over her bare arm like a patch of heat, and shut her eyes against the darkness. Slowly, he rubbed his lips against the side of her face, like a wolf rubbing his scent against the trees, marking his territory. His body pressed against her back and he tightened his hold on her left arm, steadying her.

"What are you doing?" she gasped, finding herself leaning back into him. Her body, quicker than her mind, was already seeking to mold against his.

"What does it feel like I'm doing?" Rowan dug his head deeper into the hollow between Dara's neck and shoulder, moving his mouth over her skin, tracing the quick beat of her blood. A hint of teeth grazed her flesh. He sucked the delicate skin into his mouth, his tongue tasting and laving over the frenzied pulse.

"Rowan, don't—" She made a faint protest, sounding unconvincing even to her own ears.

"Rowan don't, what?" he teased, and his mouth took her again.

Dara groaned and twisted against him, her breathing growing erratic. She tilted her head to the side, allowing his mouth full access, and his sharpening teeth sank deeper. The small pain stirred a hot jolt right through her core, and she drew in a shaky, hissing breath.

He fondled her right breast with a sure hand, kneading her flesh through the supple leather, and she moaned aloud and squeezed her hand over his. The surrounding shallow mounds of Tara shrank into nothingness. The only thing remaining was Rowan's body against hers.

Rowan laughed against Dara's neck, the sound low and dangerous. Gently wrestling his hand free from her grasp, he slid beneath her fingers and captured the laces tightening her corset. Dara recalled his fingers fastening those same laces back in Medb's bedchambers. She gasped as Rowan manipulated the silken threads in the valley between her breasts, and exerted a slow, gentle pull. The corset gave and hung loosely against her back, its front half-open. Her breasts heaved with her breath, finally freed from their tight confinement. Rowan cradled the curved underside of one naked orb. Slowly he shifted his hand, pressing a rough fingertip around a hardening nipple.

"Rowan..." Dara moaned, rubbing her back against his chest.

"Get on your knees," he coaxed, urging her with a thrust of his thighs, imploring her with his hands.

"'Kay," she breathed, bending forward to lean on all fours. A sluggish fog had settled upon her mind, blurring the remaining shreds of any rational thoughts.

His hands were already cajoling the tight leather skirt up her ass. She felt him shifting behind her, peeling down the buckskin breeches he still wore, muttering an impatient curse. His erection sprang free against the crevice splitting the twin globes of her buttocks. He pulled the cheeks of her ass apart, driving his hard shaft in between until his cock head was nestled against her vaginal opening. Dara whimpered, trying to push her hips back, to get him inside her, but he'd moved his hands to her hips and held her in place with a firm grasp.

"Please," she pleaded.

"As you wish," he said. He laughed then, with the same edgy note she'd heard earlier that night. Seizing her hips with a steely grip, he eased his cock inside her with wicked slowness, enjoying it every inch of the way.

Dara whimpered with frustration, lowering her damp brow to rest against her tightening fists.

"Easy," he whispered from behind, now fully lodged within her. "Does it truly matter now...sweetheart...what is happening around us?"

"No." She gave a muffled groan, feeling him flexing inside her.

"Does it matter...if anyone else is watching us?"

"No," she whimpered again. "No, there's only this... Only you."

Rowan grimaced as he struggled for control.

Eyes aglow and jaw set, he forced himself to follow a leisurely rhythm, driving into her with slow, easy thrusts. It took every ounce of restraint he had left. What he was doing to her was sweet torture, but Great Goddess, he wanted to hear her plead for more, to drive her mad enough to dare him with threats and screams. But the way her pussy was squeezing him, he'd been doing a bleedin' good job at driving *himself* out of his own mind. His eyes responded to the scant moonlight, pupils dilating, and he struggled to keep his fingers from growing claws. Thank Danu this wasn't a full moon night, otherwise he doubted that even his unique talent would have kept him from fully changing. A low growl formed deep in Rowan's throat. He dug his fingers into Dara's hips and pulled her against him with force, burying himself deep inside her.

"*Yes...Rowan!*" she screamed, her palms pushing against the ground, muddied with a paste of sweat and soil.

He started pounding into her with an almost-violent force, his mind blurred by a heady mix of fury and lust. A roar undulated inside him... *Mine. Mine. Mine.*

Her back arched. She met him with equal fervor, matching his thrusts with short, broken screams. As his balls slapped her ass and his sweat-soaked skin pressed against hers, she wasn't pleading, but *challenging* him for more, urging him to take her harder. Deeper. Rowan granted her what she demanded. He plowed inside her with rough shoves, control slipping away. Dull pressure built in his head, muscles tightening in his lower abdomen.

She cried out and squeezed down on him, her pussy tensing on his cock with a shocking, brusque force.

Harsh pleasure surged up Rowan's body, fire rushing down his loins. With a howl he forced Dara's ass tight against his body and exploded inside her, shuddering with the force of it. He came so hard that nothing else existed besides *her*... So tight around him. Hot. Wet.

Dara moaned as he jerked inside her, her pussy still quivering around his shaft.

He collapsed against her, his semen oozing down her inner thighs. Trembling roughly, Dara sagged to the ground with him. For long minutes they lay on their sides with their chests heaving, their sweat-drenched bodies crushing the already-trampled grass. Neither could utter a single word.

"You two are at it *again*! Will you give it *over*!"

Dara yelled with shock and sprang to a sitting position, struggling to pull up the corset that had been tangled about her waist.

Rowan didn't bother to do more than grunt irritably, "Go away, Brighid!"

Chapter Twenty-Three

"I hate to sound like a cliché, but we *really* should stop meeting like this!" Dara suppressed a fleeting shiver, partly provoked by the sweat cooling on her skin. She searched blindly for Brighid, the pool of meager firelight having dissolved into darkness long minutes past.

"You didn't sound like a cliché a couple of minutes ago," Brighid's voice jeered in the dark. "In fact, Dara, you sounded much more like a screeching, rutting, cat in—"

"*Brighid*!" Rowan roared a warning.

"*What*?!" the Sidhe demanded. Her fingers made a dry snapping sound as she produced a small flame between her forefinger and thumb. She tilted her hand a little, dancing the flame to the center of her palm, and brought it up against her face.

"Neat trick," Dara commented, "*if* you're a smoker." She stood up, tugging everything back into place the best she could. Drying streaks of moisture still clung to her inner thighs.

"You're just jealous." Brighid grinned at her behind the quivering flame. "Now get some clothes on, both of you—unless you call *this* dressed?" She peered at them with disapproval. "And find me a place where I can get a decent meal. Then we'll talk."

Rowan uncoiled from the grass and joined Dara, towering above the wee banshee. "Where were you, Brid?" he softly inquired. "We thought you'd finally ended up with your arse seriously bitten."

"Oh, you were worried about me! I'm touched," she chirped.

"What happened back there, by that river?" Dara asked, squinting her eyes against the enchanted flame dancing on Brighid's palm.

"The Hound shapechanged, and I crashed into him from above in my raven outfit," she answered, somewhat deflated. "I hope I poked one of its eyes, at least. The bastard cost me a couple of feathers." She gave a heavy sigh. "You two had already jumped into the river, and then I lost you. It's almost impossible for me to read anything going on beneath the water, in Mananann's realm. But now that you're standing on Tara's soil, your Power is like a beacon, easy to—"

"A beacon?" Rowan interjected, shaking his head. "In that case, we'd better bleedin' move out of here right *now*."

"I wasn't the one giving the audiovisual show here a few minutes ago," Brighid shrugged, flashing Rowan an impish grin. The play of fire and shadows over her mischievous features made her face seem even more elfin.

"Fine," Dara said, "let's head back, then." She turned to Rowan. "How *do* we get back, Mackey?"

"We got ourselves a ride, remember?"

"You don't mean Teague is still down there, wai—?"

"He is."

Dara's cheeks heated, imagining Teague's thoughts regarding the *exact* reasons keeping them from getting back to the car. He'd see their clothes… Forget the clothes, with his keen shifter senses he'd easily sniff out that they'd just had sleazy, sizzling, downright mindblowing se—

"Easy, Dara, he'll say nothing." Rowan broke through her train of thoughts. She could *hear* his grin in the dark.

The three of them turned and marched down the tortuous path they'd climbed earlier. They made a small line, with Rowan in the lead looking like an odd version of the Pied Piper, and Brighid in the back, still cradling her small tongue of fire. Dara sulked in between, trying to guess Teague's first words upon seeing them.

Teague simply started his Bronco as he saw them approach, not saying a single word. Maybe it was because he was staring at Brighid so hard, he'd forgotten the art of speech. His object of fascination didn't seem to mind—Brighid had been far too fascinated with the car to pay attention to anything else, and naturally demanded to take the front seat.

Rowan swept Dara up into the Bronco's back again, grinning at the show.

"Don't worry about Teague's driving, sweetheart," he promised. "I think he *really* likes Brighid. He's got other kinds of tricks on his mind right now."

* * * * *

"I desperately need a shower before I can eat any kind of a dinner," Dara said adamantly.

Rowan nodded, his fingertips skimming over her nape, then gliding lower between her shoulder blades.

A pleasant shiver raced down Dara's spine.

They'd been lingering on the front porch for no other reason but exhaustion, solid darkness pressing against their backs like a phantom weight. The voices of Brighid and Teague drifted from the rose garden at their rear, carried over a light breeze.

"Let me show you to your room then, Dara. I think you'll find everything in there that you need." Rowan raised his unoccupied hand to haul up the door's brass knocker.

"*My* room?"

"Aye, the Summer Room," he answered with a soft grin. "You might remember the Bantiarna asking me earlier to take you there?"

She shook her head in response, too exhausted to recall a room's name popping up in some earlier conversation.

Fiona had answered the front door this time, her astounded eyes immediately rounding upon seeing them, but Rowan quickly seized Dara's hand in his, drawing her with skill past

Fiona's as-yet-unspoken questions. Together they mounted the left staircase curving from the foyer. The broad stairs opened to a mostly vacant wing of the household, mainly reserved for the rare houseguests.

Further along the hallway, Rowan halted before a door, releasing Dara's hand.

"Maybe you should do the honors, Dara," he offered with a light teasing bow, gesturing to the door.

Dara studied the heavy door with mounting suspicion. It was solid wood, carved with complex flower designs and tiny joyous birds, same as the rest of the mansion's doors.

"Well, here goes," she finally sighed and cracked it open, flicking the light switch on.

She sucked in a surprised gasp as the single light bulb's yellowish glow spilled upon another stairway, its narrow steps climbing steeply up a short, straight frame.

"You gave me an attic room!" she exclaimed into the oblong space, her voice giving an odd resonance.

Her weariness shed for the moment, Dara leaped up the stairs with childlike zeal. She paused at the doorway, then entered the room's snug warmth with a tentative first step. Her curious gaze met an airy, vibrant space, full of warm colors and equipped with a small, convenient bathroom. The Summer Room. Its name fit it perfectly, she could tell, even though moonlight was currently shining in through the sloping window.

"You like it," Rowan stated close behind her, sounding smug.

"It'll do," she retorted, failing to conceal her growing smile.

He chuckled, not fooled by her feigned nonchalance. "Aislinn donated some clothes that might fit you."

Dara slipped into the bathroom and positioned herself in front of the mirror. She scrutinized the face reflected back at her.

Goddess, when had she grown so pale?

There were thin lines etched into her face that she hadn't noticed before, and bluish half-moons hung beneath her eyes. And her hair, it was a mess of sweat-clumped tangles and knots! Fatigue poured back in like a flood. She rested her hands against both sides of the sink, struggling against the growing lump in her throat.

"Tired?" Rowan questioned softly behind her.

She hadn't heard him approach—no surprise in that. Suddenly he was there, his firm chest propping up her back. He fitted his chin into the crook of her neck, his long-muscled arms locking around her waist.

"I'll start the water running," he said, "and get you inside that tub. Help you soap your back."

"Rowan, I'm fine, really—"

"No, you're not."

She kept her hands against the sink as his arms left her, and he turned to fiddle with the bath faucets. Water splashed with a sharp slap against the tub, and then the sound was muted as Rowan adjusted the heat.

"Come over here, princess," he commanded, a familiar grin in his voice.

"Princess?" She smiled, swiveling to face him. "Which makes you what? Han Solo?"

"That name, 'tis from an American film, right?" Rowan watched her as he crouched by the oval tub, his hand dipping into the hot water.

"You're kidding, aren't you?"

"Am I?" He cocked a flaming brow, seeming to be genuinely surprised.

'Kay, so Rowan Mackey wasn't exactly a Star Wars enthusiast. A smile flickered over Dara's lips. She swayed closer to Rowan, the top of her boots now about the same level as his chest.

"You know, I really miss my sneakers," she informed him.

"True, sweetheart, they are much easier to kick off. But not as fun."

Still kneeling in front of her, he smoothed his hands up her calves, dipping his fingers into the shallow, warm hollows at the back of her knees.

"That's not how you're supposed to take a boot off," Dara quipped.

If the man kept on touching her this way, she'd self-combust in no time...

"Thanks for the tip." Rowan sighed in resignation and climbed both his hands up Dara's right thigh, swiftly undoing the descending line of buckles and laces.

"This feels so S and M," she groaned as she watched his quick fingers working on her.

"Aye," he laughed. "I'd do it slower, but the state you're in right now—by the time I finished, you'd topple over me, fast asleep. Raise your leg for me, princess."

Dara rolled her eyes at the hint of continued role-play and clutched Rowan's shoulders for support, leaning into him as she flexed one knee. His hands left a trail of warmth in their wake as he peeled away the clinging leather. Finally, her right boot dropped to curl against the floor tiles. Dara squeezed her eyes shut, regretting the instant Rowan's hands had abandoned her skin.

"The other leg now, please," he commanded, his voice blurred by the soft sound of running water.

Dara obliged.

Both Rowan's gaze and his hands came to rest on her left thigh. He let out a soft breath, stroking the alabaster flesh that taunted him through the boot laces.

Dara bit her lip.

Rowan slowly started to work his way down her left leg.

She absently tightened her grip on his shoulders as his fingers lasciviously danced over the skin-tight leather. The way he was touching her legs threw her pulse into a fit. By the time both her boots lay like abandoned snakeskin against the spattered tiles, her breathing was as labored as if she'd run a marathon.

Rowan glanced up, instantly spying the heat in Dara's flushed face.

He reacted like quicksilver, skimming his hands back up Dara's legs. His touch lingered just beneath her skirt's hem, hesitating, and then he lifted up the tight garment. The skirt bunched into a tight belt above Dara's hips. It left her bare to Rowan's eyes from the waist down. He gave a soft hiss and dug his head between her thighs, pushing them apart, nudging his face against her damp pussy.

Dara gasped aloud, swaying.

She felt hot…shaky…lightheaded.

"Easy." He caught her naked hips, steadying her.

"I'm f-fine," she managed.

Hugging her to him, Rowan gazed up at her from between her legs. He brushed his mouth over the dark thatch atop her mons, his eyes hot with need. Shifting lower, deeper between her thighs, he darted his tongue to her clit. His splayed fingers pressed into her ass cheeks, forcing her tighter against his mouth.

Dara dragged in a hissing breath, throwing her head back, eyes closed. She clasped Rowan's shoulders tighter. Goddess, she couldn't remain standing for long. She couldn't—

Propping up her weight with one arm, his hand stroked along the cleft of her ass, sliding lower between her butt cheeks. His fingers shifted, dipping into her cunt from behind.

Dara let out an involuntary groan. Her legs began a fine tremble, almost giving out beneath her. Rowan's fingers, his tongue, felt so *hot*. As if his touch had tattooed her flesh, eternally branding her. *Oh, Goddess, she was wet.* She wanted Rowan's fingers to go deep inside her cunt. Wanted *him* deep inside. But she couldn't handle it right now, the world was starting to spin. She just felt so tired —

The neglected water was now boiling with heat, puffing a bloated cloud of steam into the tub. It bloomed into a vaporous mushroom and spilled over the tub's curved edge, swathing both of them in thickening shells of milky haze. Moist heat breathed over Dara's skin.

"Rowan," she warned, her voice strangled, and still she couldn't bring herself to move away from him, not even to cut off the scorching water's flow.

Rowan started. With a bestial growl he wrenched his face and hands away from Dara's moist skin and spun to face the tub. He avoided the hot metal valves the best he could, and broke the water's flow with a furious grip-and-jerk.

He turned back to Dara in the abrupt silence that had fallen over the room. She was shivering all over, eyes wild, her arms hanging by her sides like heavy weights. The tub was still exuding steam clouds, but the water's bellowing roar was gone. The only sound filling the tight space was their own heavy breathing.

"It'll be a couple of minutes before I can start the water again," Rowan finally said.

"It's okay," she nodded, gasping as he suddenly hugged her to him with force, burying his head in the flesh of her thighs. Rowan was taller than most men, and her height was average at best. Dara watched with shock as the big Irishman curled against her, clasping her lower body to his torso.

"No, 'tis not *okay*." He entrusted the muffled words to her flesh, dampening her skin with a sigh. "You're shivering, sweetheart, and most of it is tiredness. 'Tis far from *okay*."

His "*okay*" sounded as if he'd spat it out, too angry with himself to soften the word.

"Rowan, please don't." She reached down to him, hardly needing to bend, touching his unruly locks, fingering and unwinding the thick copper strands.

He raised cool eyes to hers, the green fire now curbed. "I swear by Danu, lass, you are going to have this bath with no more bothers by me," he said, his voice so somber that she burst into giggles.

Dara raised both her hands to her mouth, trying to contain her laughter, but the combined effect of the Irishman's bewildered expression and her own exhaustion were a bit too much for her to handle. Her body collapsed in the circle of Rowan's arms.

Rowan groaned, bowing his head to hers. He squeezed her delicate rib cage against his chest, then broke into laughter himself.

"*Mo rún*, I am a beast."

"You can sure say *that* again, Mackey," she managed, half-choking on her laughter. "And will ya stop cursing me in Irish?"

Her hands sought his skin beneath the silken vest, the last of her laughter spilling into his neck.

"Americans," he panted as he half-turned to the now serene-looking faucets. Dara would get the bath she'd been craving, nothing extra added.

Well, this one time, at least.

Chapter Twenty-Four

"Got any more of this?" Brighid demanded around a mouthful of Irish stew. She helped herself to another thick slice of soda bread, slathering it with a generous amount of salted butter. Within arm's reach, strong tea exuded soft curls of steam in its earthenware pot.

"You have room for another bite, a wee thing like you?" Fiona glared down at Brighid, hands on her generous hips.

Dara had been staring at Fiona for some time now, wondering whether she was Kanjali or a plain Mortal. Here gaze drifted back to Brighid. *Goddess, the petite banshee had a healthy appetite!*

Teague was busy offering Brighid enthusiastic comments about the spread of dishes, his honey mane tangled with her fiery one. She seemed quite pleased with his intimate attention. Aislinn sank into the farthest seat at the table, watching the show with silent curiosity. The whole group seemed to be staring, entranced, at the small-sized fairy-menace devouring her dinner.

"This is the *best* meal I've had in centuries!" Brighid announced.

"Right!" A wide smile split Fiona's rosy face. "Are you for cake, then, dear? A bite of my blueberry pie?"

"Mmmm!" The banshee gave an enthusiastic nod.

As Fiona's hurried steps faded from the dining room, Rowan leaned against the generously proportioned table, glowering at Brighid. "Didn't you have enough to eat already?" he growled.

"Oh, you in for some blueberry pie, too?"

"Not hungry." He leaned back in his chair, his fiery brows drawn to an utterly displeased red line.

Fiona came back and placed a generous portion of blueberry pie beside Brighid before leaving to tend to other business. Teague filled Brighid's teacup with cream, then poured the deep-colored tea over it.

Aislinn watched them both, openmouthed.

Dara released a long-suffering sigh.

Rowan squeezed his lips even tighter, simmering silently. Tension thickened about him in an almost tangible aura.

Finally, the Sidhe pushed her plates aside and smiled. "Now I'm fit to talk," she stated.

"Then, talk," Dara said, smiling sweetly at her.

"Here?" Brighid cast a questioning look at the other occupants of the large dinner table.

"Aye, here and now!" Rowan growled impatiently. "We have nothing to hide from Aislinn and Teague."

"Right." Brighid shrugged. "Well, there are a few things you'd better know. First, your Hound and Prince Donn. For now they're still stuck down Below, but I think they're waiting for *Beltaine* night to cross over here. The Veil between the Realms will grow thin then, same as during *Samhain*, making the passage easy."

"And Tara holds a Gateway to the Lower Realm, right?" Rowan asked. "When we were still Below, you wanted to take us to some Gateway leading straight to Tara, didn't you?"

"Aye, you remember right," Brighid gave a dramatic sigh. "Indeed, there's a direct Gateway to *Lia Fáil* in the city of Khree, in Midhe. If Donn makes it there, he'll use it for sure."

"'Kay, that's easy." Dara shook her head. "All Rowan and I have to do is stay clear of the Hill of Tara on the night of *Beltaine*."

"Right." Brighid opened her mouth and closed it, then burst into laughter.

"Yeah?" Dara glared at her. "Mind sharing the joke?"

"Well," Brighid gasped, wiping tears from her eyes. "Well, 'tis impossible for the both of you to stay away from Tara on that particular night...since you two will be *at it* again, only this time against the Stone!"

"We'll be *at it*?" Dara echoed, arching her brows.

"Aye," Teague grinned, breaking in. "She means you and Rowan-boyo here will be doin' the bold thing. Gettin' a ride. Fucking like crazy against the—"

"Look, I know what she damn well means." Dara scrambled up, her chair screeching against the wood planks. "And I already told your Speakers I wouldn't do it!"

"So, Niamh truly asked you to do it, did she?" Teague's grin broadened appreciatively. "That oul' lady, she's still got juice in her bones!"

"Shut your mouth, Teague!" Rowan was up on his feet as well.

Teague rolled his eyes skywards.

Aislinn shrunk in her chair in a failed attempt to appear invisible.

Brighid leered at them all, sliding a sticky finger against her plate to scoop up any whipped cream remains left there.

Dara and Rowan exchanged embarrassed glances, before slumping back in their seats.

"Niamh told me about Amergin," Dara finally told Brighid.

"Mmm-huh." The banshee nodded, sucking on a cream-sweetened finger.

Teague watched her oral manipulation, spellbound.

"You know, Brighid, for someone who is supposed to *guard* a family, *my* family, you're doing a pretty lousy job at it," Dara snapped, unable to stop herself.

"Och, now *that* hurt!" Brighid pulled her finger out of her mouth, snapping Teague out of her spell. "Mind saying why you think so?"

"Well, take my parents, for one. And Aidan." Dara's cheeks burned and her eyes were beginning to sting. "Oh, and another thing. You've turned badgering me into a damned art form!"

"Right, then, let's get that one over with first." Brighid returned a calm gaze, counting on her fingers. "I know no rule saying that the family's guardian spirit can't badger a family member! Second...truly, I am the Sidhe guarding Amergin's descendents. Your father was the only one of Amergin's blood, Dara, your mother and your husband were *not* under my protection. At some point, I was made to choose... To either save Cuinn O'Shea, or save his daughter. I chose to save *your* life, Dara."

An awkward silence fell upon the small group of diners. By now Brighid's eyes had lost their mischievous twinkle, making everyone else at the table squirm with unease.

"Maybe 'tis time I told you the full story," the fairy went on unhurriedly. "Straight from the beginning."

"Go for it, Brighid," Dara replied, still shiny-eyed.

"Fine," Brighid replied, unabashed. "Maybe you asked yourself at times, why did the Kanjali shifters stay upon the Upper Earth when all the rest—the *Tuatha dé Danann*—escaped down Below? Or why did the *Cú*—the Hounds—hunt down the Kanjali folk? Or, better yet, who was the one who set the ancient Law thousands of years ago, to begin with?"

Dara stared at Brighid, saying nothing. Rowan leaned forward against the table, his expression rapt. Teague was shaking his head as if trying to shake away the throes of a bad dream. Aislinn remained a silent statue, just a bit paler than before.

Brighid's smile broadened as she spoke. "Well, once upon a time, when the Realms were still young, Danu, the Goddess of the Rivers and the Land, and Bilé, The God of Life and Death, Ruler of the Otherworld and Guardian of the Sacred Oak, were still lovers. 'Twas from this union that three sons were born,

Dagda, Nuada and Dian-Cécht. This was the beginning of the lesser gods, the race of the *Tuatha dé Danann*."

"Go on," urged Rowan.

Brighid sighed. "The Upper Earth belonged then to *dé-Danann* and to Mortals, and the Lower Earth belonged to fairies and spirits. That was the natural order of things, before all bleedin' hell broke loose."

Teague cocked a brow. "I need a pint of Guinness before I listen to any more of this blather," he muttered.

Brighid ignored the interruption. "See, 'twas all grand 'til a fight broke out between Danu and Bilé. These two weren't exactly faithful to each other. Bilé had lain with others, and sired Miled—aye, the same King Miled of Spain. Danu took her own sons, Dagda and Dian-Cécht, for lovers, giving birth to more sons and daughters of the *dé-Danann* bloodline."

"Goddess, this is becoming quite the soap opera!" Dara exclaimed, dropping her face into her hands. Her head was pounding with a blossoming migraine. She had never suffered from migraines before meeting Brighid or Rowan—come to think of it, before this entire farce had started!

"The truth is far worse than any soap opera, eh?" Brighid appeared smug, eyes twinkling with mirth.

Rowan uttered a colorful curse.

"And then what happened?" Teague demanded.

"I thought *you* were already gone for your pint of Guinness," Brighid teased him. "What happened then...right. King Miled's sons invaded the island of Erin, declaring war on the *dé-Danann*. The rumors say Danu paid Bilé a visit, demanding he tell the Milesians off. He refused. Things got even uglier."

"I'm not sure I can take any more of this," Dara mumbled. "I mean, I can't even bring myself to watch *Days of Our Lives*, and this is—"

"Well." Brighid tilted her head. "Too late, you started it. As I said, Danu and Bilé got into an even uglier mess. Bilé swore to destroy the *dé-Danann*, even though his own blood ran in their veins. He used dark magic, enchanting sand grains into Hounds, and then sent his Hounds to roam the Upper Earth and hunt down the *dé-Danann*."

"Hounds…" Rowan said softly.

"Aye," Brighid replied. "Only, Danu had a say in this, too. She couldn't undo Bilé's dark enchantment, so she set the ancient Law to protect the *Tuatha dé Danann* from the Hounds." Brighid pulled close another mostly empty plate, found nothing she fancied there, and pushed it back aside. "As most of the *dé-Danann* fled to the Lower Realm, Danu chose a few to stay upon the Upper Earth…as sentinels against Bilé's vileness."

"The Kanjali," Dara nodded. Here, finally, was something she'd managed to figure out all by herself.

"True," Brighid went on. "The Kanjali guarded the Gateways on the Upper Earth, acting as sentries against Bilé's Hounds, preventing them from reaching the *dé-Danann*. Kanjali folk and Hounds were both shifters, able to change between human form and *mac'tir* form. 'Twas against the Goddess's Law to use any other form of magic but this one upon the Upper Earth."

"And Kanjali Guardians?" Rowan demanded. "What, exactly, are they?"

"Guardians?" Brighid flashed him a riveting smile. "Guardians, such as yourself, are no more than Kanjali shifters with more Power in them, able to defeat the Hounds better than most." She propped her pointed chin against the palms of her hands, elbows flexed against the table, rocking her feet below.

"Is there a bit more blueberry pie in there, Fi?" she yelled towards the dining room's entrance.

"You'll explode," Teague warned.

"*You—*" Brighid poked his broad chest with a well-aimed finger, "—should have gone by now for your pint of Guinness!"

Teague captured her poking hand, his eyes igniting with a sizzling smile.

* * * * *

Dawn's gray-pink glow was already peeking through the foyer's French doors when their small bunch finally left the dining room. Awakening birds' thready chirps sounded from the garden, accentuating the quiet of the sleeping manor.

Aislinn bade them all good morning, red-eyed and wearing a half-smile, and crept out a French door to the back gardens. Teague boldly slipped his hand around Brighid's narrow waist, waiting to be slapped or chastised. When neither happened, he drew the redheaded fairy away with him to "show the lass around", or so he claimed.

"If I wanted to be mean, I'd say good riddance." Dara smiled wearily at Rowan, as they stood at the foot of one staircase. "Luckily, I'm way too tired to be nasty."

"Aye, lucky indeed." He grinned, watching as her mouth gaped in a huge yawn. "You should get some sleep," he said, capturing one rebellious raven lock between gentle fingers. "You remember the way to your room?"

"I'm just a bit tired, Rowan, not demented." She let out a small laugh, and another yawn. "You led me there only hours ago."

He tugged the captive lock and then released it to bounce right back. "Prove to me you know the way, then," he teased.

Dara shrugged and turned to climb up the staircase, too tired for a stingy retort. Rowan followed closely behind, whistling a cheery tune she remembered from their warehouse adventure. The light melody followed her as she sidled along the hallway's cool-shadowed walls.

"Well, Mackey, believe it or not, I've found it." Dara gave Rowan a dazed smile of triumph. She leaned heavily against the carved doorframe, seeking support.

"So I see." Rowan flashed a roguish grin and bent down, snatching her from her feet and into his arms.

"Put me *down!*" she protested, struggling in vain.

"Shhh. You'll be waking the dead with those screams, lass! *I'm* the one giving the orders here," he informed her in an uncompromising tone.

"Oh, yeah?"

"Oh, *aye*. Now use that shapely hand of yours—since mine are occupied—and turn that doorknob."

His brogue had grown biting, he was no less tired than she. Dara stopped struggling and quieted in his arms, reaching to open the door as ordered. "What are you going to do to me when we get there?" she inquired in a small voice.

He chuckled, low and raspy and warm.

"Oh, I'm about to carry you up these stairs," he spoke through a smile. "And then, I'm going to throw you straight into that big bed...and..." He leaned to whisper into her hair. "And then, sweetheart, I'm going to pull a big blanket over you and make sure you're safely tucked-in."

"Moron," Dara mumbled, a smile touching her lips.

Rowan grinned as his eyes fell to Dara's face. She was already dozing in his arms, her head lolling against his shoulder. He carried her into the dawn-lit room and crouched next to the king-sized bed, allowing her yielding body to sink against the mattress. To his surprise, her arms curled against the back of his neck.

"Stay," she whispered in a bleary voice.

He stilled, his body stretched above hers, his arms still enfolding her. *Could she be talking in her sleep?*

"Don't go yet."

Dara's arms tightened on his neck. He glanced down at her face just as her eyes fluttered open, hazy and dark. Her fingers slipped from his nape and fluttered over his recently shaved jaw.

"Smooth," she murmured, giving him a slow, simmering smile.

Rowan bent the few inches to Dara's lips and closed his mouth over that lazy, catlike smile. She sucked in a soft gasp as his tongue sank into her mouth, her fingertips trembling against his cheek. The wet heat that his tongue was dipping into made Rowan think of another wet, tight place. His erection was already straining against his denim. With an effort he pulled out of her mouth, studying her face.

"Dara, sweetheart, are you sure?"

One of her hands trailed low, stroking his hard cock through the rough cloth enclosing it. Rowan groaned with sweet agony. He gently shifted above her, sinking heavily between her parted thighs. She was wearing one of Aislinn's light dresses. Rowan easily yanked the trapped cloth from between their bodies and pushed it up Dara's hips until it huddled, crumpled, above the sweet cream of her breasts. Her nipples knotted as he watched, peaking beneath his gaze. He pressed both thumbs against the pink, pert buttons and Dara drew in a deep, shaky breath beneath him. Her hands pushed under his shirt and made a slow, heated climb up his bunching abdominal muscles.

"*Dara.*"

He started to move between her legs, clothed as he was, rubbing his bulging erection against her damp, hot panties. Dara cried out and clamped her legs on his ass, undulating with him, squeezing him tighter against her soaking pussy. His hands were kneading her breasts, like they could never get enough of the supple, creamy flesh.

"Dara — give me a sec, sweetheart."

Somehow, he tore Dara's drenched panties off her legs. Somehow, she unzipped his jeans. His heavy cock bobbed free, its tip dripping moisture. He sank into Dara again, moving between her thighs. His hips gave a soft forward thrust. He felt the slight jerk as her tight inner muscles gave before his swollen cock head, gradually opening up before his slow advance. She moaned low as he penetrated her, clamping her legs even harder on him. Their bodies rubbed against one another, hot and sweaty, giving each other a tight, rough massage. Dara gasped and moaned as Rowan moved inside her, running ravenous hands up and down his arms. He tightened his fists in her tangled hair and pulled her up, kissing her hard.

They rocked steadily together, both half-caught in sleep, sultry dreams mingling with lust's sweet aroma and the feel of slick sheets. Rowan, panting heavily, hovered above Dara's face as she cried out at the height of her pleasure. Dawn's mellow light deepened her rosy cheeks. Her eyes blazed with fire, and her lips parted around a scream. He growled as her cunt clamped down on his shaft, and he finally exploded within her. The tight squeezing waves traversing her inner walls kept milking him, pumping him to the last pearly drop.

After a while Rowan sank against Dara's body. She mumbled his name, snuggling against his chest. At some vague moment they both fell into full sleep, still half-clothed and tangled, oblivious to the golden pour of sunlight through the window.

Chapter Twenty-Five

Dara's eyes fluttered open. She turned onto her stomach and pushed against the mattress, finding herself trapped within a cage of jumbled sheets. Her mind was in similar disarray, humming with the last shreds of a fading dream. From the slanted attic window sunlight spilled, painting the upturned side of her face with light.

Where was Rowan…?

Funny, her body had been missing his beside it, even though they'd never woken up together… Not counting that morning on the dusty warehouse floor.

Damn the brazen Irishman!

Dara dug her face into the mattress with a groan, then managed to snake her way out of her soft-walled prison. She sat up on the bed, her borrowed dress falling back over her exposed breasts. Her gaze toured the sunlit room and found a couple of breezy summer dresses — the kindly Aislinn's again, most likely — neatly draped over the back of an armchair. Heaving a resigned sigh, Dara finally slid across the rumpled bed and touched her bare toes to the planked floor.

"Hello, dear," Fiona greeted Dara as she ambled down the stairs. The plump housekeeper had just stepped in from the back gardens, her cheeks rosier than usual and wind-tugged wisps of hair curling from her loose bun. "You'll have a bite to eat?"

"I was thinking of grabbing something from the kitchen," Dara admitted. "If you'll just point me in the right direction…?"

"There'll be no *grabbing* around here!" Fiona wiped her hands against her jeans, then tugged down her loose tunic. "Sit yourself down, Dara, I'll fetch you something that'll put some meat on your bones."

"No, no need to—" Dara started, then gave up talking to Fiona's receding back.

Fiona returned quickly, escorted by a young man burdened with trays of food. "Go on, Killian, put those in the dining room," she urged him with a quick nod.

"What time is it?" Dara asked.

"A bit past four in the afternoon, dear." Fiona flashed her a broad, knowing smile.

Dara blushed, her thoughts instantly hopping to Rowan again.

Where was he?

"Say, Fiona, where's everybody gone?" she inquired, following Fiona to the dining room. She scarcely missed crashing into Killian, on his way out of the room.

Was Killian a plain human? What about Fiona?

"Off to Tara," Fiona replied, her quick, chubby hands clattering saucers and silverware against the broad table. She shot a shrewd glance at Dara. "Rowan, Teague, and…Brighid she's called, right? They're preparing for something grand tomorrow, is what they said."

Dara slouched down against one of the chairs. Her fingers lingered above a plate of summer fruit garnished with cheddar and a thick piebald wedge of blue cheese. She finally snagged a May peach amidst succulent melon slices and smooth-skinned nectarines, bright-red raspberries and blueberries pouting in bluish-purple.

"*Bain taitneamh as do bhéile!*" Fiona granted Dara a hearty smile. "That's *bon appétit*," she added, her French spoken with a thick Irish accent.

Dara laughed behind her peach, her teeth already dug deep into the fruit's yellow flesh. After a while she laid the peach's stone aside, absently poking a silver fork against a neglected trout, fried to a golden-brown.

"Didn't your mother teach you not to play with your food?"

Dara started, dropping her fork with a chink.

"The food is supposed to go into your mouth, see?" Rowan elaborated as he detached himself from the doorway. "Besides, Fiona will have a heart attack if she sees you treating her fish that way."

"Why did you let me sleep so late?" Dara demanded.

"You needed it." Rowan paused in front of her, his heated gaze ravishing her from across the table.

She studied him with matching heat, remembering him wedged deep inside her as dawn broke.

"Are you going to eat that?" He finally gestured towards the desecrated fish.

"I already ate a peach."

"A whole peach? And you call that a lunch, aye?"

"*And* breakfast," she lifted her chin. "Stop mothering me, Rowan, my own mom tried and failed!"

He sighed and sat himself into a chair opposite her. A shadow crossed his face, as if he were about to tell her something, and the intensity of his gaze turned up a few notches. Unwittingly, Dara tensed. His face smoothed in an instant and he leaned back in his chair, flashing her his usual grin.

"Are you up for a little walk?" He reached a long arm across the table and nabbed a melon slice, skillfully spearing it on knife point. "Thought about showing you a bit around Trim, if you like."

"I would." She gave him a perky nod. "Very much."

Dara didn't mind Rowan snagging her waist as he walked her through the quiet hallway. Sauntering down the front porch's steps, he reached out and caught one spaghetti strap, sliding it back up her shoulder.

"Want to see a real castle?" he offered. "They shot an American film there, I think it had an Aussie actor in it—"

"*Braveheart*, with Mel Gibson," she laughed. "Yeah, that would be great."

"Come then," he captured her hand and drew her across the rose garden, bright with colors. She noted Teague's Bronco wasn't parked by the white pebble lane.

"Teague said he was taking Brighid out for a pub tour," Rowan chuckled.

"I'm scared to imagine Brighid intoxicated." Dara mulled over the image. "She's volatile enough when sober."

"Aye, that she is, a true banshee!" Rowan's laughter rang out about her. "Let's head for the Boyne, sweetheart. We need to cross the river to get to the Castle of Trim."

They picked their way through the greenery, finally coming across dark green trees that crowded along the riverbank, extending their tangled roots to shallow piles of river-smoothed pebbles.

"We used to borrow inner tubes from the local garage, me and Teague, and ride them down the Boyne," Rowan chuckled. "Either that, or climb up and down Trim Castle."

Dara nodded, unspoken questions burning on her tongue.

Fiona had said that Rowan, Teague and Brighid had been to Tara earlier today—"preparing for something grand tomorrow" had been her exact words. What the hell had she meant by that? And what had Rowan tried to tell her earlier at the dining room table?

Thoughts adrift, she almost tripped on the sloping grass, Rowan swiftly catching her arm.

Straight ahead, a wooden bridge arched across the Boyne. Dara lingered at the tidy metal sign affixed to its timbers.

"*Trim Town Motto*," she read aloud. "*Ever Kindly Welcoming the Stranger.*"

She gasped in surprise as strong hands caught her arms and slowly spun her about. Grinning softly, Rowan bent his mouth to Dara's and tasted her fully with a slow, fierce kiss. He planted his fingers in her hair, drawing her tighter against him. Dara moaned breathlessly, trapped between the bridge's solid wood and Rowan's firm body. Her nipples peaked against his hard muscles. His tongue was searching her deepest crevices, stroking her inside-out. He was plundering her mouth with the same ardor he'd been fucking her this morning. She felt his cock, hard and bulging against her stomach. Her pussy was damp and tingling again, ready for him. When he finally broke their kiss Dara was out of air and weak at the knees, clinging to his shoulders with hooked fingers. Her eyes fluttered open, as if waking from a dream.

"So, sweetheart, did I welcome you good enough?" Rowan's soft laughter breathed over her lips, warm and full of his arousing, undeniable scent.

"You're not fishing for compliments are you, Mackey?" Dara finally uttered. A blush colored her cheeks, and her lips curled into a soft smile.

"Mmmm," he rumbled, entranced at the sight.

That low, male sound had set her afire time and again.

Rowan chuckled once more and withdrew a step, allowing Dara space enough to climb up the bridge's planked floor.

To her right stretched the first squat houses fringing the city of Trim, and to her left the Boyne flowed and wound its way through meadows and trees.

Keenly aware of Rowan's searing gaze on her back, Dara stepped off the wood girders. Before her stood the castle's broken outer wall, assembled from uneven brown-gray bricks. Damaged and desolate, burdened with the load of centuries past, the surrounding curtain walls were still an imposing sight. The enclosed acres of grass were overshadowed by the castle's enormous, isolated keep.

"Want to climb up?" Rowan's thumb stroked gently over Dara's wrist.

"Oh, I-I don't know—" Dara looked at the massive keep with unease. Rowan's thumb meanwhile moved to abrade her knuckles in a delightful, mind-numbing way.

He gave her a funny look. "Are you afraid of heights, sweetheart?"

"I'm not sure," Dara squirmed. "I think they just make me a little dizzy."

"Back in the Otherworld, when we had to jump into the river escaping Donn—were you afraid then?" he demanded.

"Water doesn't scare me," she gave a small nervous laugh. "Just...looking down over dry land, from someplace high—*that* scares me shitless."

Sweat made the dress cling to her back. She caught Rowan's trained eyes tracing the bulge of her dagger's rig. Since Aidan had died, she couldn't bring herself to leave her weapon behind. Rowan's gaze lifted and met hers again. He didn't say a word.

They left the castle through one of its impressive gates, ambling towards the river again. After a while Dara shucked off her sandals, borrowed from the ever-generous Aislinn. She'd been craving a barefoot walk within the green pastures. Rowan strolled a bit ahead, whistling softly. A gentle breeze fingered strands of his copper hair, and the sun set them afire.

He pointed across the river. "The Bantiarna's estate," he said.

"So you brought me *all* the way down here just for the view, Mackey?" Dara shaded her squinted eyes. "And *I* thought you did it just so you could have your way with me." She had no idea what had made her say that. Could be the mild sun had over-baked what was left of her brains.

Rowan flung his head back, his laughter roaring across the meadow.

"Guess I was wrong, then," she teased, unrelenting.

He grabbed her, tackling her to the ground.

Dara screamed.

The grinning Irishman carefully straddled her hips with his weight. He captured her wrists with both his hands and forced them against the grass, high above her head. Then he bent low and silenced both her laughter and her screams with a thorough kiss that stole the breath from her lungs. Her leather rig was chafing her flesh, but she hardly noticed. Slowly Rowan lifted his mouth from hers, and she opened misty eyes, drawing in a deep, quivering breath.

"You just kept blathering on about sex," Rowan said roughly, now holding both her slim wrists with one hand. "There's only so much a man can take."

With a devilish smile he slid his free hand up one thigh, beneath the light summer dress. One red eyebrow quirked with surprise.

"How come you're wearing panties again?" he demanded with some disappointment, shifting above her.

Dara's heart fluttered madly as his hand teased her through the cloth, but she managed a smile. "How come you're always on top?" she retorted, her voice breathy.

"You want it the other way around, lass?"

Meanwhile his fingers dug beneath the scanty barrier, stroking over damp, curly hair. Dara struggled to hold back a moan, but her treacherous body yielded, as always, to Rowan's touch. Her thighs slackened, parting a bit more. When his finger pressed deeper into her slit, commencing a gentle search, she couldn't curb the half-sob that slipped from her mouth. Rowan let go of her wrists completely, shifting further between her legs. The stretching panties now made a tight band against her upper thighs.

"I should have a word with my sister about lending you needless undergarments." He grinned, but his breathing came out labored. He snapped her panties with ease, and she gave a tiny yell.

"Do you have *any* idea how many of my panties you've ruined by now?"

"Maybe some sheep might like them better than I do," he smiled as he chucked her ripped undies.

Forcing one hand beneath Dara's ass, he kept kneading her slick clit with the other. She was moaning and moving beneath him, intent on his touch, slowly rocking herself against his hand.

By Danu, he needed to taste her...

He dipped his head between her thighs, his wild mop of hair teasing her already-sensitized flesh.

"*Rowan,*" she gasped.

He manipulated both of Dara's feet over his shoulders, then grabbed her ass and forced her tighter against his face. She yelped and arched sharply against the grass as his mouth pressed against her wet entrance. His tongue drove through her thick, velvety heat, exploring her cunt with a probing kiss. He shifted one of his hands back to tend her clit and she jerked against him, crying out. His growl vibrated through her cunt. He lapped at her pouring honey and swirled his ravenous tongue inside her, tasting her flesh with abandon. She was both sharp and sweet, like delicious dark licorice. Both his hands dimpled her ass again, hauling her up roughly against his face. His mouth slid wetly to the soft, fleshy nub of her clit.

Her hips bucked.

"*Yes, Rowan. Yessss...*"

He sucked and nibbled her until she shuddered and tightened, tearing up fistfuls of grass. Only then did Rowan ease his assault, rubbing his soaked face against her feverish inner thighs. His fingers were drenched with the tantalizing mix of his mate's juices.

"Let me up," she whispered in between quick gasps. Redness tinted her face, a combination of both sex and a mild sunburn.

He eased his arm beneath her back and lifted her into his arms.

"What're you doing?" she demanded.

"Quit making those eyes at me." He smiled as he waded with her through the grass, her arms laced around his neck. "I'm moving us to a wee bit of shade."

Closer to the river, beneath a squat, dark tree, Rowan knelt and placed Dara down again, her back touching the tree's rough bark. She turned her face to his. Her hand slid down from his shoulder, hesitant, and lingered over the dark sweat stain decorating the front of his shirt.

Rowan's eyes were hot on her face.

He didn't budge.

She turned to him fully and placed another tentative hand over his chest. Her splayed fingers began a fine trembling. Swaying, she touched her lips to his, tasting herself on him, feeling his breath falter. Slipping both her hands beneath his shirt, she pushed it up his rib cage as far as it went. Her eyes fell to Rowan's sweat-glazed skin. Her mouth sank to his smooth, hard pecs, to those masculine, coin-flat nipples.

It was time her tongue got the treat it had craved for so damn long.

Rowan groaned as Dara's lips finally touched him, searing his skin with a flood of small, burning kisses. He shivered as she gathered the nerve to take one tautening nipple between her lips, to suck his flesh into her mouth. He spread his thighs to welcome her closer. His fingers dug into her wild hair, stroking her as she moved her mouth lower. A guttural sound climbed up his throat as she kissed a long line down his abdominal wall, ending beneath the edge of his jeans. His abdominal muscles tightened in heated response, his erection throbbing painfully against the rough fabric. He felt Dara's light fingers tampering with his top button.

"Dara, you don't have to—" he began hoarsely, not knowing his own voice.

"Shhh…I want to," she hushed him, unzipping him with a cautious hand. "I *want* to."

Rowan sank back to his elbows, breathing hard. He hissed out a sigh as his erection sprang free from his jeans. He watched Dara's fascinated face as she studied his erect cock. She moved between his spread thighs, drawn closer to his raging masculinity, as her gentle fingers stroked his shaft up, down and around. Her heated breath skimmed over the velvety skin sheathing his cock.

Rowan groaned, hardly able to stand the tease.

Steadying his girth with both hands, Dara bent low and extended her tongue, teasing a wet, tortuous trail up his vein-corded shaft. She laved once—only bleedin' once—about his sensitive cock head, and he bucked his hips with a hiss of pleasure, thinking he'd go mad.

Her honeyed tongue honed into a lethal point and skillfully hunted the pearly drop budding at his tip. She gazed up at his face with hooded eyes, rolling his fluid up into her mouth with a moan full of promise.

"*Dara*—"

Merciless, she slid her moist lips down his satiny cock head, lubing him with the heady combination of her saliva and his pre-cum. She took him into the heat of her mouth and sucked him softly, like she would a sweet, using one hand to hold him against her. Another curious, small hand struggled gently against the gap in his jeans and sneaked inside to tease his heavy balls.

Oh, Sweet Danu! Rowan fisted his hands and thrust up his hips, letting out a savage groan. Sweat beaded on his brow. Dara's delicate handling was driving him out of his mind.

He sat up and grabbed her hips, heaving her up with ease and impaling her on his erection with one smooth movement.

Dara gasped out a surprised moan as he so suddenly, so *deeply*, filled her. Her pupils dilated in shock as her thighs clamped on his in an instant.

"Are all Irishmen...this short-tempered?" she demanded, her voice breathy.

"There's only so much...a man...can take!" Rowan roared, and with each word he pulled her down hard on him, thrusting up with force at the same time.

Dara whimpered with each stroke, digging her short nails into his flesh.

His bruising hold on her abruptly eased as he let her ride him, briefly granting her control.

She went slow at first, loving each drawn-out second, losing herself along Rowan's long, hard inches. She then kicked up the pace, bobbing and grinding herself against him until they were both half-gone and bathed in sweat. And then she moved on him devilishly slow yet again, her eyes squeezed shut, lost somewhere deep inside herself.

Rowan again took control of his mate's damp hips, rocking her up and down his cock with mounting need. He felt her begin to climax, her sweet cunt rippling with tight waves around him. Her scream was stifled by his neck. He followed close behind, clutching her to his chest, her name scorching his lips as he burst deep inside of her. He kept holding her close, still buried within her wet heat, both of them hardly able to breathe for long, sweet minutes.

"Dara," Rowan at long last mumbled, gently squeezing her precious form in his embrace. "There is something I need to ask of you."

Dara shut her eyes with a sudden fear. This was what he'd been trying to tell her earlier this afternoon. "Ask away," she whispered at last, her mouth still buried against his feverish, salty throat.

Rowan nodded, his jaw sinking into the darkness of her hair. "Tomorrow is *Beltaine* night. You and I are..."

He paused, hesitating. Then, shaking his head and swallowing nervously, he tried again.

"Dara, how do you feel about me?"

"What do you mean?" Dara withdrew a bit and searched Rowan's face, confused.

"I love you, Dara O'Shea–Neilan." Rowan's sea-stormy gaze shackled her eyes to his. "How do *you* feel about me?"

And suddenly, there was only one right answer.

"I love you, Rowan Mackey," Dara whispered.

Rowan let out a long-held breath. His taut fingers loosened against her back.

"Then..." He once more hesitated. "Will you consent to forge this bond with me as the ancient Law demands?"

She stared up at him, dumbfounded, as he softly repeated, "Will you join with me at sundown tomorrow, Dara, on the eve of *Beltaine*, against the Destiny Stone?"

That was the Kanjali equivalent of popping The Question.

Dara dropped her eyes from Rowan's.

A thing, oppressive and icy, was again swelling within Rowan's chest, making it hard for him to breathe. Dara knew well what his request meant. If she said yes, then tomorrow she would have to mate with him against the Stone. The Hill of Tara would be crowded with Kanjali folk, some she already knew, but most would be strangers—and in front of the entire crowd she would have to accept him, body and soul, against the Stone of Fal. Making love the night before, after the Speakers had vanished from their Gathering locale, had been different—there had been no audience then. But tomorrow... There was no way she was going to willingly go through with it.

"Yes," she suddenly whispered.

"What did you just say?" His gaze jerked up.

"Yes," she repeated a bit louder.

Dara's answer multiplied to a thousand echoes in Rowan's mind. He squeezed her with a frenzied hug, almost crushing her slim form against his chest.

"Rowan, you're nuts! I can't...damn...*breathe*!"

She squirmed in his arms, and he eased his embrace, burying his face in her hair. Her heavy tresses were drenched with the sweet aroma of summer meadows, and layered deep down beneath, was all *her*.

Rowan took Dara's face in his hands and lowered his mouth to hers, his passionate kiss sealing the bargain.

Chapter Twenty-Six

Dara started, pushing up against the soft mattress. The tangled bedclothes held the pooled warmth of shared body heat. The tilted roof window let in the new day's brightness, along with the promise of a soft breeze. She absently felt around her, sweaty palms sliding against the disheveled sheets. Her hand bumped into a warm body. Slowly she peeled away the white, thin sheet, uncovering a muddle of copper-red hair.

A soft grin curved her lips.

Rowan was sleeping next to her, drowning his soft snores within one clenched, squashy pillow.

Dara tilted her head. *He actually looked rather cute like that.*

During the night he had reached for her more than once, and each time she had matched his need with an equal passion. The first time he'd lured her away from a light slumber, taking her slowly, working her with endless patience to a shuddering, soft orgasm. The second time he hadn't been gentle. She hadn't wanted him to be. He'd crushed her against the sheets, pounding into her with uncurbed want until she'd tightened around him with a violent climax. The third time, he'd turned her on her stomach and taken her from behind, thrusting into her with such force that he'd almost driven both their heads into the headboard. The fourth time... Dara smiled, flushing intensely at the oven-fresh memory. The fourth time he'd taken hold of her waist and impaled her atop his erection, making her ride him to a mutual, sweaty-hot climax.

He'd then smoothed a mass of tangles away from her eyes, coaxing her to try and get some more sleep. And she couldn't, because the cats had been yowling all night in the gardens, and Rowan had laughed in her ear, low and soft, telling her that the cats were all in *Beltaine* heat. Finally her body had succumbed to Rowan's whispered advice, and she'd fallen asleep.

Dara studied Rowan's red mop of hair and the lump his body made beneath the covers. A body she had come to know as well as her own.

Rowan Mackey. Her Chosen One.

Dara tugged carefully on the sheet and slid to the edge of the bed, trying not to jiggle the mattress too much. She didn't want to wake Rowan yet, he seemed so innocent and harmless in sleep. She was sore all over, but it was a good kind of sore… A making-rough-love-all-night-long kind.

She padded to the bath naked, quietly shutting the door behind her, then gingerly approached the mirror. She leaned against the sink and studied the face reflected back at her. It had big, dark eyes, shining with the previous night's adventures, pouting rose lips, puffy with hours of kisses, a slight blush to naturally pale cheeks, and thick, black hair, tugged at by a lover's hands and tousled against wrinkled sheets. For the first time in many mornings, Dara liked the person staring back at her.

And then it hit her.

She had promised Rowan she would have sex with him tonight against the dick-shaped stone, while the rest of the world watched.

Early summer already breathed its heat over Dara's skin as she sneaked out of the dormant manor house. She was running barefoot, clutching nothing but a thin dress against her nakedness. Her eyes widened as she moved past the rose garden and into the green fields. The meadows were alive with travelers that hadn't been there the evening before.

They were trickling into the pastures in singles and pairs, some in larger packs, most with no children accompanying them. The bulk chattered gaily with a clear Irish brogue, or conversed in fluid Gaelic — but other accents were present, and other languages were being spoken, as well. As Dara picked her way among them, it gradually became clear to her who or what they truly were—Kanjali folk, her own people, gathered here for the *Beltaine* celebrations. Their tents were strewn across the meadows among grazing sheep and occasional cows, painting both banks of the Boyne with all the colors of the rainbow.

Dara trembled as the weight of their gazes suddenly shifted to her, their whispers surging about her as she hurried past. She hugged her thin dress tighter against her flesh, almost breaking into a run. There was something she had to do before she could fulfill the promise she had made Rowan.

* * * * *

"Aislinn, have you seen Dara?"

Rowan's sister raised her gaze from her lap. She had been sitting in the back gardens, occupying the same stone bench she had shared with Dara the evening before yesterday.

"No," she replied shortly.

"Did she tell you where she was heading, then?"

"Rowan, I don't *know*."

He nodded and turned, driving his hand through his hair.

"*By Danu, that bleedin' woman!*" he suddenly roared, kicking over an innocent garden trellis.

Aislinn leaped to her feet in alarm. "Rowan, what's wrong?"

"I don't bloody know!" He spun back to her, arms spread wide. "All I know is, this morning I couldn't find her, and nobody else has seen or heard anything. She might as well have been swallowed up by the bleedin' earth!"

"What's all the shouting about?"

"No business of yours, Teague."

Rowan squinted his eyes past Aislinn, scowling at the couple that had just staggered out of the mansion. When the two of them strolled closer, they appeared more deeply involved with each other than truly drunk. Teague could hold his Guinness pretty well, Rowan could testify to that himself, and as for Brid... Were banshees even capable of getting drunk?

"You're looking fit to be tied." Brighid beamed her good-morning at him.

"Aye, what's wrong?" Teague said. His hand rested on Brighid's backside, draped in the blazing flood of her long hair.

"Dara's been missing since this morning," Aislinn volunteered. She flinched as Rowan speared her with a hot look.

"Right." Teague scratched his head, bemused.

"I should go look around the airport." Rowan shook his head.

"This is mad, bud. She could go to Dublin, but there's the Shannon airport, too..."

"Och, stop it you two, Dara didn't go to any airport!" Brighid thumped her foot against Teague's work boot. "Think, Rowan, is there someplace special she might have gone to? Someplace you took her to, maybe?"

"Aye, I can think of several such places," he softly admitted.

"Tell us where, then. We'll split up," Brighid offered in a light tone.

"We'll find her." Teague flashed Rowan a hesitant grin. "So, tonight's the big night, eh, boyo?"

Rowan only growled something incoherent in response.

* * * * *

The horizon was a rainbow of green shades as it stretched to touch the early summer sky. Wild-tufted stubby trees made darker clumps against the bright mat of the meadows and an occasional patch of yellow. An isle of red and white houses was nestled within the green—when Dara reached her thumb forward she could hide a whole tiny house behind it.

Yeah, if she kept thinking this way, it would all seem like a huge board game, and she wouldn't be too afraid to look down.

Boldly, Dara lowered her gaze, glimpsing grass and trees, and the Boyne's dark, shimmering band...

Which felt waaay too high for someone suffering from acrophobia.

Her frantic gaze darted to the colorful assembly of tourists' cars parked by the castle, which appeared more like toy cars set up for a child's play.

That felt even worse!

Dara squeaked and her hands pressed harder against the clammy stone balustrade. She squeezed her eyes shut, attacked by a sudden wave of nausea, and her breath came too quick and too shallow. Goddess, she must be a pathetic sight right now, pale-faced and hyperventilating...

She could handle it.

Why else had she fled Rowan's bed and climbed up the Castle of Trim, if not to prove to herself once and for all that she could do it?

Dara forced her wild panting to gradually ease. She swayed lightly, her fingers involuntarily twitching against the ancient stone. She lifted her head carefully and cracked her eyes open, looking straight ahead. She was staring at blue summer sky again, a fluff of white clouds stretched loosely just above the skyline. It looked almost like an ocean dappled with the froth of waves—almost, if she imagined it hard enough.

Dara let out a slow breath.

Yeah, that kind of view she could handle.

And there was another thing she'd wanted to do up here.

"Aidan?" Dara whispered, her gaze lost in the sky.

"Aidan, I think...I *know* that if you're anywhere at all, then...you must be here."

Her eyes were starting to burn. She didn't know if it was because she'd forced them wide open, or because she was determined not to cry.

"'Cause, see…this is your home. Finally found it."

Her whisper broke, but she took a painful swallow and tried again.

"You never told me much about your life, but…I bet you rode inner tubes down this river, too, even though Rowan never said you did…and, I just *know* you used to climb up this castle, maybe even stood right here."

She squeezed her eyes shut and drew in a deep breath, an escaped tear streaking down her cheek. Damn the tears! She'd decided not to weep like a little girl. She thumped one fist against the stone and it did the trick, the brief pain helping her ignore the tight ache in her chest. The words kept pouring out in clipped sentences, squeezed between quick gasps of the balmy air.

"You know, I always thought we would be together, forever…and I want you to know that each moment we had — each second — felt like forever to me."

She paused.

"When you took that arrow instead of me, I wanted to die with you. The thing is, Aidan, I didn't."

She shook her head. Another tear rolled down, hot and heavy.

"I didn't…"

She swiped an angry hand at the flowing tears.

"I love you, Aidan, always will. *Forever*. But now I need to let you go…and please, please don't hate me."

She closed her eyes again and waited, not knowing exactly what she was waiting for. It wasn't like she was really expecting Aidan to answer. Soft wind brushed the drying tears off her cheeks and gently tugged at tendrils of her hair.

"He doesn't, you know," a familiar voice sang behind her.

Dara jerked her eyes open in surprise and swiveled away from the stone balustrade. "How come you're so sure?" she asked the banshee. Her words didn't come out angry or biting anymore, just…tired.

"Aidan could never hate you, Dara." Brighid strolled closer.

"Oh." Dara was loosely hugging herself. "Well…" She let the word linger, not knowing what else to say.

"Mmmm, nice view!" Brighid called in a typical change of subject, her shoulder brushing Dara's arm as she leaned against the stone. "You know, you threw Rowan into a fit this morning, vanishing like that."

"I didn't mean to."

"We played Scissors-Paper-Stone to decide who went where looking for you, and I got the Castle of Trim. I tricked them though—Rowan, Teague and Aislinn—I used a wee bit of Glamour 'cause I wanted to get the Castle myself."

"You don't play fair, do you?"

"Not really."

Brighid swung something shiny above the void. It caught the sun and sparkled, hurting Dara's reddened eyes.

"Silver," she gasped as she shaded her eyes. "Cut that out, it hurts!"

"Och, quit being such a *babby*, you can at least look. You have, before."

Dara withdrew her hands from her face. "Why are you showing your raven birth charm to me again?"

"Why do you always think I have a reason for everything?" Brighid frowned. "Maybe I just think it beautiful?"

"Well?" Dara demanded.

"Well." The banshee sighed. "'Tis because I want you to have it."

"What!" Dara cried.

"Just for tonight," Brighid went on with haste. "I'll wrap it up in leather so it won't hurt you. You're going to need it, Dara, I swear to it!"

"Only if you tell me why." Dara's fascinated gaze clung to the glimmer coursing through the forbidden silver.

"Why? Right, that's easy." Brighid shrugged. "It'll be a full moon night. And you're going to have sex with Rowan...beneath the full moon...in public. See the problem?"

Dara suddenly did, and her face paled even more beneath the sun, her expression bordering on shock.

"Now Rowan, he's a Guardian. He can control himself well enough. You, however... You need extra Power, unless you *want* to grow fur and claws. My charm will give you such Power. So, will you accept it, Dara?"

Dara gave a slow nod.

"Rest your mind." Brighid's tone softened. "I'll be there, too, helping the others keep control as they change. All will be grand, you'll see!"

"Sure, just grand," Dara muttered.

Brighid grinned, snatching the silver amulet from the air and sliding it back over her head.

As the both of them made their way back to Niamh's estate, a dazed shifter escorted by a cheerful redheaded banshee, they soon came across the colorful assembly of newly arrived travelers. Their whispers followed Dara and Brighid as they twined their way among their lines.

"*May Queen*," someone murmured from behind.

"*Bonny, she is*," another echoed.

A woman stepped gingerly into their path. She handed Dara a handwoven basket brimming with spring wildflowers, streamers wound through its wickerwork.

"'Tis a May Basket," she told Dara. "These are all freshly picked. Wanted to put it in your hands myself, 'stead of laying it on your doorstep and runnin' off."

"Just say thank you," Brighid advised Dara in a whisper.

"Thank you." Dara's flush deepened. She pulled the loaded basket against her breasts.

"'Tis nothing." The woman stepped back, a wide smile splitting her face. "You just bring us *Samon*."

"Summer," Brighid told Dara with a slight grin. "She wants you to bring her Summer."

"I fear I'm under qualified for *that* particular mission," Dara mumbled quietly, her face still hot.

"What's that?" Dara looked at the mansion's door with wide eyes as she stepped up to the front porch. A flowering branch of hawthorn had been affixed against the dark wood.

"It means somebody fancies you." Brighid reached forward, stroking over the white blossoms. "'Tis an ancient custom called 'May Birching'. On the day of *Beltaine*, before the fires were lit, young lads used to fasten a garland or a bough to the doors or windows of the lasses they fancied."

"Hawthorn." A smile curved Dara's lips, as she recalled her Lower Realm romp with Rowan beneath the white blossoms.

"Aye, hawthorn is a fine sign, 'tis! If you get thorn hooked to your door though, you aren't that lucky."

Soon after, Dara discovered a wreath of red roses slung over the attic room's doorknob. She bent down to rest her laden basket against the floor and disentangled the blazing garland from its tethering string. Her hands trembled as she lifted it for a closer inspection, and a stab of guilt pierced her insides. Rowan must have assembled all this wild beauty for her while he was searching for her around the gardens, finding her gone from his bed. With sudden resolve Dara raised the intensely fragrant wreath and planted it in her hair. Accepting Rowan's gift was the least she could do to show him how sorry she was. She turned away from her room, leaving her basket where it lay, not wishing to go inside and tackle the rumpled bed.

Not when she knew it was empty.

Her legs walked her dazed body around the house, and, as if waking from a dream, she startled to find herself facing the closed door of Niamh's study. She gingerly touched the gleaming doorknob, then turned it on an impulse.

The door wasn't locked.

Dara stepped inside and flicked the light switch on, shutting the door behind her with an unpleasant stir in her stomach. She felt like a thief, an intruder upon a forbidden territory. The soft light hadn't utterly banished the room's shadows. They lurked among the burdened bookshelves and lingered against the walls, and she shuddered. A square of daylight beckoned behind the drawn curtains and she rushed to it, pulling the curtains aside and struggling to wrench the windows open. They swung heavily to the outside and she leaned out with them, taking a long breath of fresh air.

She gasped. A familiar tall figure was making its way towards the house, the sun sparking flames in his wild hair.

Rowan lifted his eyes, sensing the weight of a human gaze. He slowed down at the sight of his willful mate in the second-story window — apparently *someone's* search had turned out successful. She had a funny look on her face, like a child caught with a hand in the candy jar. The fiery coronet he'd made for her was nestled within the rich blackness of her hair.

Thank Danu for that sweet sight!

Rowan roared with relief, storming through the hawthorn-bedecked front door and charging up the stairway.

Dara froze at the window. *Goddess, that roar!* He must be angry at her rude trespassing on Niamh's private property. She spun sharply as the study door burst open. *Oh Great Goddess, he was even faster than she had remembered!*

For a brief instant, Rowan stood framed by the doorway, a hulking shadow darker than the corridor's gloom. And then he took a few strides in her direction, caging her waist in the circle of his arms.

"So you're not mad at—" she managed, the air almost squeezed out of her lungs by his powerful embrace.

He loosened his hold considerably. Withdrawing a bit, he bowed his head to hers, planting his mouth over her lips. Dara moaned with surprise, her hands fumbling up Rowan's back. His lips demanded hers to yield. When she surrendered and opened up for him, he plunged inside with a hard kiss. It didn't feel angry, just loving and desperate, and then he ended it with the same abruptness, struggling to contain his heavy breathing.

"Did I hurt you?" he inquired softly, running his hands up and down her back.

All she could do was shake her head to tell him that no, he hadn't. Ever.

He sighed and turned her back to the view in the window, their bodies completing each other again. For long minutes they stood in silence, bathing in each other's warmth.

"I wish I could show you Tara from here," Rowan finally whispered against Dara's ear. Her crown of roses teased his cheek, and the intense fragrance was engulfing his senses. "But 'tis more than six miles northeast from where we stand, and we're facing the wrong direction."

"It's not so bad, you'll show it to me tonight, won't you?" She was looking out the window, watching the camped travelers.

"Aye, we'll be there by sundown to light the *Beltaine* fire," he told her. "In ancient times, sweetheart, the *Ard-Rí*—the High King of Erin—always lit the first *Beltaine* fire on the Hill of Tara. 'Twas forbidden to light any other fire before the High King lit his."

She nodded, trailing her fingers along his forearm. "What else can you tell me about fire?" she asked in a soft, teasing tone, her voice a bit breathy.

"A few more things, in fact," he said, smiling. He'd taken the bait, walking his fingers to the tiny round buttons at the front of her dress. "In early March, you go to the woods and start gathering the nine sacred woods used to kindle the *Beltaine* fire…"

"I should have gone to the woods, then?" Her breath caught in her throat, and she stood very still as his hands played over her.

"'Tis customary that men, with not one piece of iron on their bodies, should gather the sacred woods. Three of each kind." He undid the first button.

"Three," she gasped.

"First you have to get…" He undid the second button. "Birch." He loosened the third button, and she let out another soft gasp.

"Then, oak…"

Dara moaned aloud as he popped the fourth button open.

"Then, there's rowan."

"That's your name," Dara squirmed beneath his hands.

"Aye, 'tis also my name. But I'm not finished yet." He grinned. "There's also willow. Hawthorn. Hazel. Apple. Vine. And fir."

With each name he loosened another tiny button. Dara trembled like a leaf.

"I'm out of trees," he finally said and turned her around to face him. "But you're not out of buttons."

Dara gasped and arched back as Rowan tore the rest of the buttons open. He then slid his hands beneath the gaping sides of her dress, and pulled her naked body tightly against his clothed one.

"You're not wearing useless undergarments today," he pointed out smugly, moving his mouth against hers. One of his hands fondled the soft curves of her ass.

"I didn't have time this morning. I was busy escaping." Her heart was beating in her throat, she could barely form the words.

He laughed, making that soft rumble she liked feeling against her skin. Her fingers dug into his shirt as she tried to wrestle the obstinate cloth out of his jeans. To her confusion, his rough whisper stopped her.

"Dara, sweetheart. Not *now*..."

Rowan's breath was labored. She could smell his sharp arousal, feel his hard cock pressing against her bare flesh. What was she doing wrong?

"The ancient Law," he said hoarsely without her asking. "For couples joining at *Lia Fáil*, 'tis forbidden to mate after the dawn of their Day of Joining." His voice sounded painful. "They may mate only once that day, against the Stone."

"Oh," she said, letting out a hissing breath. Defiance boiled inside her, but she said nothing more.

Suddenly, it was dawn that mattered? Why, dammit, when everything else went by sundowns?

Rowan tried to soothe her with gentle caresses, but his touch only inflamed her more. She finally tore away from him with a wild growl and pulled her torn dress tightly about her body. Her rose garland lay slanted across her dark mane. Arduously, Dara regained her breath and composure. Rowan stood watching her, appearing more flustered than she.

"Thank you, Rowan," she whispered at last, "for teaching me about fire."

Chapter Twenty-Seven

"Well, are you nervous?" Aislinn asked shyly. "Because of tonight?"

After replacing her ruined dress, Dara had fled from Rowan's presence to one of the garden's cool sheds, wishing to chill the fire searing her insides. She had quickly run into Aislinn, and was grateful to find her there.

"I'm trying not to think about tonight," Dara admitted.

"Sorry," Aislinn said, tilting her head, but she continued to smile.

"Oh, it's okay, really," Dara answered, smiling back. "It's funny, you know…"

"What?"

"This picture suddenly popped up in my mind—an old memory that I haven't thought of in years."

"What was it?" Aislinn pleaded.

"It was just before my family left Ireland—the last memory I have from here." Her voice softened. "I was standing in my mom's kitchen—and my mom was holding this *huge* snail."

"A snail!" Aislinn exclaimed, laughing, but something crossed her face.

"Yeah. I was up before sunrise, wreaking havoc in our garden, and I found this really big snail. It was the first of May."

"Oh please, please go on," Aislinn begged.

"Well, Mom was holding her palm flat, like this." Dara demonstrated. "She was staring at the snail sliding across her palm, and suddenly she said, 'Come, Dara, let's do a wee bit of magic'."

"Oooh grand! What did your mom do?"

"She sprinkled a plate with flour and put my snail on it—then placed a large leaf of cabbage atop the whole thing. She'd then told me to wait after sunrise and see what happened."

"And what happened?" Aislinn was brimming with curiosity.

"Well, of course I could barely wait 'til sunrise! I climbed up a chair and leaned over the kitchen table, staring at the cabbage leaf, and the tiny movements the snail was making beneath it as it slithered through the flour."

"Ick. And what then?"

"Mom came and pinched the edge of the leaf aside. 'Now,' she said, 'now you will see the first letters of your Chosen One's name traced in the flour!'"

"And what did you see?" Aislinn gasped. "Did the snail draw Rowan's name?"

"I don't remember," Dara admitted, embarrassed. "I was four years old. Last thing I recall is Mom holding the edge of the cabbage leaf, about to lift it from the plate."

"Oh Dara, you are so *bad*." Aislinn yelled with frustration, then settled back again, laughing. "You know, I remember that kitchen, too."

Too late it occurred to Dara that Aislinn's family had moved into her parents' house shortly after they had left.

"Oh Aislinn, I'm *so* sorry, I didn't mean to—"

"No." Aislinn vigorously shook her head. "I loved your story. Thank you for giving me a good memory of that place, Dara."

As the sun began to slant in the sky, Teague made his way into the garden shed's cool shadow. Dara turned away from Aislinn, casting a questioning look at the intruder.

"Nice outfit," she remarked, scanning his short green robe.

"'Tis time to crown our May Queen," Teague smiled, then bowed lightly. "Would you join us, Highness?"

"Oh, Goddess, I'm not good at this kind of thing," Dara mumbled, going pale. In high school she had never been Head Cheerleader, Homecoming Queen, not to mention Prom Queen. Baton twirling had been out of the question. She'd gladly settled for a swim team championship.

"You'll do just fine," Teague grinned and snatched her hand. He hauled her out of the shed, squirming and protesting desperately. Aislinn, blushing with excitement, gathered her dress and dashed out after them into the open meadow.

The colorful throng of Kanjali folk split and parted before the three of them, the crowd humming with wired anticipation. An improvised dais had been erected further back into the meadow, far enough to allow the crowd to move comfortably around it. Words and bits of sentences passed the huddled trio as it made its way through the general buzz.

"May Bride…"

"The Queen of May…"

"Bringer of *Samon*…"

"There's already a crown on her…"

"Can picture *her* sky-clad…"

On that last remark she'd picked up speed, her face flaming brighter than her wreath of roses. She laced her fingers tighter within Teague's, and he returned a comforting squeeze. Before she knew it, they were standing before the dais, and Rowan was turning to meet them. Seeing him, Dara's already fluttering pulse skipped a beat or two. He looked like an ancient king, the setting sun crowning him with copper flames, his green attire complementing the stormy sea-green of his eyes.

"All yours, she is." Teague tugged on Dara's hand 'til it rested within Rowan's sure grip.

Rowan leaned down briefly. "*Beautiful*," he whispered in Dara's ear, just before turning and leaping onto the platform. He crouched low, leaning over the platform's edge, Dara's hand still clasped in his. She gasped sharply as Teague seized her waist and easily swung her onto the stage and into Rowan's arms.

"*Your May Queen and her King,*" Teague hollered, his cupped hands making an improvised megaphone against his mouth. Brighid suddenly tore away from the horde, joining his side with a laugh.

The crowd broke into wild cheering, discordant hand clapping and piercing whistles. There were a few shouts, too.

"Kiss her!"

"Show us a good one..."

"*Kiss. Kiss. Kiss. Kiss. Kiss.*"

The crowd gradually fell into accord and became a single chorus, the same word shouted in unison from hundreds of mouths.

Dara pressed tighter against Rowan, her body throbbing with the crowd's pulsating command. "They're not going to just shut up and leave, are they?" she joked over the mayhem.

Rowan shook his head, then bent to his May Queen's mouth and gave the masses exactly what they wanted. Shocked, Dara moaned into his kiss, the crowd's roar fizzing through her blood like a stimulating drug. Her mouth started to work against Rowan's. She climbed her fingers to his nape, entwining them in his hair and pulling him down against her. He instantly responded, deepening his kiss, his hands roving over her back. Dara made a sound low in her throat. The earth was swaying beneath her, and she was falling...

She opened her eyes to find Rowan cradling her face in his hands. Her fingers were still firmly laced against the back of his neck. He spoke her name and she nodded slowly, as if awakened from a spell.

Then they were both snatched off their makeshift stage and hurried away on anonymous shoulders. The parade washed like a flood through tents and randomly parked vehicles — pickups and caravans, road-dusty cars, slim motorcycles and a skeletal horde of bicycles.

The May Queen and her King were loaded upon the back of Teague's faithful Bronco, and slowly the procession set off in a tumult of engine roars, loud honks and earsplitting human applause.

Rowan steadied Dara against him, laughing.

"Next stop, the Hill of Tara," he said.

She didn't answer, suddenly filled with a vague foreboding.

The long train of vehicles plowed through acres of green farmland, leisurely advancing along narrow country roads. The sun, on its way down, was occasionally winking at the travelers from behind dense roadside foliage. Laughter and loud singing echoed across the fields. The long, north-to-south ridge of the Hill of Tara was low enough for Dara to have missed if Rowan hadn't pointed it out to her. Finally, the royal couple slumped down against the Bronco's trunk floor.

"We're about to skirt the Hill's south side," Rowan told Dara.

She smiled vaguely at him, her mind adrift.

After a short while Teague pulled off and hopped out of the car, and Brighid leaped down from the passenger's side. The never-ending motorcade rumbled to a full stop behind them, sparking another flare-up of cheering, wailing and wild honking. The cars were abandoned along the road, blocking lavish miles of it, as their occupants flowed unhurriedly up a gently sloping pasture.

No one dared undermine Dara and Rowan's honorary position at the head of the lively parade. The colorful ensemble flowed and gathered behind the two like a human river. As the keyed-up crowd marched on, voices and laughter slowly died down. Tall grass whispered around them, swayed by a passing breeze. Dara briefly shut her eyes, sensing sluggish magic settling over her skin like fine dust. Then Rowan gently tugged her hand and they halted.

"All old Irish roads lead to Tara," Rowan said softly, squeezing her hand in his. "Look, sweetheart. What do you think of Tara in broad daylight?"

The Hill of Tara stretched boundless before them, and the crowd finally scattered, spreading through the wide-open, grassy plain. Dara watched them, inhaling a deep, excited breath. Butterflies fluttered in her stomach. Rowan hugged her to him, leading her to a secluded spot. He guided her west 'til the Hill started to slope down.

"Look, Dara."

Rowan gently rotated her in his arms towards the vast panorama. He was speaking softly against her hair, hugging her from behind. She turned to feast her eyes on the view.

"Oh, Rowan," she gasped, her hands tightening over his.

Just beyond her feet the Hill's west slope dropped steeply. Behind it, the whole world opened before her with sharp clarity, a vast tapestry of variegated greens. The land's farthest rim was already shadowed. The sun's red sphere now hung low above the horizon.

"'Tis getting dark," Rowan whispered. "On a good day, you can see as many as thirteen counties, just looking down from Tara. There, to the north—that white mass—that's Newgrange."

Dara's gaze traced Newgrange's white quartz front, bright against the looming dusk. She squeezed her arms over Rowan's.

"So, Highness, how do you like the view so far?" Rowan inquired, a smile in his voice.

"I feel like I can see half my 'kingdom' just standing here," Dara replied, her dark eyes glittering with mirth. Then a sudden fear chilled her. Something utterly hateful and dark was still lurking within all this beauty.

Chapter Twenty-Eight
The Hill of Tara
April 30, Sundown

The *Beltaine* fire was about to be kindled.

Dara could feel the crowd's tension surging about them.

The majority of the crowd huddled within the confines of the Royal Enclosure, a vast earthwork encircling the hill's crown, and the others spilled about the rest of Tara.

The enclosure held two linked ring forts. Dara and Rowan had been positioned within the eastern of the two. From its center jutted *Lia Fáil*, the Stone of Destiny, making a phallic silhouette against the flaming sunset.

"I thought *Lia Fáil* was much larger," Dara shyly admitted. She glanced nervously north, towards the shallow Mound of Hostages, where the Speakers had the Gathering, touching the enclosure's inner rim.

"The Stone only seems short because 'tis half-buried in the ground." Rowan gently squeezed Dara's hand, raising it to his lips. "Truly, *Lia Fáil* is a dozen feet tall."

Dara nodded, her hand climbing to the small leather pouch slung about her neck.

Brighid's raven charm.

A faint chill coursed through her as she thought of the thick chunk of silver dangling so close to her heart. It would give her more Power to stay human, Brighid had told her. She glanced at the dark mass of eager shifters, acutely relieved that Aislinn wasn't standing among them. Rowan had ordered his sister to keep to the estate. Knowing she would be the only Mortal amidst a crowd of Kanjali shifters, he refused to take her with them on this unsure night.

The red orb of the sun was now kissing the western horizon. There was a sudden stirring within the crowd, and a collective gasp breathed in unison from hundreds of mouths. Thick rows parted to make a clear path for a slim figure at the assembly's edge.

"Niamh!" Dara whispered.

"Aye, the Bantiarna has a liking for a bit of drama," Rowan chuckled.

The leader of the Speakers circle cut through the crowd with sure strides.

"Where are the rest of the Speakers?" Dara demanded quietly of Rowan, watching Niamh's advance. As she neared, the elongated wooden staff in her hand became visible.

"The circle's leader is the only one to show his face," Rowan replied. "*Her* face, for that matter. The other Speakers are scattered within the crowd, their true identities hidden."

Meanwhile, Niamh moved between the two joined ring forts and made a smooth climb up the barrow, facing the assembly beside Dara and Rowan. She was carrying her wooden staff in both her hands, as if presenting it for viewing. Dara noted with surprise that the staff's end had been sharpened to a finely honed point.

Niamh then began a slow, measured walk, making a full circle around Rowan, Dara and *Lia Fáil*. Her gaze flowed calmly over the crowd that pressed against the ring fort's edge. As she finally halted, all random chatter subsided.

"The Bearers of the Nine Woods shall now climb." She spoke into the silence, making no attempt to raise her voice.

The nine woods…

Dara recalled Rowan saying that nine sacred woods were needed to kindle the *Beltaine* fire. From all around them the nine Bearers made their way to the barrow's top. Each was a sturdy man, leather-girded and clad with a short green robe. Upon their right shoulders they carried a bundle of rough logs. Teague was in the lead, flashing Dara a soft grin. She recognized Killian among them as well, and he gave her a knowing wink as she caught his gaze. The Bearers huddled together, then crouched, each laying his treasured load at his feet.

In the west only half of the sun's red orb was now visible above the skyline, and the sky around it had erupted in seething hues.

Niamh nodded in approval. She stepped closer to *Lia Fáil* at the barrow's rough center, and touched her sharpened staff to the grassy soil.

"She's preparing the Sacred Grid for the kindling of the *tein-eigin*," Rowan whispered to Dara. "*Tein-eigin* means need-fire, or forced-fire."

Niamh had begun to work her way carefully around the grass, her white robes flapping about her in the twilight breeze. She cut a large, square grid in the yielding soil, her movements practiced and confident. When the last line had been cut, the sun had already slipped below the skyline. A pale, perfectly round moon skirted the eastern horizon, and the striped sky behind it moved from pale blue to deep indigo.

"The sun has set," Niamh spoke over the reverent silence. "Bearers, cut out the turf!"

Eight of the nine men drew pointed sticks from their belts, short versions of Niamh's sharpened staff. They approached the Grid, their dark shapes moving across the sky's shifting blue radiance. Teague, with oak at his feet, hadn't moved with the rest. Each of the others took his place within one of the Grid's squares, leaving vacant only the ninth, central one. The Bearers dug out the turf, each skillfully tending to his own grassy domain. Within a surprisingly short time they had all stood up, their work done.

"Return to your woods," Niamh softly commanded them. "Bearer of the Oak, step forth into the ninth square."

Teague picked up the oak branches and moved forward. He carried them over to the square in the Grid's hub—the only one still covered with turf. Kneeling in the grass, he fitted one of the oak rods, fashioned like a spindle, into a socket carved beforehand in an oak plank. He then started to rotate the spindle against the plank, muscles swelling in his powerful arms.

Niamh, meanwhile, untangled a small bag of leather from within her robes.

Suddenly, the violent friction of wood against wood sparked, and the crowd made an audible gasp. Niamh stepped over to Teague and peppered the fire with her bag's contents. The unsure spark brightened and swelled, blazing into a steady flame. Quickly, Niamh and Teague leaped away from the spreading flames, and Teague fed his remaining log to the fire.

Rowan and Dara pulled back from the heat, the Destiny Stone's chill presence breathing closer against their backs.

"What did she sprinkle over the fire?" Dara murmured.

"'Tis crushed agaric, a kind of mushroom that grows on old birch trees," Roan whispered back. "Easily combusts."

As if on a cue, the other eight Bearers stacked their logs upon their shoulders and advanced to the blazing fire. Each fed his three logs to the flames in turn, and the fire hissed and crackled like a living thing. The crowd, which had kept silent through most of the kindling ritual, roared for each man, waving and shouting the Bearer's name. When the nine men had finally scrambled back down the barrow, the Hill of Tara shook with the loud ovations.

At last, Niamh raised her staff high into the air. Ruddy patches of light shifted on her body as she moved, curbing the ecstatic Kanjali folk back into silence.

"Almost four thousand years ago, on *Beltaine* eve, the *Tuatha dé Danann* invaded Erin, landing first in Connacht."

She spoke into the dawning quiet, disturbed only by the fire's soft hiss and snap. Slowly she moved, gazing upon the illuminated, raised faces.

"*Beltaine* falls halfway between the first day of Spring, when day and night are equal in length, and Midsummer, when the day is the longest of the year, and night is the shortest. *Beltaine* takes us from Dark to Light."

Dara absently tightened her grip on Rowan's hand. He glanced down at her and smiled at her rapt expression, watching flames and shadows play over her face.

"*Beltaine* has also a second name," Niamh went on. "'Tis also called *Cestsamhain*, 'Opposite *Samhain*'. And, truly, *Beltaine* falls exactly opposite to *Samhain* on the Wheel of the Year. The two split the year in half. Dark and Light. Death and Life. Winter, *Garn* — and Summer, *Samon*."

Dara felt that Niamh had named the seasons both in Gaelic and in English mainly for her sake. An excited hum rose from the watching crowd, broken off by Niamh's raised hand.

"And because both *Samhain* and *Beltaine* are intermediaries, they are both times of no-time, and the Veil between the worlds grows thinnest. At these special times, passage is easy between the Upper Earth and the Otherworld. At these times, we should take extra care guarding the Gateways."

The crowd hummed its agreement.

"Tonight we celebrate Light, Summer and Life," Niamh went on. "We celebrate the union between the Great Mother-Goddess and the God, He Who Guards the Sacred Oak. Tonight we also bless the joining of Rowan, the son of Breandan, and Dara, the daughter of Cuinn."

The dusky air thundered with cheers. Dara's heart pounded, and her stomach clenched. Rowan squeezed her hand and leaned over to her ear, whispering something that made her cheeks flare hotter than the flames' heat. Niamh half-turned to them and smiled, allowing this round of applause to last longer. Finally she turned back to the roaring Kanjali folk, and shouts dwindled and abated beneath her gaze.

"For the first in many years, this night of *Beltaine* is also blessed by a full moon," she said, swinging her arm to the east sky. "The Speakers and I will walk among you and do our best to aid your own control of the transformation. The weaker among you, and those traveling with young ones, are requested to leave now, while there's time enough. I will not tolerate bloodshed among my own kinfolk. I assure you, the punishment will be grave for those left alive."

There was movement within the mass of shifters, and an escalating muddle of whispers. Niamh watched the crowd closely, missing nothing. Her gaze alone made some flinch and withdraw of their own free will. A few others gathered up a child, winding their way out of the knot of shifters. Niamh gave them all time enough to make up their own minds, hoping each would come to the right decision.

At last, there was no more movement within the crowd.

"Now," Niamh spoke again, "if this were an ordinary *Beltaine* eve—if we didn't have a full moon—I would have asked Fiona to pass around her special *Beltaine* Cake. I personally witnessed her charring the bottom of one slice."

Laughter broke from the listeners as Fiona raised high a dish burdened with a large round cake, scalloped around the edge and split in four. "I got more of these for you right here!" she bellowed, pointing at a plump, bumpy bag leaned against her legs. The crowd roared louder with laughter and screams.

So, ruddy-cheeked Fiona was as Kanjali as the rest of them.

"Why are they so worked up over a cake?" Dara turned astounded eyes to Rowan.

"'Tis not a simple cake—'tis called *boinneóg*, and made of oatmeal," Rowan raised his voice over the ruckus. "The cake is passed around in a bag, to men and women brave enough to draw out slices. The unfortunate bastard who draws the slice charred at the bottom is pronounced the *Beltaine* Fool."

Dara giggled. "What happens to the Fool?" she asked, curious.

"He has to leap through the fire three times, if he's lucky," he told her.

"That's if he's lucky? And what happens if he's unlucky?"

"Then he gets pelted with eggshells, as well."

"No!" she gasped with laughter.

"Oh, aye. And usually there are some nice lads grabbing him, pretending to throw him into the fire," Rowan grinned. "Then all through the rest of the celebration everyone speaks of him as if he's dead."

"Now, that's just cruel," Dara protested, though her eyes were squinted with laughter.

"Living thousands of years among the Celts, you pick up odd habits." Rowan shrugged.

Then they both quieted, suddenly aware that Niamh was again addressing the crowd.

"This *Beltaine* eve we have no time for cakes," the Speakers' leader stated. "By now, you must all feel the pull of the full moon. At midnight its Power will be at its peak. None of you will then be able to resist transformation. But I want all of you to be able to keep as much control as possible. There is no reason for anyone to go full *mac'tir*, not when the weak have left, and the Speakers are walking amongst you."

A hum of agreement drifted from the assembly. Dara found herself clutching the small leather sack dangling from her neck, silently thanking Brighid for forcing her to accept her precious raven charm.

It will help you draw on my Power, the banshee had told her as she'd tied the leather thong around Dara's nape.

"There will be no dancing around the *Beltaine* fire tonight," Niamh spoke. "There will be no passing of cakes. But tomorrow at sunrise we will erect the Maypole, and by Danu, we'll have our Maypole dancing!"

Again there were shouts and waving, but the audience seemed dispirited. Full moon or not, *Beltaine* with no fire-dancing?

The general mood cheered considerably as Niamh turned away from the whispering throng and approached Dara and Rowan. The two of them stood pressed together with their backs facing the Stone, watching Niamh with the fire's glow in their eyes. Halting a short distance from them, Niamh stabbed her staff into the ground with a sudden thrust. The wooden pole remained erect, its upmost end still quivering.

Dara flinched unwillingly at the abrupt violent gesture. Rowan hadn't stirred. Niamh turned to Dara, her soft tone contrasting with her harsh action.

"Dara, the daughter of Cuinn O'Shea. Give me thy left hand."

Dara hesitated, then extended her left hand, and Niamh accepted it with a gentle, firm grip. Next she turned her eyes to Rowan.

"Rowan, the son of Breandan Mackey. Give me thy left hand."

He extended a steady hand, and she took it.

"Dara, will thou take Rowan as your lifemate for as long as thou shalt live?"

"Yes," she said.

"Rowan, will thou take Dara as your lifemate for as long as thou shalt live?"

"Aye," he said.

"I bind you both together, body and soul, and your bond shall be forged by joining against *Lia Fáil*. As ye join your hands, so your lives are joined. The earth and sky, the moon and stars, the fire and air shall be witnesses to this joining. The four winds shall carry the word. Now clasp your left hands together."

Hot silence breathed from the crowd as Niamh joined both Rowan's and Dara's hands beneath hers. She untangled from her left wrist a three-strand braid of red, black and green. Carefully she wound the cord three times about Rowan's wrist, three times about both clasped hands, and three times about Dara's wrist, and tied the loose ends together with three knots.

"Ye shall now forge this bond as avowed by the ancient Law set by the Mother Goddess," she declared. Employing the same methodic care, Niamh unwound the cord from their wrists and pulled back.

Rowan gently turned Dara in his arms to fully face him.

"Rowan." Dara gazed up into his eyes as he took her face in his hands.

"Aye, sweetheart?"

"Rowan, what…what am I supposed to do now?"

The night made her dark eyes even blacker. She spoke in a voice too small. He wanted to wipe the lost expression off her face, to banish the shadows and leave only the flames.

"Just look at me, Dara."

He wrapped his arms tighter about her, enfolding her slender form with hungry, long caresses. His kiss moved from her brow, lower, touching her mouth, and she faintly responded. Her hands weren't clinging to his body, weren't stroking him back. She stood still and shuddering in her thin dress, breathing fast like a captured gazelle. He had to make her forget the white-hot tension wafting from the surrounding Kanjali folk.

"Look at me," he demanded again with a scorching whisper, and she opened her eyes.

"Does it truly matter now, sweetheart, what is happening around us?"

She gave him a stunned look, his words forcing up a recent memory — Rowan making love to her against the damp grass, at the Speakers' abandoned place of Gathering.

"Does it?" He wrapped her face again with the heat of his hands.

"N-no," she finally managed.

"Does it matter if anyone else is watching?"

"No," she whispered a bit more steadily. "There is only you."

Rowan crouched and lifted Dara so that her legs were now hugging him. His hands supported her buttocks, crushing the gauzy cloth of her dress. As her arms locked around his neck he touched his mouth to hers again, pressing harder. Dara's lips parted. Rowan curled his tongue between her lips to tease and stroke her own tongue, to thrust deeper into the welcoming heat of her mouth. She responded with a sudden move, bracing his head to hers. Her silky tongue finally twined with his. He felt her gasping into his breath, wringing his hair with clenching fingers.

Rowan gently pulled back, and Dara gazed up at him with dark, hazy eyes. She ran her tongue over her misted lips, in between quick gasps for air. Her face dug into his chest, taking cover from everything around her, like a little girl playing hide-and-seek.

Slowly, Rowan turned them both away from the crowd, and carried Dara the last few steps to the Stone of Destiny. He knelt with extra care, like he'd done the first time he'd held her in his arms in a land strange to him. He laid his mate against the grass with her back touching the Stone, feeling her brief shudder at its chill.

The Stone stayed silent, oblivious to both their touches.

Rowan's broad back made an almost-perfect shield against the spectators as he crouched between Dara's legs. He drew her dress higher up her thighs, his touch gentle. Dara held her breath as he moved, her flesh burning beneath his hands. His fingers skirted her moist pubic curls, and she jerked with a shudder. Rowan's erection was making an obvious bulge beneath his breeches. Dara twisted with unease, trapped between his body and the Stone, trying to shift against him. Her hands desperately clamped over his forearms.

"Rowan, don't. Wait…"

He instantly froze, his hands framing her naked hips, struggling to control his breathing.

"Rowan, I'm…" Dara took in a deep, shaky breath, her voice imbued with unshed tears. "I don't think I can do this." Her hands shot to her face, stifling a half-sob.

Rowan gazed down at her, wrapped around him half-naked. She was quivering in silence, her hands pressed tightly against her face. *By Danu, she was falling apart.* He pulled back and hauled her against him, crumpling her dress as he hugged her.

"Stop, stop, sweetheart, I'm not good with a crying woman. Stop, *céadsearc*, we are not going to do this."

"But I promised—"

"Shhh, no more crying, aye?"

He rose to his feet, cradling Dara in his arms, and turned from the Destiny Stone with dire resolution. The Stone was a mocking, living presence at his back. The moon was almost topping the sky, its Power rapidly peaking. Dara curled tighter into Rowan's chest. His eyes found Niamh, a white-clad shadow watching silently from a distance. The crowd below began to simmer with a soft hiss, like a dragon with numerous heads. Rowan took a hard swallow, his throat aching with dryness.

"There will be no mating against *Lia Fáil* tonight," he announced, confronting his kinsmen. His golden eyes dared them to say otherwise.

And then an icy gust burst over the broad plain, flattening the tall grass. A howl echoed across the Hill of Tara, spilling down over the night-black farmlands. The sound was a familiar blend of a man's cry and a bestial wail, Rowan had heard it before. But back then it had been far away, rolling towards Dara and Brighid and him from distant purple mountains.

But now...now it was less than a mile away.

Dara screamed in panic, her fingers digging into Rowan's flesh. She fought him as he lowered her to the ground, and he caught her with a steely grasp, forcing her to quiet down. The crowd below erupted with a jumble of baffled shouts, its dense mass swaying and twisting beneath the fire's glare. Niamh wrenched her staff from the ground and leaped to the edge of the barrow.

"Quiet!" she ordered the crowd seething beneath her feet. "Keep your silence!"

The tempestuous Kanjali shifters gradually yielded to their leader's cool command. They now stood in silence, their burning gazes cast northward. They were staring in the direction of the Mound of Hostages, and further, to the night-dark north.

Brighid scrambled up the ring-barrow, her gown and cape clutched and raised in her hands, and Teague hurried up after her. The two of them took their places beside Rowan, with Dara still quivering in his hold.

"They've crossed through the Veil," Brighid said, her voice controlled.

"You are Dara's guardian Sidhe," Niamh stated after sparing her a brief glance.

Brighid jerked her head in affirmation.

The air suddenly filled with the clatter of horses galloping. Shadow-riders washed in from the north, showing as slightly blacker masses against the darkness. Moonlight shone harshly on a silver pommel, and Brighid whispered, "*Donn.*"

Chapter Twenty-Nine

Shouts sounded from the shifters' outermost rows, and Rowan couldn't tell if they meant fury, panic or pain — nonetheless they testified to the first physical clash between the attackers and his gathered kinfolk. A dark-clad rider tore ruthlessly through the crowd on a foaming white horse. Firelight glittered and bounced from his short sword as he wielded it left and right with sharp accuracy, stabbing and slashing his way through.

"Donn is heading here," Brighid called over the shouts.

Rowan had already forced Dara behind him, and was standing as a live shield between her and the mayhem.

"No," Dara yelled in protest, her voice desperate. "I want to—"

Rowan swiveled to her for a half-second. "Go to the Stone, Dara," he roared. "Go back to the Stone, and do not move from it!"

His eyes were molten amber. She withdrew from his unfamiliar face until her back pressed against the chilly Stone. She then gave her head a violent shake, steadying her feet against the grass. Reaching a trembling hand beneath her left armpit, she clasped a familiar bone hilt. The drawn dagger drank light from both the fire and the moon, its silver etchings erupting with raw brightness. Dara swayed, sinking back against the Stone. Her right fist tightened on the dagger's hilt with a painful, sweaty grip.

Niamh readied her staff, her eyes set on Donn. "Teague! Bearers of the Nine!" She bellowed over the confusion. "Each take command over your own! The Speakers are fighting among you, you will keep control even if you shift fully!"

"I will make sure of that," Brighid said and vanished in a swirl of fog. A large raven tore out of the mist into the surrounding dark.

Teague mumbled a curse, likely at seeing her change for the first time. His eyes were as golden as Rowan's as he forced his gaze away from her fading form. He leaped into the crowd with a growl, taking charge of his group of shifters.

Rowan and Niamh had been left standing side by side on the ring's edge. The Kanjali shifters had separated into nine smaller groups under the Bearers' command, following their ancient traditional alignment. Their dark shapes twirled and twisted, painted ruby and gold by the blaze. Instead of merely reacting, they were now fighting back. They fought with hands and stones and sticks, since iron had been forbidden on these sacred grounds on the night of *Beltaine*. Transformation rippled through their lines like an advancing front, setting fire to their eyes and lengthening their clawed fingers. Many of Donn's riders were pulled down from their horses to be ripped apart by the raging shifters. On any other night the mounted shadow-warriors wouldn't have been more than wraiths, but *Beltaine* made the denizens of both Realms substantial to one another. Now and then firelight shone on an oversized raven as it made brief dives over the crowd, expertly evading weapons.

"Donn is mine," Niamh shouted, her burning eyes fixed on the approaching rider.

Her voice was a half-growl. She had slipped out of her white robes and was standing naked, staff readied. Fair fur, as bright as her hair, washed over her skin, painting her flesh gold. She leaped down, aiming her staff for a stab. Donn's short sword met the oak, failing to cut through it but breaking the blow. Niamh's weight heaved him out of his saddle, and both of them rolled on the trampled grass. They tore away from each other and leaped to their feet, barehanded. Each coolly studied his opponent as they circled one another with measured steps.

Donn's lips twisted into a rough smile. "Women seem to turn into wildcats whenever I'm around," he said.

"They just grow fangs and claws," Niamh snarled back. "'Tis not the same."

The smile vanished from the rogue prince's face. "I'm going to kill you," he said.

"Can you fight as well as you talk?" Niamh's transformation deepened. Her words trailed into a menacing growl as she dropped to all fours, fog swirling about her.

Mist exploded around Donn as he shapechanged into a black leopard and leaped towards the golden *mac'tir*, aiming for her throat.

Rowan's gaze toured the battling throng, his fists clenching and relaxing by his thighs. He couldn't make out the Speakers among the fighting Kanjali, but he was searching for something else entirely. He closed his eyes, extending his Power, half-blinded by the moon's bright force. Carefully, he reached out further...

There.

Rowan turned a half-circle to the south and opened his eyes, locking gazes with the blank-faced Hound.

Adam let go of a limp Kanjali female as Rowan watched him from atop the barrow, and her body sank to lie motionless at his feet. He smiled and raised a bloodied, clawed hand to his lips, tasting the female's blood with a long, wide lick. He then reached behind his back and pulled forward a wooden bow, stringing it with a silver-tipped arrow.

He wasn't aiming at Rowan.

"*Dara!*" Rowan tore towards *Lia Fáil*.

Dara had been standing against the silent Stone, making an unconscious target for the Hound's arrows. She raised dark, confused eyes to Rowan as he rushed to her. Her dagger glittered in her right hand, and her left was clutching a small leather sack threaded about her neck.

The Hound let go of the arrow, sending it spiraling into the air in a wide, lethal arc. Haze solidified around him as he began to transform.

Dara screamed as Rowan crashed into her, throwing them both against the dark grass at the Stone's foot. She hit the ground with violent force. Her dagger flew out of her hand and lay an arm's reach away, a band of light against Tara's night-black soil. She yelled again as Rowan heaved her up and turned her in his arms, shouting her name with urgency.

"Are you hurt?" Rowan's hands roughly skimmed over her body as she panted and struggled. "Is there blood on you? Answer me, Dara!"

"*No!*" she cried in response, panicked and infuriated. "No! Rowan, you're hurting me! Let me go!"

"Stay down," he ordered in a husky voice, loosening his steely grip on her. His hands slid away from her body, and he slowly climbed to a crouch. His head snapped back to the south.

Dara pushed backwards with her feet. Her fingers felt oddly slippery against the grass, daubed with something sticky and warm. She raised her hands to her face, staring with shock at the dark liquid staining them.

"Rowan, you're bleeding," she whispered, her trembling fingers widely splayed.

Her eyes shot to his bent form, watching his back heave with a hissing breath. His face was hidden behind a spill of tangled hair. He twisted his left arm with a furious growl and clutched something at his side.

"Rowan, don't!"

He tore the Hound's arrow from his left flank with a savage howl and let it plunge to the grass, almost collapsing with it. A dark stain was rapidly spreading over the small of his back, flowing down his left thigh. It shimmered bright red in the firelight. Rowan dug his bloody left fist into the ground, steadying his squat. Flimsy threads of mist formed about him, slowly thickening, as he twined his Power with the moon's cool force.

"You're too hurt to change," she pleaded with him.

"No choice. The Hound has changed fully," he answered. His voice rumbled thick and inhuman from within the white fog that surrounded him.

Dara's eyes followed his gaze, and saw something huge and dark making its way up the barrow. Its glowing eyes were staring directly at them.

The Hound.

Dara whimpered and scrambled to all fours, crawling on scraped hands and knees in a blind search for her dagger. A sob flew from her mouth as her fingers fell upon its hard Damascus steel. The blade's embossed silver singed her fingertips, but she refrained from jerking her hand away, instead sliding her grip further onto the cool hilt. She snatched her dagger from the grass, gasping with relief. The blade had been muddied by Tara's soil. Dara didn't bother to wipe it off, swiveling to look for Rowan.

Her breath caught.

He stood, huge and magnificent, pale mist still bathing his feet. The fire's ruddy glow touched his fur with molten copper. The deceitful darkness made his wound difficult to recognize, a dark, wet stain tarnishing his fur's perfection.

She could hear his voice in her mind. *Dara, stand back*, he was begging of her.

He thundered a low, ominous growl at the black creature facing him, and limped forward.

The transformed Hound crouched slightly, barely a leap away from him. His yellow eyes scorched the both of them, as hungry as the fire's flames. He launched himself into the smoke-thick air with startling abruptness, smashing into Rowan's *mac'tir* form with brutal force. His steely claws scored bloody, ragged lines in Rowan's flanks, ripping his arrow-wound wider.

The two *mac'tir* beasts rolled against the crushed grass in an intimate tangle, copper and black alternating, tearing at each other's flesh with fangs and claws.

Dara screamed, stumbling away from the violent duel. Her hand was so tight on her dagger, it hurt. Her knees gave way and she sank down at the Stone's foot, hot tears blinding her.

The Hound was killing Rowan.

She swung the back of her left hand against the tears. Her vision was still tear-blurred, and angrily, she wiped the remaining wetness from her eyes. The night grew sharp again. Then all of its gory details snapped into place, like the pieces of a puzzle.

A bonfire.

A white, round moon riding high, on its way to the western horizon.

A dark line of blood slanting across the Stone's pale face... Rowan's blood.

Aislinn had seen it all in her dream.

Further away, against the crushed grass, Rowan was losing control fast over his *mac'tir* form. Dara felt his Power shuddering and slipping away from his desperate grasp. The arrow's poisonous silver had already spread in his blood—an arrow meant for her, just like the one that had hit her on All Hallows night back in Oregon. Just like the one that had killed Aidan.

"Not again," Dara whispered, clutching her searing dagger against her breasts. "Goddess, please, not again!"

Fog was finally dispersing over the battle scene, revealing two nude, humanoid forms. The Hound was bending over Rowan's still body.

"*No!*" Dara shrieked. Her eyes widened as the Hound raised burning eyes to her, his pale face framed by the black spill of his hair.

"He's not dead," the Hound said flatly as he stood up. "Yet."

She froze as he stepped over Rowan, approaching her leisurely. She found the strength to back away from him until her back touched *Lia Fáil*. The blood smeared over the stone covered her sheer dress with warm stickiness. She trembled, forcing her numb fingers to keep hold of her dagger. She had to grip the bone hilt with both her hands just to keep it from slipping down.

"Any weapon is useless against me without a Guardian's Power backing it," the Hound said.

He was now standing above her, his face smooth of emotion. Moonlight washed silvery over his naked skin, and bloodied slashes slanted in dark, ragged lines across his chest and abdomen. He was erect.

He crouched between Dara's thighs with deliberate slowness, trapping her chin with one hand.

"After your Sidhe poked one of my eyes out I had to grow a new one," he said softly.

His claws grazed her skin. Dara stifled a sob, her eyes wide with fear. The Hound leaned further into her and brushed a cool cheek against the side of her face, holding her lower jaw captive. A whimper slipped from her lips, though she tried to stop it.

"I seem to take all your men from you, mixed-breed," he whispered tightly against her ear. "Maybe it's better that I haven't killed you...yet."

His bow-hand was moving between her legs.

Dara tensed.

"You're wrong," she said coldly. "*This* weapon *can* hurt you."

She turned her dagger with both her hands, its hilt pressed against her chest, and drove the soil-tarnished blade deep between the Hound's ribs. She felt the blade sliding against the rim of his breastbone. Groaning, she pushed it deeper inside, to the hilt. Her mind was screaming.

Mom had always said when Tara's soil touches a Hound's heart, it will die...

The Hound tore away from Dara with an anguished howl, then stumbled back to the ground. His hands wrapped around the ritual dagger's hilt protruding from his chest. Surprise slowly washed over his features, the first emotion he'd displayed.

"Either way," he whispered, "it ends here."

His hands slipped from the bone hilt. Swift change rippled through his motionless form, turning flesh to pale sand. A breeze fanned over the fine white grains, as if aiming to banish a texture so odd to Tara's soil. Thunder crashed over the Hill of Tara, blue light splitting the dry sky. The sounds of battle transformed to a muddle of surprised cries as Prince Donn and his shadow riders vanished from the face of Upper Earth.

Dara shot up from her crouch and raced the short distance to Rowan. He was slumped over, naked and unmoving, his face veiled by sodden hair. She dropped to her knees beside him, afraid to touch him. He was still breathing, she could see the faint movement of his sweat-washed back.

A large raven circled thrice above Dara's head and landed beside her with a ruffle of feathers.

"'Tis close to the night's end," Brighid said quietly, smoothing hair and clothes back to order. "The Hound's death ended it sooner, before dawn. Donn and what was left of his men have been all pulled back Below. 'Til next time they manage to open a Gateway, that is."

"Rowan," Dara brushed soggy hair away from the upturned side of his face. "Rowan, please…"

Shadows fell over her, and she raised feverish eyes to Niamh and Teague standing above her.

"He's alive," she pleaded.

"He's badly hurt, and there is Hound's silver inside of him." Niamh arduously crouched beside Rowan. Her staff was missing. There was a deep slash across one of her thighs, and she was supporting her left arm against her rib cage. Her face was a tight mask, disclosing no emotions.

"Lads, help me turn him over to his back," Teague ordered a few of the closest men. He, too, was bloodied and ruffled. "Let's carry him over to the Stone. Easy, you *amadáin*!"

Rowan groaned as they lifted him, another faint sign of life.

"Dara," Teague said softly, supporting his friend's back against *Lia Fáil*. "The full moon hasn't set yet, but 'tis already kissing the horizon. There's only one thing you can do now, and be quick in deciding."

"Yes," Dara whispered, stroking Rowan's face. "I can try *Slánú*. Help me hold him."

She'd do *Slánú*—use sex to heal him. Back in the Oregon warehouse, Rowan had told her *Slánú* would work for those meant to be together. Well, Rowan was her Chosen, they *belonged* with each other.

She wouldn't let him go.

Dara shifted above her unconscious mate. Her knees burrowed damp holes in the grass, framing Rowan's thighs. Her unsteady fingers unbuttoned what was left of her dress and she shrugged off its thin shreds. Now she was as naked as he. Cradling one of Rowan's hands in both of hers, Dara placed his palm over the roundness of one naked breast.

"Feel that?" she whispered, pressing his hand harder against her flesh.

Bowing over him, she covered his mouth with hers. She ran her tongue over his lips, gently probing the slack gap in between.

"Kiss me back, damn you," she whispered, releasing his hand to slide limply down her stomach.

She kissed him lower, down his neck, lingering over his thready pulse. His skin tasted of salt, seasoned with sweat and blood. She dipped her tongue into the shallow hollow at the base of his neck. Her hands hesitated over his chest, afraid to cause more pain. He groaned and stirred as her gentle touch found the gashes traversing his ribs. *At least he was responding,* she thought with desperation. Her mouth followed her fingers' path, kissing every inch to make it better. For a brief instant she thought she felt him move again beneath her.

"Damn you, you stubborn Irishman." Her words breathed hot over his flesh. "I can't do this alone, Rowan. You've got to help me!"

She climbed up his body again, her sweaty skin tight against his. Teague's arm made a solid support beneath Rowan's back. Dara cradled Rowan's face in her hands and breathed life into his mouth with a deep kiss, bruising his lips. Her breasts flattened against his chest as she pressed their bodies closer. He moaned as she kissed him, and a wild surge of hope shot through her. She started to rub her naked pussy against his semi-hard cock, moving slowly back and forth.

"Feel *that*?" she exhaled into his mouth. "I'm all wet for you, Rowan. Kiss me back. Kiss me back."

His tongue brushed hers in his mouth. His hands curled weakly against her bare thighs. She felt his chest heaving beneath her breasts, swelling with a deeper gasp. Teague carefully withdrew his supporting hand from Rowan's back. Dara dropped her hands to Rowan's and laced their fingers together, breaking their kiss for air. Rowan's eyes fluttered open. He tightened his hold on her. Biting energy shot from their linked hands, and Dara groaned as she felt Power surging through her body.

"*Yes*!" she cried out. "Rowan. Yes."

This time Rowan's mouth found Dara's. His lips were fever-hot, moist. She moaned as he dipped into her mouth and drank from her with a thirsty, endless kiss. His deep, slow tongue-strokes enhanced the flow of Power between them. She felt him drawing on her life force, twining it with his. From mouth to pussy she clung to him, wanting him to take whatever he needed. Rowan's hands gently unwound from hers and traveled up her damp back in a tight caress. He wrapped his palms against the back of her head, warming her nape, drawing her tighter against him. Finally, they tore their mouths from each other, breathing heavily. Their eyes locked, amber flecked-brown hotly clinging to ocean-green.

Dara shifted once more above Rowan, her movements still slow, careful. She felt his cock stroking her damp nether lips. She placed her hands on his shoulders and moved against him until all their parts matched.

"Dara," he whispered with effort, a brief tremble stirring him. His cock head was nudging her entrance.

She lowered herself on his erection, taking him all the way inside her. Slowly, inch by inch. She felt him taking in air with a loud hiss.

"Move," Rowan whispered. His hands dropped to her hips.

Wordlessly, Dara started a slow ride, undulating up and down his shaft. Her hands tightened on his shoulders. She watched Rowan's face as he leaned his head back against the Stone, watching her sway above him. His hands roamed up her stomach, caressed and cupped her breasts. Her body instantly responded to his touch, her nipples wrinkling and tautening beneath his palms.

Dara moaned aloud.

It didn't matter that they weren't truly alone. It didn't matter that they were fucking in front of an engrossed audience of shifters atop the natural stage the ring made. Rowan felt so *good* inside her. Dammit all, he felt so good *alive*. His cock was kneading every wet, hidden part of her as she rode him... Stretching her hungry flesh... Reaching the very end of her.

A cry tore from her mouth.

"*Dara.*" Rowan's grip tightened on her hips. His grasp had already regained its natural strength. He started to dominate their rhythm, moving her faster and harder on his cock.

Dara trembled all over, her back arching sharply. Her eyes squeezed shut until red fog was dancing behind her quivering eyelids. She let Rowan rock her above him, answering each of his deep thrusts with a broken scream.

Goddess. Oh, Goddess. She needed to come.

Her sweaty hands slipped down from his shoulders and reached between her thighs for her clit. Her fingers parted her nether lips with a burning search, sliding over warm, thick wetness. She found the slick fleshy nub, erect and throbbing like a tiny cock.

"*Rowan,*" she gasped.

Her fingers pressed and kneaded her engorged clit as Rowan's cock slid in and out of her in long, sharp thrusts. She came on a scream, her inner flesh rippling with tight contractions. Rowan groaned and heaved his hips, spearing her deeply. He pulled her down hard on him as he burst deep within her, shooting his semen deep into her womb.

Dara arched her neck, crying out again as waves of pleasure rocked her body. Spent and still quivering, she sank against Rowan's chest, her thighs still clutching his waist. His large hands fumbled against the small of her back, loosely pulling her to him.

Rowan felt Dara's tender touch searching his chest, her light fingers tracing the lines of his ribs. She moaned with relief, finding his flesh whole beneath the caking of mud and blood.

"You can touch me harder, sweetheart," he whispered against her tousled dark head.

She mumbled something against his shoulder, but Rowan couldn't make out the words, only feel the hot moisture dousing his skin. She was crying in silence.

Niamh rose to her feet in a laborious climb, aided by Teague. The first shafts of morning sunlight dusted her bright hair with gold.

"This bond is now forged by the Stone of Fal as demanded by the ancient Law," she declared, and a wild burst of joyous screams exploded from the battered crowd.

Brighid gently undid the leather thong from Dara's nape as she rested in her lifemate's embrace. She then took her amulet out of its protective pouch and tied the naked charm back around her own neck. The silver flashed once sharply in the morning sun before vanishing beneath Brighid's gray cape.

"I wish you both happiness," she whispered, lightly touching Dara's naked shoulder. She vanished within a cloud of mist, and a large raven soared from the haze and aimed for dawn's flaming sunrise.

"*Brighid!*" Teague shouted. "Brighid, wait!"

Niamh laid a restraining hand on his arm. "Let her go," she said.

"Aye, Bantiarna," he whispered and bent down to where the redheaded banshee had last stood. His long fingers uncovered a small leather sack from within the muddied grass. He pressed it tight in his fist. "'Tis not the last we'll see of each other, wee one," he promised, touching the leather to his lips.

"Are you okay, sweetheart?" Rowan caught Dara's face in both his hands and studied her pale expression.

"Yes," she told him. "I just had a busy night."

He laughed.

She lifted her hands to his hair, stroking the damp, copper tangles. She still couldn't believe he was alive and whole again. The image of him naked and bleeding over the grass had been burnt into her retinas. Her hands slid down further to flatten against the Stone, framing her lover's face.

A rumble started, so deep that the earth itself shook.

Dara cried out, keeping her hands against the Stone's face for balance.

"What's happening?" Teague bellowed, thrown to the ground. "Are the bleedin' riders coming back?"

From everywhere around them frightened voices cried out as shifters stumbled upon the shuddering earth. Rowan and Dara had been tossed away from the roaring Stone and lay in a tangled heap.

"No, Teague, 'tis the voice of *Lia Fáil!*" Niamh shouted, struggling to rise to a crouch. "The Stone is roaring!"

As if compensating for over a thousand years of silence, the Destiny Stone's first roar was a fierce and long one. It roared two more times, making the Hill of Tara quaver from south to north. When its last echoes had faded, the Kanjali folk struggled back to their feet in a jumble of bewildered shouts.

Rowan crouched above Dara within the tall grass fringing the Stone. Gently, he stroked her face.

"'*Lia Fáil* will again utter a cry, the first and the last in one and a half-thousand years,'" he softly recited.

"But why did it cry now?" she whispered, eyes wide and stunned. "When I touched it before, it stayed quiet!"

"Only now, Dara, when you touched *Lia Fáil*, you had new life growing inside you," Niamh said, her blue cobalt eyes bright with sunlight. "The Stone didn't cry for *you*. It cried for your unborn child."

Dara gasped with disbelief.

Rowan flashed her a weak grin from above.

Teague groaned. "I need a drop of Guinness," he muttered.

Circling high above, unseen and unheard, an oversized raven crowned with a blazing feathery tuft squawked with mirth.

Enjoy this excerpt from
Ordinary Charm
© Copyright Anya Bast, 2004

All Rights Reserved, Ellora's Cave Publishing, Inc.

She walked back to the entryway where she'd seen a table with a phone. "It's here." The message light blinked five messages. Cole came to stand beside her. She hit play.

A sultry, breathy female voice filled the foyer. "Darling, this is Monique. Call me. I'm missing you." Pause. "Darren is out of town on business this weekend. Come see me. *Please.*"

Serena rolled her eyes. The woman sounded like she needed a fix. Maybe Cole *was* a drug dealer...of the carnal variety.

Beep

A perky cheerleaderesque voice was up next. "Hey, Cole, baby. This is Cynthia. I had a fantastic day with you last Saturday." Pause. Her voice lowered, got huskier when she spoke next. "Saturday night was even better. Wanna repeat? Call me back."

Beep

"Yeeeech." Serena turned away and walked toward the living. She couldn't take any more. It was nauseating.

"I guess I have a few women," Cole said, sounding mightily pleased with himself.

Was it any surprise? The man was stunning. Serena looked back in time to see him push a hand through his hair. The action defined his biceps perfectly and made hunger twist through her body. She looked away. "Yeah. Guess it hasn't really been a long time, like you said."

He frowned. "Guess not. Sure feels like it, though."

There were two hang-ups. Blessedly, the next message was not from a woman. Instead, it was an older sounding man. Serena wandered back to the answering machine.

"Hey, Cole, just wanted to let you know that we received *Fire of the Ancients*. We love it and only want a couple changes. You did a fantastic job on this game. You're the king of adventure games, man. We'll be getting back to you with more details, but you've done it again. This'll be a hit!"

"Well." He slanted her an unsure look. "I'm the king of adventure computer games, I guess."

"Apparently, that's not all you're the king of," Serena muttered.

He appeared to not have heard her. "So," he said to almost himself. "I design computer games. That explains all the equipment in the living room." He frowned and glanced at her. "Designing computer games is kind of geeky. Do I seem like a geek to you?"

"What?" She turned toward him. "First of all, there's nothing wrong with geeks. I happen to be one myself. Second of all—" She took him in from the top his head to his feet, every luscious well-defined muscle in-between, and tried not to swallow her tongue. "No, you don't look like one." Suddenly uncomfortable, she turned away. "Anyway, what the hell does a geek look like?" she finished, irritably.

"Let's explore the rest of the apartment." He turned and walked into the living room.

"Don't you want to call *Monique* and *Cynthia* back?" She mimicked their voices when she said their names. It was childish, but she couldn't help herself.

He turned back toward and fixed her with suddenly hooded and heated gaze. It was the calculating and measured gaze of a predator. Like shark that had just scented blood in the water, or a lion on an African plain that had spotted a wounded zebra.

Shit.

She took a step back involuntarily and bumped into the telephone table. "Are you jealous, beautiful?" he purred as he came closer.

"Uh." Oh, *that* was an intelligent response. Mentally, she smacked her forehead with her open palm.

"Because you sound jealous," he murmured. He reached her and cupped her cheek in his hand. "Maybe I should kiss you again and reassert the fact that I desperately want you in my bed, Serena. It was *you* that balked, remember?"

"I-I'm not jealous," she replied, tipping her chin up a little. "I just don't like to see women make idiots of themselves over a man." *Just like she was doing.* "I just don't...shit—"

His mouth came down on hers, completely stealing the rest of her thought. He seduced her lips to part and kissed her deep. All the while he rubbed his thumb back and forth over her cheek. He broke the kiss and set his forehead to hers. After making a little purring sound in the back of his throat, he closed his eyes and clenched his jaw. "Your skin's so soft," he murmured thickly. "I can't help but wonder if you're as soft all over."

Serena's breath caught. She used the table behind her to take some of her weight because her knees weren't doing a very good job of it.

He set his hands on either side of her, resting them on the table, and gazed into her wide eyes. "You need to leave, Serena. I mean it. You're not safe around me...for so many different reasons. I want to lead you to my bed, lay you out and take you over and over until the morning light breaks the night. I want to strip you, beautiful. I want to sink myself inside you."

A whimpering sound reached her ears and it took her a second to realize it was coming from her.

He pushed away from the table and turned. "If you don't want any of that, you should leave now. Because you're tempting me something awful."

Serena glanced at the door and back at Cole. He stood with his back to her. Suddenly, he shot a hand out toward the door and it opened.

She stared at the open door, her ticket out of here, out of this whole dangerous mess. If she left now, she'd be free of the whole Ashmodai thing, presumably.

But she couldn't seem to move.

She did want Cole. Of course, she did. She was just surprised, and more than a little wary about the fact that *he* wanted *her*. In her mind, she was still the fat girl in school all the boys ignored. It was hard for her to wrap her mind around the fact that this perfect, beautiful specimen of manhood—this man who could have any woman he wanted—found her attractive. No. Not even that. Cole professed to find her *irresistible*.

How could that be?

She wanted to find out if it was true, however, so instead of walking to the door and out of it like she *should*, she stood staring at Cole's broad shoulders, his tight ass and the back of his head. She *liked* this man as well as found him attractive. He was compelling, mysterious and more than a little dangerous. She found *him* irresistible.

But...what would happen when he got her clothes off and he discovered her overweight body naked? Would the fire in his eyes dim? Serena shuddered. That was something she *didn't* want to find out.

Something Brian had told her once came back in a rush, *You'd be so pretty if you just lost some weight.*

She glanced at the door, then back at Cole. She *should* leave. It would save them both some pain and anguish. She moved to take a step toward it.

He flicked his wrist. The door slammed shut.

Crap.

Suddenly, her mid was awhirl. What kind of bra and underwear had she put on this morning? She flushed as she remembered donning the serviceable blue briefs that sported tiny pink flowers and the boring white cotton bra. Not exactly alluring lingerie.

She just hadn't expected to be seduced today.

A wild laugh rose up in her throat, but it was choked into submission by the look on Cole's face as he turned toward her. A dark, predatory light graced his brown and green-flecked eyes. "You're mine now, beautiful," he murmured.

About the author:

Dawn is a hopeless romantic and a Gemini, a tricky combination to handle. During daytime she's moonlighting as a medical doctor, but at nights...oh, at nights...at nights she's fervently hammering steamy scenes on her moaning keyboard.

A secret identity...sort of like Catwoman, right?

Simply put, Dawn finds penning Erotica/Romance for EC so much more stimulating than writing boring medical articles! After all, daydreaming of alpha werewolves, sexy, dark vampires and muscle-bound futuristic warriors is by far a more invigorating pastime than listening to your patients complaining!

Dawn welcomes mail from readers. You can write to her c/o Ellora's Cave Publishing at 1056 Home Avenue, Akron OH 44310-3502.

Why an electronic book?

We live in the Information Age—an exciting time in the history of human civilization in which technology rules supreme and continues to progress in leaps and bounds every minute of every hour of every day. For a multitude of reasons, more and more avid literary fans are opting to purchase e-books instead of paperbacks. The question to those not yet initiated to the world of electronic reading is simply: *why?*

1. *Price.* An electronic title at Ellora's Cave Publishing and Cerridwen Press runs anywhere from 40-75% less than the cover price of the <u>exact same title</u> in paperback format. Why? Cold mathematics. It is less expensive to publish an e-book than it is to publish a paperback, so the savings are passed along to the consumer.

2. *Space.* Running out of room to house your paperback books? That is one worry you will never have with electronic novels. For a low one-time cost, you can purchase a handheld computer designed specifically for e-reading purposes. Many e-readers are larger than the average handheld, giving you plenty of screen room. Better yet, hundreds of titles can be stored within your new library—a single microchip. (Please note that Ellora's Cave and Cerridwen Press does not endorse any specific brands. You can check our website at www.ellorascave.com or

www.cerridwenpress.com for customer recommendations we make available to new consumers.)

3. *Mobility.* Because your new library now consists of only a microchip, your entire cache of books can be taken with you wherever you go.

4. *Personal preferences are accounted for.* Are the words you are currently reading too small? Too large? Too...**ANNOYING**? Paperback books cannot be modified according to personal preferences, but e-books can.

5. *Instant gratification.* Is it the middle of the night and all the bookstores are closed? Are you tired of waiting days—sometimes weeks—for online and offline bookstores to ship the novels you bought? Ellora's Cave Publishing sells instantaneous downloads 24 hours a day, 7 days a week, 365 days a year. Our e-book delivery system is 100% automated, meaning your order is filled as soon as you pay for it.

Those are a few of the top reasons why electronic novels are displacing paperbacks for many an avid reader. As always, Ellora's Cave and Cerridwen Press welcomes your questions and comments. We invite you to email us at service@ellorascave.com, service@cerridwenpress.com or write to us directly at: 1056 Home Ave. Akron OH 44310-3502.

NEED A MORE EXCITING WAY TO PLAN YOUR DAY?

ELLORA'S CAVEMEN

2006 CALENDAR

COMING THIS FALL

COMING TO A BOOKSTORE NEAR YOU!

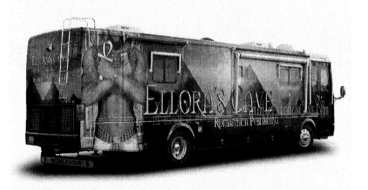

ELLORA'S CAVE
2005

BEST SELLING AUTHORS TOUR

ELLORA'S CAVE
ROMANTICA PUBLISHING

Discover for yourself why readers can't get enough of the multiple award-winning publisher Ellora's Cave. Whether you prefer e-books or paperbacks, be sure to visit EC on the web at www.ellorascave.com for an erotic reading experience that will leave you breathless.

www.ellorascave.com